Lilian Carmine is the wr[...]
plans to live in places all[...]
settles for the worlds and places inside her head.

She currently works with illustration as well as the next
book in *The Lost Boys* series.

Also by Lilian Carmine:

The Lost Boys
The Lost Girl

LOST
AND
FOUND

LILIAN CARMINE

EBURY
PRESS

1 3 5 7 9 10 8 6 4 2

Ebury Press, an imprint of Ebury Publishing
20 Vauxhall Bridge Road,
London SW1V 2SA

Penguin
Random House
UK

Ebury Press is part of the Penguin Random House group of companies whose
addresses can be found at global.penguinrandomhouse.com

First published in 2015 by Ebury Press

www.eburypublishing.co.uk

A CIP catalogue record for this book is available from the British Library

ISBN 9780091953430

Typeset in Times LT Std by
Palimpsest Book Production Ltd, Falkirk, Stirlingshire

Printed in Great Britain by Clays Ltd, St Ives plc

Penguin Random House is committed to a sustainable future for our business,
our readers and our planet. This book is made from Forest Stewardship
Council® certified paper.

MIX
Paper from
responsible sources
FSC® C018179

To the fans
My everlasting gratitude for making my dream
come true.

Chapter One
Witchy Boot Camp

"How about now? Are we there yet?"

"Harry, dude, this stopped being funny three hours ago," Tristan grunted from the driver's seat.

It was the twelfth time Harry had asked since we'd set off on the road trip. He had been squirming in his seat for the past hour, fizzing over in excitement.

Seth sat in the passenger seat, repeatedly turning the map upside down and back again, his tongue poking out in concentration.

"We should be getting near a small side exit now. The camp is really close, I think," he stated.

"Are you sure? You don't seem to know the right way to read that thing . . ." I muttered from my seat next to Harry in the back.

"Shut it, Skippy. In this car I'm the second in command. I'm Chewbacca to his Hans Solo. I give the instructions to the captain of the ship here!" Seth said smugly.

That was Mr. Seth Fletcher, my hardcore nerdy blond friend.

"Fine, *Chewie*," I grumbled under my breath. I had been demoted to the back seat because even if my life depended on it, I wouldn't know how to read a map and give the right instructions, therefore Seth had been allowed the seat next to Tristan to assist him as the official navigator.

"Are Josh and Sam still following us?" I turned round to look at the road behind us. Sam and Josh had most of our luggage and instruments in their car, and were following us close behind. Nobody had wanted to sit in the back of their car because of Rocko, Sam's new dog. Rocko, an English Mastiff, tended to get car sick quite easily, and I couldn't think of anything worse than a barfing hyperactive dog on such a long journey.

"Man, this trip is going to be *friggin' swell*!" Harry exclaimed, imitating the Fifties slang that Tristan sometimes used when he was excited. "We are going to rock the fans' socks off with this new album. I can feel it!"

We were heading out of state to a private camp in the woods. A secluded cluster of cabins in the middle of nowhere was the perfect place to start working on the new album and brainstorm some new songs and lyrics in privacy. We'd be semi-incognito, so wouldn't even need a security guard, which was a relief after the way the last one had turned out.

The girls had been left behind. Seth and Sam's girlfriends, Tiffany and Amanda, were used to the band's private get-togethers whenever we had a new album to work on, and Robin, Harry's new girlfriend, was having a vacation of her own with a couple of friends. But this trip wasn't just about work, although the girls weren't aware of our ulterior motives for this week away.

"I'm just happy to be free of the press right now," Tristan

mumbled, staring at the road ahead. Ulterior motive number one.

After getting engaged on a small island off Italy, Tristan and I had announced our marriage to the press a couple of weeks later, once we'd arrived home and signed the official papers. As we'd expected, the local media went nuts at the news. We couldn't go anywhere without being hassled by photographers and harassed by the paparazzi. A photograph of the happily married rock-star couple was currently worth big bucks, and the vultures were fighting for a chance to snatch that one golden picture.

Tristan resented this invasion of our privacy; he hated the exposure that came with the band's fame and success. This week away was the perfect chance for us to have a break from all the nosy reporters for a little while.

"Here's the entrance! Turn here." Seth pointed to a metal sign at the side of the road. "It says 'Misty Lake Woods'. That's the name of the place, right, Joey?"

"Yep. That's the place." I nodded as Tristan slowed the car. He flicked on the indicator so Sam, in the car behind, wouldn't miss the entrance. For good measure, he also thrust one arm out of the window to point in the direction we were headed.

It took a few turns down a narrow graveled road before we finally reached a small cabin that looked promising. From its roof hung a big wooden plaque with "Misty Lake Camp" carved on it in big yellow letters. A guy came out of the cabin as soon as he saw our cars approaching, and introduced himself as Craig Simms, the camp caretaker. He was middle-aged, short and a bit chubby, with grizzly brown hair and a bushy moustache. He wore round, thin-rimmed glasses and was dressed in khaki adventure shorts and a shirt.

Craig instructed us briefly about the directions to the camp itself and handed Tristan a small map, circling the two cabins that were reserved for us with a red Sharpie.

He told us the main house was right down the road, and our cabins were further up the hill into the woods. "Miss Harker has asked for Mr. Joe Gray to check in at the main house as soon as he arrives. She is waiting for him," Craig informed us, peeking inside the car to see which one of the boys was "Joe".

"It's *Mrs.* Joe *Halloway*," I corrected him.

"But Joe is a boy's name . . ." he countered, despite the fact that Seth and Tristan were trying to give him subtle *please don't* looks.

I guess the last name could change all it wanted, but the curse of the boy's name still continued, firm and strong. Whoop-de-doo.

"Oh, I beg your pardon . . . *Mrs. Halloway*," Craig apologized, with a frown, after finally noticing the boys' reproachful glares.

"Yeah, yeah. Joe is a boy's name," I said, slightly annoyed. "Fair mistake. Happens all the time. Let's get a move on."

Tristan thanked Craig for his assistance and drove up the hill for a couple more minutes, turning left on to an even narrower trail before we reached our final destination: two wood cabins nestled cozily amongst the tall pine trees. One cabin was considerably smaller – for Tristan and me – and, a few meters away, the other was significantly bigger, for the boys. Everybody started getting the bags, backpacks and musical instruments out of the cars the minute we had parked.

"We can quickly drop our bags in the cabin and I'll

drive you to the main house to check in," Tristan proposed, but I dismissed his offer.

"It's all right, Tris, you can go inside and relax now. We've had a long journey; you must be tired from driving. And it doesn't seem to be too far to the main house. Plus, I need to stretch my legs. You take the bags inside, and I'll go meet Celeste, okay?"

He leaned closer and pecked me on the lips. "Okay, buttercup. Have fun with Celeste, then." I snorted loudly at that remark, and he arched one eyebrow in reply. "Be nice, Joe. You promised you'd try, remember?"

"Yeeeah, I remember. I will, don't worry. It's mostly force of habit. 'Celeste' and 'fun' don't fit in the same sentence. Ever," I said, but quickly followed up with, "I know she's trying hard to be more patient with me. I must try to be, too."

Celeste was the second reason for this trip. Ulterior motive number two. I wasn't here just to work on our next album and to escape reporters, but also to attend a Gathering for witch apprentices. This year, the Harker sisters were coordinating it.

Celeste Harker, the eldest of the three Harker siblings, had taken over Miss Violet's role as my occult mentor, after the whole situation with Tristan in the first year we met. Miss Violet had assisted during those hard times – when Tristan was brought back from the dead – and Celeste had taken on her mantle afterwards, tutoring me in the occult arts of witchcraft.

It hadn't ended well. I was too short-tempered, and Celeste was too strict, bossy and a gigantic pain in my ass, so one day I quit after a heated argument and left her house, determined never to return again.

Until a couple of months ago, when I had, as I've tended to do, waddled into murky magical waters. I had got myself into big trouble by accidently switching powers with my other-worldly friend Vigil. Celeste had helped me through the whole ordeal and had been there for me when I'd needed her most.

We had both agreed to give the mentor-slash-tutoring thing another chance. We had even shaken hands. I promised to be more focused and zealous with my studies, and Celeste was going to be more patient and understanding in return.

When Celeste had called to invite me to this Gathering for young apprentices, I'd agreed to go. But not just to honor my promise to Celeste to take this occult thing seriously – there had been another reason for my quick acceptance.

Ulterior motive number three.

For the last couple of weeks, my mother had started acting very strangely. At first, I'd put it down to some sort of shock that I'd almost died after my last turbulent magical mess, which had left me in a hospital bed – or to my secret marriage to Tristan after that. But then she'd invited me back home to Esperanza and dropped the biggest bomb since I found out that Tristan was a ghost.

"I can't believe you're only telling me this now!" I'd exclaimed, shocked at the news she had just given me.

"I'm sorry, munchkin. I have always had my suspicions, but I didn't know for sure. The first inkling I had was that New Year when you brought a boy back from the dead. I wanted to wait to see how things went with Tristan before saying anything, but after this last scare with Vigil, I realized I'd waited too long."

"You mean you've known something was up since the day I brought Tristan back?" I said, and then gasped as realization hit me. "That's why you handled things so well, wasn't it? I did think you were being outstandingly understanding at the time . . ." I narrowed my eyes suspiciously at her. ". . . *too* understanding."

She squirmed in her seat, looking flustered and all guilty. "It was only a small suspicion but, deep down, I've had it since you were very little. You could see – *can* see – people's feelings so clearly; you can read people like open books! But then I thought maybe you were just a very sensitive and perceptive girl. Some people can be that way, you know. But that craziness with Tristan happened in the new year. You had a lot to deal with. I didn't want you to be even more scared than you already were. I even tried to convince myself it was something to do with Tristan rather than you. I used my time at work to track down his background history and dig through his past, while you were at home busy worrying if he was going to go to school with you or not."

I tried to protest, but she shushed me. "Oh, you know it's true, Joey, stop it! Your only concern back then was to keep him by your side, and you know it. You didn't stop to think about any of this magic nonsense happening to you! But I was trying to figure it out while you were away boarding at Sagan. Only I didn't find anything suspicious or dark about Tristan's past, so I was stuck again. I had no idea how to explain what was happening to you.

"And then Tristan was gone, and you were devastated. You were hurting so much, I . . . I . . . couldn't bear to talk to you about it. I thought you needed some time first to heal, mend your broken heart. I thought this magic craziness was finished, with Tristan gone." She sighed deeply, passing a frustrated hand through her hair. "How naïve I was, to rely on wishful thinking. You managed to bring him back again. And then you had magic forever in your life, constantly by your side, in Tristan's presence.

"You were so happy, living a normal life," she said, her eyes full of apology. "You had a boyfriend who adored you, and you had your band. Everything was good and back to normal. I thought all the magic troubles were over. I didn't want to put any doubts in your head. They could stay only in mine. But the truth is, your father—"

At this I couldn't help but interrupt. "You think this magic I have comes from *Dad*?"

She paused. "I don't know for sure, honey. I told you, your father never said anything to me. He was very secretive about his past, and I suppose that's kind of a giveaway. As far as I know, he didn't have any family. He would get very upset when I asked him about it. He'd tell me to leave the past behind and live for the future. It was one of his conditions, in fact, before we started dating: that I had to stop asking about his family. That he alone should be enough.

"One day he gave me an ultimatum. If I couldn't let the past stay buried, and if I couldn't accept him on his own, then things between us were over. I loved him very much. So much that I agreed. The past didn't matter, as long as I had a future with him . . ." She shook her head and glanced down, her eyes brimming with tears. "I didn't know I would get such a brief future with him, though. I didn't know that my decision to stay ignorant could put you in harm's way now."

She wiped the corners of her eyes and took a deep breath, in an effort to compose herself. "The thing is, honey, your father always had this kind of . . . magical aura about him. A little bit like Tristan has. I thought I was romanticizing things, because I was so in love. And he was a musician. You know how it is. They all have a special glow about them . . . But small things – weird things – sometimes happened around your dad. And then weird things started happening around you, too . . . Well, let's just say I don't believe in coincidences. I'm worried about you, Joey. I don't know how much more weird this can get. Last time, you ended up hospitalized!"

"You think something happened to Dad, Mom? Did he die because of magic?" I asked, scared. "Did something strange happen?"

"No, no, honey. What happened was an accident. Your dad was in the wrong place at the wrong time. Magic had nothing to do with it, just bad luck. The guy that robbed that convenience store is locked up for the rest of his life; he won't hurt anyone ever again." She put her hand gently over mine, trying to comfort me. "But I need to tell you this now, about your dad and magic, in case you want to look for answers yourself. Miss Violet said she'd found magic connections to the name Gray when she was trying to help with the New Year's spell, but she can't confirm if they have any relation to you. You could investigate a little, maybe try to find out more about your dad's family? Maybe your friend Celeste might know more?"

My mother's eyes had been filled with hope – and regret.

And that's really why I was attending the Harkers' Gathering: to find out more about my magic heritage, my dad's past – and maybe some family secrets.

The boys had agreed to help me. I could work on the

album half of the time, and study magic the other half, while surreptitiously digging up secrets about my father's history. Everybody was in agreement, and now here we all were.

The Lost Boys had arrived at Misty Lake Camp!

Chapter Two
Blind Sighted

I stopped in the middle of the road to check the map that Craig, the camp caretaker, had given us. I seriously sucked at reading instructions; no wonder I had been demoted to the back seat of Tristan's car.

The directions seemed pretty clear, though: it was one squiggly trail from our cabin to a big straight road that went all the way down to the main house. Figuring it out wasn't exactly rocket science, but I had been walking down this graveled road for a while, now, and the main house still hadn't come into view. It seemed the proportions on the map were a tad incorrect, and the main house wasn't as close as the map indicated. Either that or I'd screwed up and managed to get seriously lost in the camp already.

The second option was going to be so embarrassing if it was true.

"Hi, there, happy camper!" A small hand pulled the map I'd been studying away from my face to reveal a beaming girl wearing big glasses. She had frizzy brown hair and looked like a little bunny rabbit: all frail and skittish. "You seem lost. Are you heading to your cabin? I can help you find it, if you want," the girl offered, with a kind smile.

"Oh, thank God. I was getting worried. Do you know if this is the right way to the main house?" I asked, with a sigh of relief.

"The main house? Yeah, you're heading in the right direction. Just keep following this road. There's literally no way you can lose the main house in this camp: all trails lead there. Are you here for the *Gathering*?" she asked, whispering the last word in a spooky voice to make it sound more supernaturally impressive.

"Yes, I am. You're attending, too? Celeste Harker is actually waiting for me at the main house, or so I was told."

The girl widened her eyes. The effect of her bugged-out eyes through her thick lenses was quite impressive. "Miss Harker told me to come see if her apprentice Joe Gray had arrived yet. A-are you by any ch-chance . . .?"

"Yep, nice to meet you. I'm Joe Gray. Actually, it's Halloway now, not Gray." I beamed, extending a hand towards her.

She looked at my hand as if it were a two-headed snake. "You're really *the* Joe Gray?" she whispered. "I thought Joe Gray was a boy!"

"Doesn't everyone," I mumbled tiredly. "It's not a big deal. Sometimes girls have boy's names and vice versa. Why are you looking at me like that?"

"Oh, my God! Are they really true, all those stories about you?" she said, her easy demeanor returning. "Are you really an empathy seer? People are saying you're the best one there is! Can you really enter people's heads and mess with their minds? Like, for real? I can't believe I'm talking to you! No one believes you're really coming to this Gathering. Everybody thinks you're the greatest." She squealed in full-on fan-girl fashion. I would recognize those high-pitched notes anywhere. The sound was embedded in my memory from all the fans screaming at shows we played.

"Where did you hear these things?" I crossed my arms and glared at her.

She caught sight of my guarded expression and rushed to explain, "Oh, no, you don't need to worry! We all swore to secrecy; only witches are allowed to know these things, if you know what I mean." She tapped the side of her nose in a Mob-like secret signal. "A witch's vow is a serious thing. There are grave consequences if someone breaks one. You have my word: I will never say a thing." She raised a hand and placed it over her heart.

"Okay, I guess," I muttered, still watching her suspiciously. Her expression seemed to be genuine, though, so I let myself relax. "These rumors have been completely blown out of proportion, by the way. Most of it's not true at all, so you can understand my worries. If this story leaked to the press, it'd be a nightmare for the band."

She looked at me with the most puzzled expression. "What band?"

"Hmm, you know . . . my band?"

"You have a band?"

"You don't know about my band?" Go figure. She knows about my empathy-sight but doesn't know a thing about me being in a popular rock band. Okay, fine, we weren't internationally famous yet, but we were fast heading in that direction. How could she not know I was Joe Gray from The Lost Boys? "I'm in a rock band. It's my main occupation. This witch thing is just a hobby, at the moment."

"Oh, okay. That's cool. Rock 'n' roll! Whoohoo!" Her awkward cheer ended with a weird snort, and she added a feeble fist pump into the air in an attempt to look cool. "I'm Liza, by the way. But my friends call me Lizzie, so call me Lizzie. Not because I'm assuming you'd want to be my friend, no one ever does. I mean, you can, if you want to, but I'm not forcing you, so you don't need to be, but you can call me Lizzie, or whatever you want . . ." She trailed off, shuffling her feet on the gravel road.

"Nice to meet you, Lizzie. My friends call me Joey, so call me Joey." I extended a hand once again for her to shake.

This time, she took it and shook it vigorously. "All right!" She was clearly exhilarated that she was officially my friend now. She made the rock 'n' roll hand signal, trying to impress me, but ended up failing miserably, looking even more awkward than the first time.

"Come on, Lizzie. Show me the way! We have a Harker sister waiting, and time's a-wastin'!" I chuckled.

The main house turned out to be bigger than I expected. The walls were all made from a dark wood, but inside it had a cozy feel, very welcoming. There were fake bearskin rugs scattered around the floor, and paintings and photographs of the camp adorned every wall. Above the front desk in the lobby was a big map of the camp, the main house at the center, with small cabins dotted across the surrounding area.

Lizzie pointed at the entrance to the cafeteria, telling me that if I ever decided to sample a bit of the camp "cuisine", this was the room to head for. Then she pointed out the meeting hall, explaining that it was where travelling groups and their tour guides usually congregated; then she showed me a few recreational games rooms where people hung out in their free time, when they were not hiking or exploring.

As we walked back to the main entrance lobby, a frantic girl hurried up to Lizzie, asking for help solving an emergency regarding the room-sharing list for the cabins. She also asked me if I could do her a favor by taking a plate of cookies to the meeting hall for the first introductory lecture, which was due to start.

Lizzie was completely appalled by her friend's lack of ceremony towards me; the girl clearly had no clue who I was. She tried to apologize on her friend's behalf, but I waved her off and took the tray of cookies, telling her it was completely fine.

Before I started this trip, I decided that I would face this Gathering with an open mind. Tristan had once taught me, several years ago at school, that the way we perceive a situation can change everything about that moment. If you see it as fun, it ends up being truly fun. And I was choosing to see this Gathering as a great opportunity. Nothing and no one was going to upset me here; I wouldn't allow it.

"Excuse me, you!" Someone standing at a table within a circle of girls snapped her fingers in an annoying fashion to get my attention as we entered the meeting hall. The girls all looked to be around my age, early twenties. "We've been waiting for these damned cookies for ages, here! What have you been doing all this time, making them from scratch? I have a low blood-sugar level; I could have fainted waiting here this long!" The voice came from a fake-blonde girl. She continued to berate me, while her cluster of friends tutted.

I raised my eyebrows in puzzlement. For a moment, I thought I had travelled back in time and this was high school all over again. They were sure behaving like the cast of *Mean Girls*: bratty, rude and immature.

Okay. So far, not a very good start – at least, not if I were going to manage to maintain my good-natured self. But, like I said, nothing and *no one* was going to upset me while at this camp.

I bloody wasn't going to let it.

I forced a smile and placed the cookies calmly on their table. "Here you go, ladies. No need to faint any more." No one in their group seemed to recognize me from The Lost Boys, which did make me wonder about the skill of our marketing team, to be honest. Maybe it was my comfy road-trip sweats that were distracting them: it didn't look like an outfit a rock star should be wearing, after all. "Go ahead!" I continued. "Gobble up these fattening cookies. They look like the type that go straight to the hips, if you ladies know what I mean."

I gave them a cheeky wink. They looked like the sort of girls that went in for crazy diets. The type that thinks a good reflection in the mirror determines their real worth. They should worry less about appearance and more about what was inside, I thought. In other words, they should stop being superficial twats and start treating people who brought them cookies a little bit better.

As I expected, my comment had the desired effect. The low-blood-sugar girl, who was about to snatch up a cookie, faltered. She began to glare at the sugary treats as if they were a long-sworn enemy.

I grinned, seeing her reaction. She looked like she was starving, but the fat-to-the-hips-cookie threat had been a complete turn off. I know, it was mean for me to point it out; I could have let her have her cookie, guilt free. But, hey, she started it!

"What are those things made of, anyway? They look stale to me. I'm not eating that crap," she muttered, searching for an excuse to reject them.

"They look fine to me," a younger blonde girl, who resembled the older, teased. "And taste even better!" She munched one cookie in an exaggerated display of enjoyment.

"Ah, Felicia. No wonder you can't find a boyfriend, dear sister. Boys don't like fat girls, you know," the grouchy older girl jibed at the younger one, in clear sibling rivalry.

Felicia stuck her tongue out, and her sister blew her a kiss in provocation, while the rest of the girls giggled.

"Hey, Alicia, speaking of boyfriends," one of them piped up, "do you really think this Joe dude is coming to the Gathering?"

"Of course! He's Celeste star student, after all, isn't he? And she's organizing the damned thing. He'll be here, don't worry," Alicia stated, before adding smugly, "I've come prepared. The boy will be putty in my hands by the time the day is over, you'll see."

I was fighting hard not to laugh out loud by this point. So the rude blonde girl named Alicia thought Celeste's star student was a boy named Joe.

The curse of the name struck again. *The joy.*

If I had a penny for every time someone has mistaken me for a boy because of my name, I'd have all the pennies in the world.

"Do you think he's really done everything people say he has, Alicia?" another minion asked. "I mean, it all sounds very far-fetched to me. I know you said you heard your grandma talking about it, but I don't think all those stories can be true."

"Well, you know how those old bats are, they do tend to exaggerate. We can't be completely sure . . ." Alicia murmured, and pulled at her black velvet tank-top so that more cleavage was showing. "But you've heard the wild tales about Miss Violet's protégé. No wonder Celeste Harker rushed to snatch the Gray boy out of the old hag's wrinkled hands. She's always been the greediest – and smartest – of the sisters."

Still hovering nearby, I perked up at this. Wild tales? What was that all about? How much did these people actually know about me? How much had Miss Violet and Celeste let on?

"Do you really think this Joe can conjure up Death?" Felicia asked. "That he has free passage into the Land of Lost Souls, and that he can go there and leave as he pleases?"

Apparently, rumors of my visits to Sky's home (also known as Death's domain) had been circulating here.

It was true I had passed through Death's scorching desert a few times, albeit not on purpose. At the time, I had been trying to save Tristan from the deadline of his New Year's spell. And then, very recently, I had met Sky again in an encounter that had been particularly gruesome and had ended horribly for me. The purple scar on my stomach was still fresh and constantly reminded me of that terrible night at the warehouse.

A few weeks ago, I also received a special wedding

present from Sky herself, which I kept safely hidden in my apartment: a translucent glass coin that gave me free access to her home. So I suppose I did have a free pass into the Land of Lost Souls, come to think of it. But no one except Tristan knew about this gift. We hadn't told anyone, and I was glad about that now. It turned out that witches were not a very secretive bunch, and I feared what people might do if they knew the truth.

"Oh, I'm sure those are just stories, Felicia. No one even knows where these rumors come from, anyway." Alicia waved her ringed fingers, which caused around a dozen metal wristbands to clang noisily on her arm. She also had loads of moon-and-star pendants hanging from silver necklaces around her neck, wore dramatic earrings and a multitude of bracelets and rings. The witch image she was trying so hard to project was painfully obvious. She even had a huge pentagram design printed on the front of her velvet tank-top, for God's sake. All that was missing was an "I wanna be a witch" flashing neon sign on her forehead.

"You know how boys can be, bragging about stuff they can't really do, puffing out their chests to impress us girls. He's probably come up with some clever incantation that got the old hags in a hustle, that's all," Alicia mused in dismissal.

"Do you think he's cute, Ally?" one of her minions asked giddily, and I pretended to be clearing used plastic cups from their table as an excuse to keep hovering around while I eavesdropped on their conversation.

"I heard Celeste saying this Joe can charm his way around anyone!" Felicia chirped excitedly.

"He may be a charmer, but he won't be expecting this

little concoction, here!" Alicia waved a small purple flask for her group of minions to admire. "A love potion. I just need to put a little of this in his drink, and he will be the one charmed into submission. He'll be *all over me*, you wait and see."

I grimaced in disgust. Dear Lord, how low can a girl go?

"I don't know, Alicia," her sister cautioned. "This Joe fellow doesn't sound like a fool you can play that easily."

"Trust me, I'm more cunning than any boy will ever be, little sis."

"Wouldn't be so sure, if I were you," Felicia continued. "People are saying he's a very powerful empathy reader. He'll see right through you the second he lays his eyes on you. He'll know you're up to something."

Alicia tucked the flask in her jeans pocket and turned to glare at her sister. "I'll have you know, I've come prepared for *everything*, Felicia. See this?" She waved a crystal ball, which hung from one of the many silver chains around her neck. "I got this from a very powerful witch. It will deflect his eyesight, blind him so he won't be able to see any of my intentions. I'll be a beautiful and intriguing mystery to him. Boys love that!" she said triumphantly.

I looked intently at the crystal. It seemed like a worthless piece of glass, if you asked me. It wasn't blocking my sight at all.

I had this strange gift called empathy-sight that gave me the ability to read other people's emotions just by looking into their eyes. Some people were really strong broadcasters, and the insight I got from them was almost close to a mindreading experience. Some people had pretty strong defensive walls, though; it was very hard for me to read anything from them. But most of the time I could see right through people's intentions without even realizing I was doing it. It was so easy for me that I couldn't make it stop – at least, I hadn't been able to at first. It was like trying to stop seeing with your eyes open. It was only after the latest incident – when I switched powers with Vigil – that I'd learned how to control this ability. And I'd also vowed never to use my sight on close friends and family. Especially not Tristan. For the majority of our relationship, my empathy-sight had been a problem. It was hard for Tristan to have his privacy, and keep his feelings to himself, when I kept reading him.

Now I only used this ability on strangers, and only for my protection. At the moment, it was working at full capacity. I could read Alicia as clearly as a cloudless day: she had barely any protective barriers whatsoever, and that "amulet" was as ineffective as plain old glass.

There was a sudden stir amongst the many clusters of people around the room. Alicia and her circle of minions turned to watch as a guy around our age entered through the door.

He was slim and tall, with dark hair tinted blue at the tips, and he was dressed all in black. He was accompanied by two other boys; all three of them were trying hard to put on a brooding and mysterious act, but only the tall one – who was clearly the leader – managed to pull it off.

"It's him!" the girls around Alicia exclaimed.

"It's Joe Gray!"

Chapter Three
Presentations

"It's gotta be him!" Alicia squeaked, and rushed to grab a drink she could spike with her potion. Then she sashayed towards the couch where the brooding boy and his friends had sat down, a seductive smile on her pink glossy lips and the cup firmly in her grasp. Her minion troupe followed, all giggling and nudging each other.

Oh, I cannot miss this, I thought to myself, and grabbed the plate of cookies to offer them as an excuse to be close by.

This was going to be epic. I could feel it!

"Hey! How y'all doing? Are you boys here for the Gathering?" Alicia purred, with her friends at her side. Groups around the room started to drift closer, trying to eavesdrop, like I was.

The impostor Gray glanced up at Alicia, his expression a mix of disgust and annoyance. "Yes. Obviously. Everybody in this camp is here for the Gathering. We've booked the whole place for the week. *Duh.*" He had a faint accent that I couldn't quite pinpoint. It gave his words a sharp enunciation.

Alicia seemed taken aback by his hostility, but recovered astonishingly fast, the creepy smile on her lips never faltering. "Well, yes, obviously I know we have booked the whole place, but—"

"Not the whole place. The cabins up the hill are being used by a rock band," I interrupted. Alicia turned round, a flash of irritation in her eyes, but I gave her an *it's true* shrug.

"So, as I was saying, do you guys need any refreshments while we wait for the Harkers' presentation? It's awfully hot in here today, dontcha think?" And Alicia shoved the drink into impostor Gray's hand without waiting for a reply.

The boy eyed the cup and the gaggle of girls with a deep suspicion. "I'm not really thirsty," he stated, handing the cup back to her.

"Of course you are," she insisted and placed the cup firmly back into his hands, waiting expectantly for him to take a sip.

His suspicious gaze skimmed across her and landed on me, standing a few feet behind: the odd-looking duck in colorful sweat pants amongst a sea of prissy wannabe Black Sabbath girls. I had been shuffling suspiciously close by, eagerly waiting for the most opportune moment to stop him from drinking the spiked drink.

"Okaaay. What's going on, here?" he said, directly at me.

Despite his arrogance, he seemed to have good gut instincts for trusting me, I'd give him that.

"They think you're Joe Gray," I told him with a wide grin.

His mood darkened considerably, and he scoffed at the whole room. "Oh, come on! Not again! I've been hearing this non-stop for the past half hour! 'Are you Joe Gray? Is it you? Oh my gawd, it's Joe Gray!'" he mimicked in a mocking girly tone.

Alicia paused for a moment. "So you're not him? Give me that back, then." She snatched the cup from his hand and huffed in annoyance.

He seemed offended by that, which was odd seeing as he had just declined the offer of a drink. "I'm not Joe Gray. I'm Simon Blaine, if you must know. What's the big deal about this guy, anyway?"

I guessed the refusal of a drink had been a blow to his male ego, because he trash-talked Joe Gray in retaliation. "I've not even met the guy yet, but he's pissing me off to unreal levels already! I'll teach him a lesson in humility, if he ever shows up."

"You can try, but Joe has black belts in two martial arts, you know," I chirped, with a knowing smile. "Cookie?" I offered, extending the plate towards him.

Boy, this was so much fun. It was like watching a live comedy show. It was a shame there wasn't any popcorn around . . . The cookies were good, but popcorn would have been much better.

"So, are you by any chance related to Cillian Blaine?" Alicia asked, instantly perking up at the mention of his surname.

He rolled his eyes, seemingly used to that kind of reaction. "Yes, Cillian is my older brother."

"On second thought, you do seem parched. Here's your

refreshment back." She made to push the drink in his hand again but stopped midway as the crowd around us stirred.

We all turned to see the Harker sisters entering the room, with dorky Lizzie tagging behind them. Celeste took the lead, dressed in her usual formal white attire, as petite and pristine as ever. Celeste looked like a Disney ice princess: cool and collected, her perfect hair so blonde it appeared almost white, and flawless skin as pale as a snowflake. Brooding Luna was by her side, dressed as usual in black, and lovely Arice flanked her left, typically wearing a flower-patterned summer dress.

"Joe Gray!" Celeste beckoned, stopping right in front of me, her blue eyes twinkling in the bright light of the meeting room. "Lizzie told me you'd arrived. I'm so glad you came! Welcome."

Aww. Okay, I guess the fun had to end some time. Sad it had to be over so soon, though. I smiled back at Celeste and saluted playfully. "Aye, aye, Captain. Joe Gray reporting for duty."

She rolled her eyes at my jest and turned to see a score of faces staring at us with unblinking eyes and gasping mouths. "Erm . . . is everybody all right?" she asked.

"*This* is Joe Gray? B-but . . . you're a girl!" Simon protested accusingly.

"Okay, yes. But just so you know, you owe me a penny for my 'Joe-is-a-boy's-name' penny jar. It doesn't have to be right now, but, you know, whenever you can . . ."

He blushed, embarrassed.

"I'm kidding, couldn't resist, sorry. You don't owe me anything," I told Simon, with a chuckle. "Oh, but speaking of owing . . . Alicia, darling. About that drink you spiked . . ." I turned to face her, frowning. "Gross, dude. You don't do that to people. That's seriously messed up."

She gawked at me in fury. "You *can't* be Joe Gray!" she shouted.

At the same time, Simon asked, "What did she put in that drink?"

"Wait a minute, I can't believe it! Isn't she Joe Gray from The Lost Boys?" Alicia's younger sister finally connected the obvious dots, her realization accompanied by an audible gasp. "Oh, my God, she is! They are the rock band she said were staying in the cabins up the hill. There's talk about her everywhere in the news. She's just got married . . ."

"Good to know at least one of you figured it out. I was seriously worrying about the band's public profile," I muttered.

At the danger of sounding rather conceited, this was the longest I'd been in a crowd of so many people without anyone recognizing me, especially with the media stalking me day and night. It had been making me kind of anxious, because I'd been waiting for the penny to drop, but that familiar gasp of recognition hadn't come. Until now.

"But, yeah. That's me. I'm Halloway now, though, by the way. Not Gray any more."

"Excuse me, sorry to interrupt . . ." Simon bellowed over the excited shouts of the gathering crowd. "I don't care if you're a boy, girl, a Halloway or whatever. What I would *really* like to know is *what the hell was in that drink?*"

"I think she's spiked it with a love potion of some kind," I told him, nodding to Alicia, who was clearly having a hard time concealing her guilt.

"And you were all going to let me drink it?" he asked, appalled.

"Of course not. I was merely observing to see if she'd actually go through with it. I was going to stop you, but you kept refusing the drink, so I didn't bother," I said, then turned to Celeste. "What *I* really wanna know is what's this place's policy for people slipping 'love roofies' in other's people's drinks?"

The room was in uproar. Alicia and her minions protested vehemently, saying these were ludicrous accusations; Simon and his friends were shouting in indignation about the attempt to poison him; and people everywhere around us argued fervently, taking sides in the debate.

"All right, everybody, settle down!" Celeste's commanding voice boomed through the room, making the waves of excitement dissipate instantly.

She rubbed her temple and gave me a look that said, *I knew you'd end up in some sort of trouble here, but I didn't imagine it'd be mere seconds after your arrival.*

"Miss Collins, is there any truth to Joey's accusation?" she asked sternly.

"Of course not! It's obviously a lie. There's nothing in the drink!" Alicia squeaked in outrage, glaring deadly daggers my way.

"Really? Why don't you give the drink to one of your friends, then? If there's nothing in there, it shouldn't be a problem," I dared. It would be a good lesson to her minions for supporting this kind of thing. I hoped this would serve to teach them not to try this ever again. Although I wasn't really worried – if Alicia's love potion was anything like her crappy crystal ball, it wouldn't have any effect, anyway.

"Sure. Of course. No problem at all," Alicia conceded and, with gritted teeth, turned to face her friends.

Her sister took a significantly large step back, clearly not wanting to swallow that drink for anything, not even her "dearest" older sister. The other girls watched in horrified silence.

"You. Drink this." Alicia forced the drink into the hand of a girl who seemed to be the least inclined to disobey. The trembling girl took the cup, looking pleadingly at her leader, who showed no signs of mercy. *"Drink. It,"* Alicia hissed. The girl obediently gulped the drink in one go. "See? No problem at all."

"Of course. My apologies, then. I might have misheard things." I mock-bowed graciously in apology. "I'm sure nothing strange will happen to your friend after that drink," I said, with a knowing smirk playing at the corner of my lips, which didn't pass by unnoticed.

I knew everyone would be looking for signs of poisoning now. Alicia had better pray for her potion to be utter crap, or summon an antidote fast, or her farce would be exposed for everyone to see.

"All right. It seems that the matter is resolved," Celeste said, clapping her hands to dismiss the topic before turning to address the crowd. "We can start this meeting now, since everybody's here. Welcome all to the Misty Lake Annual Gathering!"

She motioned to her sisters, who took their seats at a long table at the head of the room, while everybody else shuffled around to fetch chairs and find places in front of the Harker sisters.

I decided to linger away from the crowd, perched on the arm of the couch, as Alicia, her friends – and even

Simon – kept giving me dirty glares, and I didn't feel like sitting anywhere near them.

"Thank you all for coming," Celeste continued, moving to stand between her sisters. "It is a delight to see so many lovely faces this year. We've never had so many attendants before!" I noticed a lot of people kept glancing sideways in my direction, and I was betting the rumors about Joe Gray – the infamous Death Conjurer – had something to do with the big turnout this year. I sure had already caused an impactful introduction for the first meeting of this witchy boot camp.

So much for keeping a low profile, like Tristan had asked of me . . .

"This Gathering is about exchanging experiences; it's about communing knowledge. You'll get to know other forms of practice from your colleagues here. 'Sharing' is the key word. Now my sister Luna will say a few words."

"All right, people," Luna began, taking over from Celeste. "This is the start of our first official meeting. You've been chosen by the most influential mentors for the privilege and the opportunity to attend this Gathering, so listen closely now, because I'm going to give you the rules: break any of them and you'll be asked to leave, immediately."

By the looks on everyone's faces, they were taking Luna Harker very seriously. She was the scarier and snarkiest of the sisters; with her long straight hair, heavy make-up and gothic style, she did look pretty intimidating.

"To clarify the first question raised: the policy for 'spiking' drinks with any kind of substance is zero tolerance. If any of you are caught doing so, or if there's any hard evidence that you did, the penalty is immediate expulsion from this

Gathering. Your mentors *and* parents will be duly notified, too. The same goes for hex bags found in your possession, as well as dark magic enchantments of any kind."

She shot a cold glare at Alicia and her minions. "Also, Joey really is with The Lost Boys at this camp, and they will be staying in the cabins up the hill. Which leads me to my first rule of the Gathering: it is strictly forbidden for any of you to go anywhere near those cabins to stalk or harass the band. If we catch you up there, it's one strike down. You get three strikes for misbehavior and you're in for detention hours. There's a lot of work to do around this place that the camp employees will gladly hand over to you."

There was a series of disappointed grunts from all around the room.

Arice continued after Luna, her round, beaming face the direct opposite of her moody sister's. "Okey dokey, folksies. Now, on a lighter note, the following are some camp rules set mostly for your safety and wellbeing. It is important that you follow them so that you all have a nice stay, all right? First, you shouldn't wander round the woods at night. If there is an emergency, or something urgent that demands you leave your quarters, never go unescorted. Take a cabin room-mate with you, and notify me or either of my sisters immediately, okay? It's very easy to get lost in these woods, and it isn't safe." Then, jokingly, she added: "We'd have to organize a search party, and it would be a hassle all around. So please, just don't."

The rest of the meeting went on for quite some time, along the same lines of safety in the camp, telling us what we could and couldn't do. I zoned out and stopped paying attention after rule number two, to be honest.

I dangled my legs from the arm of the couch while

humming a tune that had suddenly come into my head. It was rather catchy and felt very promising, potentially a single for the new album. I was musing to myself, when Arice called out my name.

"Hmm, sorry, what?" I snapped out of my musical reverie to notice a sea of faces staring at me, waiting for an answer. Celeste rolled her eyes, knowingly.

Oops! Busted by the teachers while daydreaming in class, again. Bummer.

"Could you repeat the question, please?" I asked with a smile.

"As I was saying, it is time to form the groups that will be assigned to each head monitor," Arice explained again. "My group will be discussing White Wiccan dealings, Luna will be handling the hidden powers of the Mists and the Moon, and Celeste will be tackling advanced theory in Occult Philosophy."

"So which group do you pick?" Celeste asked impatiently, giving me a pointed look that clearly indicated I should choose her, for obvious mentoring reasons.

I saw that most people had already formed clusters around the sisters. I was the last one to pick a team.

Alicia, Felicia and her minion friends had chosen Luna's group. That alone was a very good reason to stay as far away from that group as I possibly could.

Arice had a gleeful bunch of her own; one of her girls had epic blonde dreadlocks with dyed pink ends, and the friend by her side had a nose piercing and wild auburn hair braided with small daisies. They looked like fairy girls.

And then there was Celeste, with mousy Lizzie by her side waving at me with the goofiest grin ever, plus Simon, his two backup friends and some other people I didn't know.

"Well, it's a . . . you know . . ." I stalled, sucking through my teeth while trying to come up with a valid excuse to ditch Celeste and go roam with the fairy team. They looked like a fun bunch to play magic with.

Be nice to Celeste, Joey. You promised you'd try. I could imagine Tristan's serious voice. I scowled, but relented anyway.

I had promised, and I always kept my promises.

"I'm with Celeste," I mumbled, and let out a small, defeated sigh.

Chapter Four
Playtime with The Lost Boys

"Hey, you're back!" Tristan greeted me with a welcoming smile.

After the meeting in the main hall, we had a free afternoon so everybody could get to know the camp and relax. I had decided to go back to the cabins to check on how the guys were faring, rather than hanging out in the main house.

Okay, maybe that wasn't the real reason: maybe it was because Alicia and Simon were still giving me death glares, and I hadn't wanted to fight with them. As soon as I started walking up the hill, I knew I was safe: thanks to the Harkers' rule, this area was now forbidden territory for camp folk, Alicia Collins and Simon Blaine included. Which was epic. Now I didn't need to worry about my privacy, as anyone who snooped risked a "strike" on their naughty list.

"Whoa! This place is amazing," I said, as I entered the cabin. The main room was inviting and had a rustic style, the modest but welcoming space filled with beautiful sculptures made of raw wood, rusty metals and dry leaves. The interior design used elements of the forest in every nook. It made everything look really earthy and natural.

"You have to check out the guys' cabin. It's three times bigger than this one!" Tristan said, heading into the kitchen and selecting a bottle of water from the fridge. "How was your day? Had fun with the Harkers?" he asked, returning swiftly.

"I had a tremendous amount of fun," I confessed.

Tristan beamed and came to give me a proud peck on the lips.

"But then Celeste arrived."

The smile disappeared and he rolled his eyes at me.

"I'm sorry!" I chuckled. "The joke about Celeste ending the fun never gets old!"

"Halloway! Is she back yet?" We heard Harry's high-pitched voice shouting from the neighboring cabin.

"He's been asking that since you left. They're all a bunch of comedians . . ." Tristan grumbled and leaned out of the window. "Stop shouting, Harry! This is not how we're going to communicate in this place. You come over to ask in person!"

"What? Walk all the way over there? No way!" he complained, still bellowing. "Is she back or not?"

"Your degree of laziness astonishes me, man. We are literally a few steps away from each other. Come over and see for yourself!"

"He wouldn't make me go there for nothing . . . I think she's back, you guys!" was the last shout we heard.

"He's been waiting for you to get back so you can go sightseeing," Tristan explained, making himself comfortable on the couch.

A minute later, the other Lost Boys came bustling

through the cabin door, talking animatedly with each other. Harry was at the front, jumping up and down excitedly. "Yeah! I knew it! She's here! Come on, come on, Joey! Let's go!" He grabbed me by the hand and started pulling me to the door.

"Oh, hey, how was your meeting with Celeste, Joey?" I asked sarcastically. "Why, it's so lovely of you to ask, Harry. Thanks, it was good."

He rolled his eyes at me. "You know we don't talk about your encounters with the . . . erm, 'gifted people'. We know they exist; we don't need to talk about them. Let's leave it that way and keep rolling."

The boys still freaked out a little every time some supernatural event happened. To be fair, freaky unnatural things were kind of a constant in my life. The boys had eventually got used to it, but they still felt wary and avoided any discussion on the topic. As if not talking about supernatural things could magically make them less likely to happen.

They were still very skittish around Vigil and the Harkers – or, as Harry liked to put it, "any of the gifted people". The only supernatural presence they were completely at ease with was their best friend, former ghost Tristan. And also me, of course – their honorary witch girl.

Josh, Harry and Sam remained at the front door, eagerly waiting, wearing what can only be described as their adventure outfits. They had on a mix of training sneakers, combat boots, cameo shirts and sportswear. I could also hear Rocko yelping excitedly next to Sam. It was a good job the Harker sisters had left their cat, Mr. Skittles, safely at home.

"Aren't you guys coming?" I asked Seth and Tristan, who were both stretched out on our couch.

"I'm not going outside. You know what I think of nature," Seth stated, crossing his arms in defiance.

"It only wishes to kill you," we all chorused in unison, having heard this statement every time we invited Seth to take part in any kind of outdoor activity.

"In the most slow, torturous way possible," he added, shaking a can of insect repellant he had pulled from his bag and spraying it all around him. "Did you not see that TV show when that thing put those eggs in that guy and, well, let's just say, dude died in a horrible disgusting way. I'm not taking any risks, thank you very much."

I rolled my eyes. "And you, Tris? Are you going to stay to protect him from the evil wiggly bugs?" I teased.

"I'm staying to get dinner ready for when you lazy bums get back from your stroll in the woods, my darling wife," Tristan teased back. He was still enamored with our newly married status and threw a "darling wife" into every sentence he could. He was so frigging adorable! "Seth is helping me prepare dinner, so stop 'bugging' him." He chuckled. "Sorry, buddy, pun only half intended."

"All right, have fun cooking, boys!" I wasn't going to offer to stay and help, as I was the most rubbish of them all at cooking. I had won the lottery in terms of snatching up a master chef for my husband.

We left them at the cabin and went for our exploratory walk into the forest. Josh kept racing me, his competitive side ensuring he was always at the front. He kept choosing paths off the main trails, which had dead logs and rocks – as "obstacles", he said – to make the race "more exciting". Harry, Sam and Rocko tagged along behind, more interested in appreciating the sights the forest had to offer.

Rocko was having the time of his life, sniffing every

inch of forest he could stick his wet nose on, and Harry wasn't much different, poking things and picking up insects.

We would all howl to the forest from time to time – like true lost boys should – accompanied by Rocko's excited little yelps. It was a lot of fun, our first stroll in the woods, but the night soon came and we headed back to the cabin in time to see the last rays of sun disappearing through the treetops.

We were almost at our cabin's doorstep when we bumped into Craig the caretaker, who was also taking his last stroll of the day. He was glad to see we'd had fun exploring the forest and gave us a few tips on the most interesting places to discover around the camp, pointing out that the most beautiful trails were near the lake and offering to be our tour guide if we ever wished for him to show us the best spots of Misty Lake Woods.

Dinner was loud, deliciously filled with good food and a lot of laughter, but eventually, as night rolled in, the boys left Tristan and me to rest and get an early night.

Although rest and sleep didn't actually feature in Tristan's plans for the night. Our honeymoon – of sorts – of a month ago had been cut short by the sudden appearance of our friends for a surprise marriage celebration, so now he was seizing this opportunity to take back some of the "honeymoon time" we'd lost. We were still in that giddy state of newlywed excitement, and a private cabin in the middle of the woods was the perfect place to get right back to it. And back to it we went. Tristan was a very happy – and very exhausted – man when we finally settled down to sleep, the morning sun only a couple of hours from rising.

I had completely forgotten that I had an early meeting with Celeste and her group at the crack of dawn. I woke up to mousy Lizzie knocking insistently at the front door of the cabin. When I answered groggily, she greeted my pigeon's nest of hair and sleepy face with a happy and refreshed smile.

Oh, goodie. She was one of those happy early-waker-upper types.

"Miss Harker asked me to come fetch you, Joe," she explained. "We've been waiting for you at breakfast. You're a bit late. She was worrying and asked me to check on you, see if everything was all right up here."

I peeked around her, with only one eye open, to look at the dim forest in the distance. "The sun isn't even up yet!" I protested with a whine.

"Miss Harker's motto is 'the early bird catches the worm'. And the sun is up, trust me; the trees are just in the way."

"If I pass on the worms, can I sleep some more?" I asked grumpily.

"Uh, there's no worms . . . it's just normal breakfast," she said, shuffling nervously from one foot to the other. "What should I tell her? You're not coming, then?" She looked like she was about to have a seizure at the prospect of having to explain to Celeste why I wasn't attending breakfast.

"No, tell her I'm coming. You go ahead, I'll get ready and be with you guys in a sec."

I left Tristan sleeping peacefully in our bed, and a few minutes later – after a quick shower and an even faster toss of clothes over my tired bones – I was entering the main house cafeteria like the agonized dying zombie that

I was. I even had the shuffling walk, moan of agony and deadened gaze to fit the undead description.

Why did I have to stay up all night? It was all Tristan's fault, the handsome, irresistible bastard!

"Oh, finally! The mighty Gray rises from her precious bed and decides to grace us mere mortals with her presence," Simon greeted me, with a provocative sneer. "We've been waiting for ages, you know."

You'd think he'd have been more thankful that I'd saved him from a spiked drink. Men can be so ungrateful, sometimes.

"You only arrived five minutes ago, Mr. Blaine. That can hardly be described as waiting for 'ages'," Celeste interrupted, greeting me with a short smile. "You two were the last of the whole group to arrive. Please, have a quick breakfast and join us outside by the front doors as soon as possible," she instructed before quickly departing, with a bunch of people following at her back.

"Ages," I scoffed at Simon.

"It was more than five minutes," he mumbled, as I passed by him and made for the breakfast table.

Minutes later, I was heading outside, a Styrofoam cup of coffee in one hand and a muffin in the other. People were mingling around the entrance, bleary eyes and sleep-deprived faces everywhere you looked. At least I wasn't the only one.

I leaned against the doorframe and watched as Celeste huddled in a circle with her sisters, discussing the day's events and schedules. Their designated groups shuffled in flocks nearby. Simon appeared at my side, watching the groups' movements with the same curiosity as I was.

"I'm sorry your chances of joining their group were

shot to hell after what happened yesterday," he mused, sipping from his own Styrofoam cup. "The famous Joe Gray should be dying to be part of the Glitter Coven. They are all about the glamorous lifestyle; you'd fit right in." He gave a short nod towards Alicia and her minions.

I glanced quickly at him and took in his gothic, brooding style. He looked like he was trying as hard to make an impression as Alicia's girls were with their "witchy" outfits. "You are the one fitting right in, dude. Stick a silver moon on your shirt and you're good to make a pledge to the sisterhood of sparkly witches right away." I looked down at the colorful attire I'd picked for the day: a vivid orange hoodie over blue jeans, and converse shoes. "I think I might fit in better with Arice's group, to be honest. They look more tolerant of color."

"Hmm . . . yes. The Daisy Braiders are painfully colorful," he concurred. "Too much hippie for my taste, but I can see why a rock star would be interested in their 'herbal' knowledge."

"Hey!" I turned round and flicked him on the forehead. "The Lost Boys don't do drugs. We're all about the music, not the 'herbs'," I said, affronted by his insinuation, but then added as an afterthought, "Although, we do fancy a nice cup of herbal tea in winter time, so you're not totally wrong, there . . ."

He gawked at me. "What are you, ten years old? Adults don't flick other people on the head!" he rubbed his forehead, scowling at me.

"Oh, I'm sorry. You were acting juvenile, so I thought I should join in. My bad. What are you and your friends even doing here, anyway? I thought this Gathering was for witches. Can guys be witches, too?"

"No," he scoffed indignantly. "There's a male term for it. Sorcerer, if you must know." He puffed out his chest, trying to look cool.

"Right. Sounds very manly. Not geeky at all," I said, trying not to laugh at him. "So, tell me, what are we?"

"Excuse me?"

"Our group? What are we called? There's the 'Glitter Coven' for Luna, the 'Daisy Braiders' for Arice. What's Celeste's group called?"

"Nothing! We aren't called anything."

"Come on, you can tell me. Of course we're called something!"

Right on cue, Simon's friend separated from the cluster of Celeste's group and walked towards us.

"Hey, Blaine! This Lizzie girl here is asking a bunch of questions about that last book you read. You've been studying it for longer, tell her what's it about," he said.

I had seen that same excited expression before – on a very familiar face, belonging to a very geeky blond lost boy of my own. "Oh, Jeez . . ." I exhaled in realization. "We are the Cool Nerds."

Chapter Five
The Cool Nerd

Celeste's first plan for the early morning of witch boot camp was to lead our small group to a clearing in the middle of the woods, where we could sit on the grass and share our learnings with each other.

Why that sharing needed to be so freaking early in the morning, I had no idea, but apparently "communing" in the early hours of the day was better for the "craft". It certainly brought the group closer, since we all felt like sharing the same awful bout of sleep deprivation we were experiencing.

We walked down a narrow trail, Celeste taking the lead, while the rest of the group shuffled sleepily behind. I noticed Simon dragging far behind at the back and slowed until I was walking beside him.

"So, Simon, do you come to these Gatherings often?" I began nonchalantly.

He eyed me suspiciously but responded anyway. "No, it's my first time. I've lived in Russia with my dad for the past four years."

"Oh, that's where the accent comes from."

"I grew up here, but my mother always made a point of speaking Russian inside the house, so I've always had a faint accent, hardly noticeable," he replied. "It's slightly accentuated now because I've been living out there since graduation."

"I'd accentuate it more, if I were you. It's a cool accent," I said honestly. "Russian is a beautiful language. I wish I knew a few words."

"You're in a famous rock band. Haven't you ever played in Russia?"

"Not yet. I hope we can go some day. How do I say, 'Thank you for coming to our concert'?"

He gave me a small smile before replying. "*Spasibo, chto prishli na nash kontsert!*"

"Ugh. That sounds hard to say."

"It just needs practice, is all."

"Are you here on vacation?"

"No, I'm staying with my mother full-time now. I thought I should take the opportunity to see how these things are done here. Gatherings in Russia are very dull. This seems promising already, with the 'famous' Joe Gray attending," he said, with a hint of provocation in his voice.

"Dude, come on, stop with the hate," I protested. "You're angry for no reason. I didn't do anything to you."

"You were going to let me drink that potion!"

"I told you, I was not! I was going to stop you. You shouldn't be so upset; even if you'd taken a small sip, nothing would have happened, anyway. Alicia's spells are utter crap."

"I'm not so sure about that. The girl who drank the potion was acting exceptionally smitten this morning, following Alicia around like a love-struck puppy, you know."

I widened my eyes. "Shut up! She was? Really?"

He turned to face me and nodded, a small grin tugging at the corners of his mouth. We stared at each other for a second before our shoulders started to shake with laughter. "That's awful! We shouldn't be laughing," I admonished between giggles.

"She deserved it. It was a good punishment. Miss Harker was pleased with your way of settling the problem."

"She was?" I hadn't noticed; I had been so focused on Alicia.

"My room-mate told me Miss Harker doesn't usually let students hand out punishments, but yours was so creative. She looked impressed by your quick thinking yesterday at the meeting. No wonder she made an exception to take you on as her apprentice."

"An exception?"

He quirked an eyebrow. "You mean, you don't know? Are you serious? Celeste Harker has never taken on an apprentice before. No one is ever good enough for her. At least, that's what I've heard from the gossip mill. I know more than you just from one day of asking around. That's priceless!"

I frowned. "Well, excuse me. This is all new to me. I haven't been aware of this magic community up until recently. And Celeste has only taken me under her wing as a favor for an old witch friend of mine. She was my neighbor, once, and felt sorry for me and decided to help me. I'm mostly a charity case. Don't need to mock me for it."

"So, are you saying the rumors about you aren't true, then?" he asked curiously.

"What rumors?" I played dumb. "I've heard quite a few wild stories lately. Some are very good, like the one where I walked through the Valley of Death, or the one where I can mess with people's heads. I can also shoot lasers from my eyes, control the weather and even burst into flames. I'm sure that, by the end of this Gathering, you'll be hearing I can make pigs fly," I mused with a chuckle.

The best way to make people discredit you is to create a story so ridiculous they will think you're only joking. The funny part was that I'd actually done a few of the things I'd told him, but I'd made it sound so unrealistic, it all seemed implausible.

He smirked, falling for my act. "People are stupid. I know those rumors are all fake."

"What about you? What's up with your brother . . . Cillian, is it? Alicia seemed quite taken by the name."

His relaxed demeanor instantly changed to tense and guarded. "He's a bit famous."

"Why? What's he done to be famous?"

"I can't really talk about it. He's a sorcerer of the Top League."

"Top League? What's that?"

"You've never heard of the Top League?" He eyed me with distrust.

"Is it like a sports thing for male witches?"

"Not 'witches', *sorcerers,*" he corrected impatiently, looking offended. "It's not a sport. Are you really Celeste Harker's apprentice? And you really don't know anything about the League?"

"Can't say that I do. Maybe I skipped that class?"

"You don't seem to know much about anything . . . What are you even doing here? This Gathering is for advanced apprentices only. What can you possibly share with any of us if you have zero experience and no knowledge whatsoever?"

"I wouldn't say I have 'zero experience'," I mumbled, feeling a little ashamed of my ignorance. Maybe I should have paid more attention to Celeste's insufferable lectures, after all.

He shot me a patronizing look. "As charity cases go, you are a very privileged one. You should be thankful to be allowed in here. And also try to step up your game. Celeste's influence won't carry you for long if you have nothing to show," he warned, and then picked up his pace so he could catch up to his friends at the front of the group.

Well, I guess that conversation was over. It had, at least, been partially fruitful:

I had discovered a lot of new things from Simon. Now I needed to find more about this secret Top League.

What worried me the most about Simon's warning was the last part: "step up your game". Whenever I threaded through magical waters, things usually tended to get murky, as Tristan often put it.

I wondered if stepping up my game was really a wise thing to do here. Last time my game was "upped", I almost burned everything in my wake . . . But if I continued hiding things, I'd have nothing to show. I'd be a burden on Celeste, a disappointment as an apprentice and a taint on her mentoring position.

I mulled this over the whole morning. Celeste and the group sat in a quiet spot in the woods and mostly talked. I listened to them sharing experiences they'd had with their mentors, and having philosophical debates about the meaning of magic in their lives.

It resembled a lot of Celeste and Vigil's conversations that I'd overheard when we were hanging out in her house while she tried to teach me how to control Vigil's powers. I had listened to the two of them talking endlessly about these intellectual things, but only ever grasped the edges of what they were saying.

I had hoped this Gathering would shed some light on the nature of magic – real, actual magic – and maybe teach me how to control my new abilities that kept appearing, but Celeste's group only talked about things. That was it. *Talking.*

There were no practical demonstrations of actual magic; there wasn't even a mention of abilities at all. Nobody showed any signs of being able to do anything "extraordinary", like I could. The whole thing seemed awfully pedestrian, like group therapy or one of those self-help lectures.

And then it struck me . . . In all the years I had been in contact with magic – through my empathy-sight, bringing ghosts back to life, talking with Death, having Vigil's powers, fighting alien magic creatures and, lately, even casting fire – I had always considered it *normal*. It was something that had been present in my everyday reality; it was a constant in my life. It was based on real facts and real evidence. I had seen it through my own eyes, witnessed it first-hand, fought and survived it. It wasn't just theoretical considerations. It wasn't just *talk*.

It was real to me.

Only after my mother's recent revelation about my father's history had I stopped to consider that, maybe, I should have started asking questions a long time ago, when Tristan first came into my life. I had naïvely accepted everything without question. My mom was right: all I'd cared about was how to keep Tristan by my side. Now I was beginning to realize how recklessly and stupidly I had been behaving.

I had learned, through Vigil, that magic always came at a price. I'd never bothered to worry about the cost, though, not until this latest power-switch incident. Now I knew better: I knew how careful I had to be around magic. It had the power to consume me and destroy everything I loved; it could leave marks that stayed forever.

I had thought this Gathering was going to teach me how to deal with my magic. That it would make me feel more included, like I wasn't alone in this supernatural world. But it seemed I was still very much alone, since nobody in this place seemed to have any actual power or practical experience whatsoever. Even Celeste wasn't showing anything to the group. If I hadn't witnessed her throwing those light balls during our fight with that evil, sneaky Nicky, I wouldn't have believed she could do anything, either. Here, she only talked, endlessly, and my patience was wearing thin.

The sun was at its height when we returned to the main house for a lunch break, after long hours of much talking. I hurried to sit with Lizzie in the cafeteria, with the intention of digging up some answers about the cryptic things Simon had said. If I wasn't going to learn anything about real magic, at least I could try to dig up some information about my father while I was here. That secret Top League seemed like a good place to start digging.

Lizzie was sitting by herself and seemed quite startled to see me slumping in the seat in front of her, with my tray in my hands. "Hey, Lizzie. Do you mind if I sit with you?"

"Y-you want to s-sit with me? Why? No one ever wants to join me." The shock on her face was quickly replaced by suspicion.

"Why not? We're friends, right?" I gave her a warm smile to prove I came in peace.

"All r-right. If you say so . . ."

"So, Lizzie, I wanna ask you something."

"Ah," she said, with a nod, my question confirming that there was really an ulterior motive for me joining her at the table, besides an alleged claim of friendship.

"I have heard some things, and you seem like the smartest person in the room. I thought you'd be able to help me."

"Well, your attempt of flattery is a bit obvious, but I'll take the bait. What do you want to know?"

"Do you know anything about the Top League? Simon told me about it, but I don't know what it is."

"Oh, is that all you want to know? That's not a big deal. Everyone knows about the League." She noticed me glaring and quickly corrected herself: "Except you, otherwise you wouldn't be asking. Sorry. I didn't mean to sound like a smarty pants. Well, it's like this: there are levels of apprenticeship. First is the Basic Level, for beginners, which I'm assuming is where you are at the moment."

I glared at her again, and she flustered in apology. "Sorry, I didn't mean to rub it in your face again. So, as I was saying: first, there's Basic. You go up the ladder with the help of your designated mentor until you reach Advanced Level. When Advanced is completed, you can continue on your own without mentor supervision. You can act in the field after that, or you can try out for the Professional

League, which is only for the most trained – the top notches. It's very hard to become a Pro."

"What is Celeste's level?"

"The Harker sisters are all Pros," she explained. "And then there's the Top League, the last and ultimate step on the ladder. Only the most gifted can enter. It is a very secretive group; they only recruit a selected few . . . Simon's brother is the recruit from Russia. It is the highest honor to be asked to join."

"Oh. That sounds . . . complicated. Why has Celeste never told me any of these things?" I mumbled to myself.

"You're still in Basic. You have to climb a few steps first to know more, I suppose. Actually, come to think of it, perhaps I shouldn't be telling you any of this, after all . . ." She was suddenly very reticent to continue.

"What's Simon's brother so famous for? Do you know what he's done in that League?"

"Hmm, erm . . . I-I don't really know."

I narrowed my eyes at her. "Liar, liar, pants on fire."

She gulped, eyes bugging out behind her thick glasses. "Darn it, I forgot about your sight. Can you really tell when someone's lying to you?"

"Yes. *Always*. Come on, Lizzie. I thought we were friends."

That seemed to hit the jackpot: her eyes glinted with remorse and even a smidgen of fear that I might stop being her friend if she didn't tell me. "I-I, well, I'm not supposed to know this . . ."

"If someone asks, I didn't hear it from you, I swear," I said, tapping the side of my nose, as she had done before, when we first met. "A witch's vow is serious business."

She eyed me in silence for a moment before conceding.

"All right. So, get this, I heard that everybody in the Top League has some special ability going on. Like, actual real super powers! I know, it sounds ridiculous; these things only happen in movies, right? But there are rumors that they can do some really freaky stuff!"

I perked up on my seat. "Freaky stuff? Like what?"

"Like control the weather, or hypnotize people with a glance of their eyes, or control fire. I heard one of them could even make you go blind with the snap of a finger. I don't know for certain what Simon's brother can do, but I heard some rumor saying that he can instill so much fear into your head that you lose your mind. He can literally make you have a mental breakdown. People are terrified of him. He must be really scary." She shivered on cue.

I had stopped listening the moment Lizzie had said there was someone who could cast fire. I was so excited. My investigations were leading to another person who could also manipulate fire. And not only that, now I knew of a whole group of people who had extraordinary abilities, just like me. I wasn't alone in this, after all!

Could this mean I may be related to this mystery League guy? Or that maybe he could have a connection to my dad? Could he be family?

My head swirled with too many unanswered questions.

And only one person could give me the answers I was looking for.

Chapter Six

Secret Investigation

"Hey, Celeste!" I shouted as I ran to catch up with her at the front steps of the main house.

"Oh, hello, Joey." She turned round to greet me, continuing to walk up to the front doors as she added, "I was heading to my room, to unwind a little before the afternoon activities. You will be working with your band during afternoons, if I'm not mistaken?"

"Yeah, that was the deal," I agreed, keeping pace with her as we entered the lobby. "We need to get the next album up and running. The record label's been on our backs, you know how it is . . . But, hey, I wanted to ask you something, before you go take your nap . . ."

"It's not a 'nap', Joey," she corrected, annoyed. "I will be meditating in my room and preparing for the afternoon meeting."

"Suuure," I agreed, trying to hide a smile. She was so going to take a big fat nap; I could see it written all over her tired face. "But before you go 'meditate', I was wondering if you could tell me something. I've been hearing a few things about these learning levels. Thanks for not mentioning any of that to me, by the way. Everybody is looking at me now like I'm a clueless idiot. But anyway, what's the deal with this Top League I've been hearing about?"

The alarm in her eyes was a pretty big tell that I had hit a nerve. "Where have you heard about that?" she asked sharply.

"Oh, you know . . . around. Why?"

I could almost see the protective walls she was raising between us, trying to block me out of her head. "This is not your concern, Gray. You will learn about it when it's time for you to know about it, and now is *not* the time."

"Celeste." I narrowed my eyes and focused in concentration. She was never very good at blocking my sight; even after much practice, she still couldn't raise a proper shield. "What are you hiding from me?"

She sighed, sensing I wasn't going to let this go. "You will learn about levels of apprenticeship in due time, Joey. That's why I've asked you to come to this Gathering, so you can advance in your lessons. You don't need to concern yourself with Top League matters for now."

"Is there by any chance a mention of a Gray enlisted in that League?" I hazarded a guess. If there *was* a guy with fire powers there, maybe we could be related, I wondered again.

"How in God's name do you know that?"

I couldn't tell her that I had discovered someone in the League had fire powers, and that this ability could connect back to me. She didn't even know I could cast fire, and, since she was so full of secrets, I decided it was best to keep this one to myself.

"I had a hunch. Plus, it's kinda written all over your face," I explained, pointing to her eyes to let her know I was reading her. She huffed, irritated, and shifted her eyes away.

"I told you to stop reading me, Joey."

"So? Is there?" I pressed.

"Maybe." She glanced around the lobby to see if anyone could be eavesdropping. "We are investigating this, Joey. They are a pretty secluded group, we don't know much about what goes with them, but we are trying to find out. I think there's been mention of an old member named Gray, but listen . . ." She lowered her voice and looked around one more time to be sure it was safe to talk. "Stop asking questions. It will only draw attention to yourself, and the Top League's attention is not a good thing to have. I'll let you know when we have something concrete to share, okay? Leave the detective work to us Pros, all right? We've got it covered. Now, focus your energies on learning. And stay out of trouble!"

"Fine," I harrumphed.

"And, for the last time, stop reading me! I told you it is rude and intrusive and very annoying when you do that," she snapped. She patted her clothes and gave an indignant pout before swiftly changing topic. "Anyway, how is Vigil doing? Have you heard from him lately?" she asked, looking everywhere but my face.

"Last time I saw him was on my wedding day in Italy. He's retired from work now."

"Oh, yes, I know. He told me."

"Did he, now?" I quirked a curious eyebrow and watched her fluster.

"Well, hmm, yes, he visited me a little while ago. To

see how things were going after that whole magic glass ball problem. He was very excited about taking some time out and enjoying his new life. Said he liked the concept of retirement very much."

"Hey, funny thing, huh? First thing he did to enjoy his new life was to come visit you." I tried hard to stop the smirk from showing on my face.

"Well, yes, it was very thoughtful of him to check on how I was doing." She kept brushing invisible specks of dust from her clothes and avoiding looking at me.

It seemed my intergalactic friend was developing a new crush after his brief stint inhabiting this little blue planet. I could picture oddball Celeste and clueless Vigil together: perhaps a strange pairing, but the most adorably weird couple ever!

"He told me he was going on a quick tour of the world now, exploring our planet and all," I said, and watched her perk up at the news. "But I reckon he will be back soon from his travels. He seemed eager to come back as soon as possible to spend some time with a friend, to drink some tea and chat about cosmic philosophical stuff." He hadn't actually said those words, but he'd hinted as much and I knew those activities where his favorite pastime as was Celeste's. "I wonder who that mysterious friend could be?" I asked, wiggling my eyebrows suggestively at her.

I didn't think Vigil understood the concept of a date yet, but he had inadvertently set himself up for one without knowing. Maybe that was a good thing: ignorance could sometimes be bliss. In Vigil's case, it certainly avoided a whole lot of awkwardness. He acted the most weird when he was trying to mimic human behavior without entirely understanding what it was he was supposed to be doing.

"Erm, well, he might have mentioned tea during his last visit, I can't quite recall," she lied blatantly. "I do love tea and good, stimulating conversation."

"I'll bet you do."

She blushed ever so slightly and cleared her throat. "So, hmm, I'll be waiting for you again, early tomorrow, Joey." The change of subject was not so subtle this time. "Do try to arrive on time for breakfast, yes?"

"Actually, Celeste, I was thinking that maybe I could switch groups? That way, I'd be able to do other activities and learn more from your sisters. I mean, why stick with only one Harker when I have two other amazing sisters available?" I had exhausted my interrogatory options in Celeste's group, but maybe I could discover more amongst Arice's buddy bunch.

Celeste paused and mulled over the idea. "That is actually a very good suggestion, Joey." She gave me a proud look that said, *I'm so happy you are taking this seriously and applying yourself.* "You can attend Luna's meeting group tonight, then!"

Luna happened to be coming through the front doors of the main house at that precise moment. Celeste called out, "Luna, come over here!"

"Actually, I was thinking more about Arice—" I tried to correct her, but Celeste was distracted, calling over to Luna.

"Luna, listen! Joey will be joining your group this evening. She wants to learn more about the secret ways of the Mists and the Moon. Isn't that great?"

"Cool beans," Luna replied. "See you at eight, then, Gray. We meet here at the front doors. Bring a jacket; it gets cold here at night. Don't be late!" she instructed, and waved a hand before carrying on her way through the lobby.

And that was how my doomed fate with the Glitter Coven was set for the night.

"So, did you find out stuff about your dad?" Tristan asked, as soon as I was back in our cabin later that afternoon.

Josh was sitting on the other couch a little further away from Tristan, and stopped air banging on his imaginary drum set to hear the latest news. All the boys knew about my secret quest to discover more about my father's history.

"Yeah, I discovered a few things, actually." I told them what I knew, and slumped down on the couch next to Tristan. "But Celeste ordered me to quit asking questions because she was already on it. She said I should stick to the program and focus on learning 'witch stuff', and let her worry about the League," I muttered sulkily.

Tristan wrapped his hands around me and pulled me into his arms. "I'm sure you'll find a way to continue your detective work without Celeste finding out."

"What? You're not going to scold me for wanting to disobey Celeste's orders?" I asked in dismay.

He chuckled. "A year ago, I certainly would have. But now I know better. You always do what you've got to do, Joey, no matter what people tell you. I've learned that the hard way. Now I know the best thing to do is leave you to it, be prepared for if things go wrong and always be ready to help you out of trouble. Knowing your history with magic, trouble will certainly come. But that's all right. I know I used to get mad at you for getting into trouble, but now I understand it's the best thing."

"It's the best thing?" I asked, astonished. "Really?"

"Of course. You always mess up when there's magic involved. But your first time messing up was the best thing that's ever happened to me, remember? I am your first magical mess. How can I complain about it now? It *was* the best thing for me!"

"You sure make life much more interesting. Things are never boring around you!" Josh agreed. "I personally think having magic like you two have in your lives is kind of incredible, to be honest. I'm hoping some of it will eventually rub off on me. It'd be cool, messing up with magic like you do."

"Seriously? I thought you guys hated it," I said to Josh.

"We don't hate it!" He laughed. "Harry and Sam get a bit scared, sometimes, but that's because they watch too many horror movies. But we all think it's cool. Seriously."

"So you won't mind if unfortunate magical accidents happen around here?"

"Are you kidding? We've been betting on how many days it will take for things to get 'bumpy' in this place! Harry's bet on day one, so please try to be careful for the rest of today. Tomorrow you can be as reckless as you wish." He crossed his fingers and gave me a hopeful look. "Don't worry, Joe. If something happens, we'll be here to help you. We've got your back. Right, Halloway?"

Tristan gave a firm nod. "You have all my support to disobey Celeste, buttercup." He gave me a tight hug. "If you want me to help you with anything, I'm here for you. I can break some rules, if you want me to. I know how you feel: I don't know anything about my father, either. If there's anything I can do to discover more about yours, I'll do it."

"I can't believe this. You, breaking rules and encouraging

disobedience . . ." I mumbled in shock. "Can you please tell me who are you? And what did you do to my Tristan?"

Both boys laughed hard at me. "*You* happened, sweetheart," Tristan said, leaning in to give me a kiss. "You're a bad influence. The best bad influence there is."

"Maaan, you are *good* with the romance crap," Josh said teasingly. "I should take notes, here; it's like a gold mine of epic lines for chicks."

"It's good ol' romance, Fifties style!" I praised, with a huge grin.

"Come on, you love fools. Let's go to my cabin. The guys are waiting for us to have lunch together." Josh chuckled, standing up.

"Oh, I already ate in the camp cafeteria. You guys go ahead. I'll take a quick nap here while you eat. I'm knackered! Celeste made me get up at the crack of dawn today; it was still dark when I left the cabin. You wake me up when it's time to work on the album, all right?" I said, rubbing my eyes tiredly. "Oh, but I won't be able to work late this evening because I have a meeting with Luna and her group at eight."

"All right, pumpkin." Tristan stood up, gave me a kiss on the forehead and left with Josh.

I dragged myself off to bed and slumped onto the mattress without even taking my clothes off.

Chapter Seven
Misty Lake

What seemed like minutes later, I felt Tristan trying to wake me with a gentle shake, and I blinked at the dark room, confused, gradually realizing it was night-time already. I looked at the clock. Eight o'clock.

Fifteen minutes later, I was arriving at the front doors of the main house, panting my lungs out, cursing myself for being late again.

"Oh, look who's joining us: the wonder fake boy," Alicia greeted me, her pack of minions at her flank as usual.

"Hello to you, too, Alicia. It's oh so very nice to see you again," I greeted in return, with the same fake enthusiasm and sarcasm as hers. "But, seriously, your *Mean Girls* act is so done. I wish you'd stop with it. Please. We're all adults here."

"You're the one acting like a prissy celebrity princess, Lost Girl, not me. I wish *you'd* stop with *that*," she snapped back childishly, while her minions shot me vehement looks of disdain.

I rolled my eyes and gave up. There was no point trying

to draw adult sense out of the brains of this bunch.

"You were pretty chummy with Simon Blaine, this morning. Are you guys having a fling?" Alicia chirped evilly. "I'll bet the tabloids would die if they got hold of this piece of juicy gossip about you!"

"And I'm sure you know we don't tolerate petty gossip," Luna interrupted. "Revealing Joey's presence at this Gathering would compromise us all, Miss Collins. Keep your mouth shut about what goes here, about Joey and anything else," she ordered, making Alicia flinch. "Now, let's get a move on. It's a few minutes' walk to the lake's shore, and we don't have the whole night. Chop, chop! Let's get rolling!"

I can't tell you how much I regretted ignoring Luna's advice to bring a jacket. During the night, the forest was indeed very chilly, and not even the tall pine trees did much to stop the cold wind from blowing right through us. All the warmth the forest held during the day was completely gone, and the golden-greenish hue of the vegetation was replaced by scary shadows. The leaves in the bushes and treetops whispered to each other across the wind, crackling and rustling all the while we followed the trail. It was kind of creepy. And by kind of, I mean a hell of a lot. The only light came from the full moon and a few flashlights that some girls were carrying.

We bumped into Craig, the camp caretaker, on the way down to the lake. Luna had informed him of all late-night activities, and he wanted to know if everything was all right and whether we needed help to get safely to the shore, but Luna dismissed his offer, saying she knew her way around the woods well, and there was no need for any assistance.

I tried my hardest to avoid tripping as we walked through the dark forest, and, with great relief, at last managed to step onto the lake's shore without a twisted ankle.

The view opened wide before us with an eerie patch of gray shore. The lake stretched beyond us at either side, with a dark silhouette of a huge boulder rising at our right.

Now I understood the name of the place. "Misty Lake" certainly had what the title advertised. I could hardly discern the other side of the lake. A thick, dense mist weaved through the air above the dark waters like an ethereal blanket of wispy fog.

"Say, what *exactly* are we doing at this lake at this hour?" I asked a girl standing next to me.

Alicia turned to face us. "Oh, you don't know? You're joining in our midnight Sabbath!" she said, with a devious smile that made her face look quite diabolical in the dark. "We are going to dance naked under the moonlight and purify ourselves in the cleansing waters of the lake afterwards. But first you must do the Sabbath blood ritual."

My eyebrows went to my hairline. "D-dance naked? Blood ritual?" I'd thought we were going to sit by the lake and, I don't know, admire the moon, or something. I hadn't signed up for any of this blood ritual crap!

Luna stepped closer and joined in the conversation. "The naked blood ritual is required for new members that are joining our group. That means you two, Joe and Felicia. You're the newbies this year. You must do the ritual before you are accepted as equals into the group."

She had quite the evil expression on her face as well. I wouldn't put it past Luna to do this sort of thing; she was known to dabble in dark, dangerous crafts like this. Everybody was pretty scared of her; I guess now I knew why.

"So, Felicia Collins, are you ready for this?" Luna asked in a chilling voice, her face hidden by the shadows.

The entire group had formed a circle around Felicia and me, shooting us intimidating glares. Felicia looked like she was about to crap in her pants, her eyes fixed on her big sister, pleading for help. Alicia didn't move a finger to come to her sister's aid. She just stood there, arms crossed over her chest and an amused smirk on her glossy lips.

"Miss Collins?" Luna pressed on, her tone cold and uninviting.

Felicia slumped in resignation, her expression tense with fear and humiliation as she prepared to start undressing. I was about to intervene, because I didn't want to be a part of this sick ritual or even witness any of it, but Luna barked an order for her to stop before I could do anything.

"How about you, Joe?" Luna turned to me, her voice slightly more menacing than before.

"Hmm, okay, sorry to rain on your 'Sabbath Parade', dudes, but that's not going to happen." I crossed my arms defiantly. "I'm not getting naked here. What's wrong with you people? And I'm not swimming in that lake, either. It's freezing cold. Are you guys nuts? And I'm *definitely* not doing anything with blood! If this is what it takes to join in, count me out."

There was a ring of dead silence for a few moments before Luna raised her head. I could finally see her expression clearly, fully illuminated by the moonlight.

She had quite a pleased smile on her face.

What?

"And *that,* girls, is how you do it." She gestured to me.

Everybody around us grunted in unison, some huffed disappointedly, others moaned in disbelief.

"Fellow witches, our Gathering group is here to study the hidden secrets of the Moon and the magic within the Mists. That is why it is required we come to the lake shore during the night," she explained, then turned to me and Felicia. "You two can relax now; there's no blood rituals or naked activities required here. That was a little initiation prank we do every time someone new joins the group. You are the first to refuse the offer, Joey, and thus, to pass the test. Congratulations."

"Wait, are you saying everybody here fell for this prank?" Felicia asked, confused. "Even you, Alicia? Did you fall for this, too?"

"Yes. They all have," Luna replied, with an amused grin. "Everybody is so eager to please the group and join in. Everyone here has fallen prey to peer pressure."

Luna turned to us, her face serious now. "There will be times in your lives, girls, where you will need to take a stand, even if the odds are against you. People will do anything to belong; you have to realize that some things aren't worth doing. You must have the courage to stand up for yourself and refuse."

Everybody shuffled their feet, mumbling in quiet agreement.

"I can't believe you fell for it!" Felicia teased her older sister, after everybody had broken the circle and started ambling around the lake shore.

"Shut up! You fell for it too, dumbass!" Alicia hissed in irritation.

I was quite impressed by Luna's first lesson that evening. I had a suspicious inkling that she had already predicted I would react that way. Luna knew I was always ready for a confrontation when faced with something I didn't agree with.

Maybe Luna's Gathering wasn't going to be so bad after all.

Maybe she was going to teach me something interesting here tonight.

Who knew, maybe even practice real magic?

How wrong my assumptions had been. I didn't learn anything practical whatsoever. There was a lot of mumbo jumbo about the moon and the many ways it could affect people's lives, and a bunch of nonsense about visions you could spot within the wisps and twirls of the mists.

As in Celeste's group, there was much ado about nothing and a whole lot of talk. They would chatter endlessly about occult powers that might exist, but in the end, they were all as normal as anyone else in the world. The only significant difference was that these people dressed all in black, with occult symbols printed on their clothing.

This whole experience of the Gathering felt more and more like a bunch of crazy people playing pretend in the middle of the woods. And I felt as clueless and lost about magic as ever.

When Luna asked me to give it a go and try to "seek visions within the mists", I complied, but with some reluctance. I knew I should be more open-minded, and I was trying, but to be completely honest, I couldn't see a damned thing in those mists. Sure, if I squinted hard and stared long enough, I'd see things forming in the fog, like in those mindless games I used to play as a kid, searching for shapes in the clouds. But like in the cloud game, here I saw mostly bunny-shaped things, sometimes a whale floating about . . . nothing worthy of qualifying as "premonitory material".

And it wasn't just me. All the other girls were lying through their teeth, declaring in fake spooky voices (to make it sound more credible) that they could see all sorts of mystical things.

"Come on, Gray! You have to concentrate on the swirls of the mists. Clear your mind and you'll be able to foresee it more clearly," Luna instructed, as we both stood at the edge of the lake, on the shoreline, the cold waters of the lake licking at our feet.

"I'm sorry, Luna, but I can't see a damned thing!" I huffed in frustration. "None of the other girls can, either, you know. They are all lying to you."

"Really? You can see with your . . . *you know*?" she asked, tapping her temple to signal my empathy-sight.

I nodded and kicked a small pebble into the lake. "Yeah. Except that Filipino girl over there. She seems like she really believes she's seeing stuff. But the rest of them, bunch of liars, the whole lot!"

"All right." Luna seemed to be mulling something over, and then she turned round to face the group that was chatting distractedly a few feet behind us. "Mayumi, darling, could you come over and give it a try now?" She motioned for the Filipino girl to approach us.

The girl stopped at Luna's side and stared into the lake. "Hmm, I'm n-not sure if I can see anything, Miss Harker."

"Well, it's a lot like meditating, you know. Empty your mind of any thoughts, don't think about having to see anything, just project your mind into the mists."

The girl squinted into the distance, and Luna was quick to correct her again. "Don't force it. You don't have to strain your eyes; you have to glaze over the mist, as if you are daydreaming."

The second time, the girl's eyes did glaze and lose focus. When she spoke again, her voice had a different tone to it. "I see . . . dark hands breaking through the water, reaching for something, trying to grab it, and . . . the lake is boiling. I see fire breaking through the water, reaching into the air." She blinked and her eyes unglazed, returning to normal.

"That was excellent, Mayumi. Well done!" Luna praised. "We will learn how to interpret those visions another night, but you did great."

The girl blushed and shyly tucked her hands behind her back.

"Now, for the rest of the group, I must say tonight's Gathering is over." Luna turned and stalked towards the Glitter Coven. "I have an *intuition* telling me that you haven't been honest with me." Her piercing, dark gaze swept over the girls, who glanced guiltily away. "I think maybe some of you may be pretending to see things in the mists that aren't really there," she stated disapprovingly. "And if that is truly the case, what a shame. What do you honestly have to learn by lying to me? I can't help you if you lie, and you can't share anything with your colleagues if you don't know anything.

"This is truly a waste of my time. Of everybody's time! We're leaving, and I suggest you *all* think long and hard about what you're doing. I hope tomorrow you all come back with a new attitude, or there won't be any more meetings with me. We're heading back to the main house now. Keep up and stay close to me." She stalked off without waiting for any reply.

Everybody hurried to follow Luna, except Mayumi, who lingered behind and tugged at my shirt to get my attention. "Hey, hmm, can I have a word with you?"

"Sure, what's up, Mayumi?" I asked, eyeing the group who started stumbling ahead up the dark trail.

"W-well, I-I wanted to thank you for what you did for me."

I turned to face her. "Me? What did I do?"

"I mean, I overheard you telling Luna about me; then she called me over and she even congratulated me! Thank you so much for helping me."

"You don't have to thank me. I didn't tell Luna to congratulate you. The merit is all yours."

"No, you don't understand. She never would've called me if it weren't for you telling. I'm so happy she gave me a chance. And it's all thanks to you."

"I'm glad, Mayumi, but I really didn't do anything. Why didn't you volunteer anyway, if you wanted a chance so much? I'm sure Luna would have let you try, if you'd asked."

"O-oh, I don't know . . . Alicia would have said I was a show-off, and I-I didn't want her picking on me and making fun if I wasn't any good at it," she mumbled.

"Mayumi, you'll never achieve anything if you let stupid people prevent you from trying out new things. Tell Alicia to go get a life and to stop bugging you!"

"O-okay." She nodded and ventured to offer a small smile.

I smiled back, and when we both turned to follow the rest of the group, we realized they had all gone.

We had been left behind, alone, in the darkness.

Chapter Eight

Lost in the Woods

"I can't believe it. Seriously, they were right ahead of us, how could we have missed them?" I complained to a trembling Mayumi, as we both stumbled blindly up the trail. I wasn't going to point out that she was the one responsible for holding us back and separating us from the group. She was terrified enough as it was; I didn't need to make her feel worse about it.

But I had to admit that my grumpiness was mostly to cover my fear. I was scared, too. Walking in a dark forest was pretty terrifying; everything crackled and rustled around us, and it was so dark, we couldn't see a thing in front of our eyes.

I tried to fake confidence while we walked through the woods. If Mayumi realized that I had no sense of direction whatsoever to guide us back, she was going to have a major panic attack, and what good that would do us?

"M-maybe we should stay put. D-do y-you think they will come back for u-us, eventually?" she squeaked in fright.

"Of course. Luna will notice we're not with the group and she'll track back to find us. But we won't even need that. We can find our way back by ourselves, right? We just need to keep following the trail. Lizzie told me that all roads in this camp lead to the main house: we can't miss it!" I tried to sound reassuring.

"B-but how do you know we're even *on* a proper trail? It's so dark! I can't see anything." Her voice threatened to break at any second.

"Come on, man! Please don't cry," I pleaded.

She sobbed in reply, and I turned to look at her, which momentarily made me lose focus on the path. I hit a big dry log, tripped and fell down hard.

"Mother fuc—" I bit back a curse and rubbed my shin, staring vindictively at the log. The palms of my hands stung from scratches and cuts as I'd tried to break my fall.

Funny thing was, I didn't remember passing by any dry logs on our way down to the lake . . . which meant we probably weren't on the trail any more. I also wasn't sure whether we should really be walking uphill right now. Wasn't this supposed to be a level terrain? It sure had been when we'd first walked to the lake . . . which was maybe indication enough that we were heading in the wrong direction.

We were very lost.

"W-what is it? Are you hurt? Did you break anything?" Mayumi had scrambled down and squashed herself next to me, patting at my legs to check for injuries.

"Hey, stop it! I'm fine!" I pulled her hands away.

"Are you bleeding? I don't know any medical emergency procedures! You are going to die and leave me all alone in this awful forest, aren't you?" She was a second away from losing her marbles, I could tell.

"Hey, no one is bleeding, here! It was just a light bump on the shin, hardly a scratch. You gotta chill, dude. Stop panicking, it doesn't help anything." I scowled, and the order seemed to make her pull herself together.

"I'm sor—"

"Listen!" I cut in sharply. "Can you hear that? It's voices! There are people talking nearby." I pulled myself up and squinted into the darkness, trying to locate the direction of the sounds. "Look! There! Flashlights, can you see?" I exclaimed.

We were running towards the light as fast as the forest allowed us, when we bumped into three very startled boys.

"Simon! Thank God!" I exclaimed, and tackled him in a hug of relief. "I'm so happy to bump into you guys!"

"We're saved! We're not going to die in this forest any more!" Mayumi shouted in joy, also hugging one of the boys.

"W-what are you doing here? Aren't you supposed to be by the lake?" the boy being hugged by Mayumi asked in alarm.

"Yeah, we were coming back from there and kinda got lost . . ." I started to say, when I caught the guilty glint in all their eyes. "What are *you guys* doing here?"

"Nothing!" one of them blurted out in panic. I grabbed the flashlight from his hand and pointed the beam at his face so as to get a better look at him. His eyes were filled with shame and guilt – a dead giveaway of whatever devious plan they'd had for tonight.

"Liar, liar," I murmured, my eyes locked on his.

"Oh, shit! That's that Joe girl with the empathy-sight, isn't it? She can read our thoughts." He looked frantically to Simon, pleading for help.

"L-look, girls, it's not what you think!" the other friend intervened.

I played up my act of mindreader. I couldn't really read people's thoughts, but I could get a good read of their strongest upfront emotion. I knew with absolute certainty that shame was the most fervent feeling, so I picked that one first.

"I see." I tossed the bait. "You should all be ashamed of yourselves."

"N-no! I swear we weren't going to spy on you girls. We didn't even know you were swimming naked by the lake!" he blurted out in complete panic, just as I had expected.

So that was what they were up to: sneaking around in the middle of the night to check out the naked girls by the lake. Typical.

"Shut up!" Simon hissed.

"I can't believe you guys," I told them, shaking my head disapprovingly. "Was this your idea, Simon?"

"Of course not! I only wanted to see what magic Luna Harker was dealing with. She's quite famous for her dark rituals. I wanted to check that out," he said in a reproachful tone. "I talked to that Alicia girl this afternoon, and she told me if I wanted to see what their Gathering was like, first I would have to participate in an initiation hazing. I was planning to skip that and spy on the activities from a distance."

I pointed the flashlight at his face and watched him squirm under my scrutiny. "Well, maybe you should have been more brave and come along for the initiation, Simon. Sometimes, you can't skip the bad parts and go straight for the good, you know," I countered.

"I'm not a coward!"

"I didn't say you were. Those are your words, not mine." *Eye roll to that.* "So, tell me, this plan of yours was only for study purposes? The part where you get to see naked girls is just an occupational hazard, is it?"

He at least had the decency to blush at that. I shook my head again.

"Who cares, anyway?" Mayumi cut in. "There weren't any naked activities to spy on! The peeping Toms here would just have seen us standing by the lake, looking into the mists, that's all. It's no big deal. I'm glad they're here! Who knows what sorts of dangerous animals we could have bumped into in these woods? We could have been eaten by wolves, if these guys hadn't shown up."

"W-wolves?" one of the boys stammered, looking around in alarm. "Nobody said anything about wolves! There are wolves here?"

"I'm sure there are bound to be one or two ambling around," Mayumi mused.

"Don't be stupid. There are no wolves here," Simon snapped.

Then, as if on cue, we heard some suspicious shuffling and crackling of twigs nearby.

"What was *that?*" Mayumi squeaked.

"That was nothing. The forest makes all kinds of rustling sounds. It's just the leaves rustling in the wind," I rationalized; everybody had decided to act like scared fools, all of a sudden.

"N-no, that was definitely something. I-I think I really saw something moving back there . . ." the boy murmured, squinting through the dark.

"Stop being idiots! It's just shadows playing tricks on

your eyes," Simon said, but his voice didn't sound so sure any more, as he glanced around, looking for possible threats. A series of sharp snaps broke close by, right behind some trees. I could even detect a faint hint of an animal growl.

"I saw its eyes! Glinting in the dark. I saw it! I told you there were wolves here!" Mayumi cried out and grabbed my arm in fright.

"Guys, come on! This is nothing, seriously. I'm sure if there were wild animals in this area, Craig would have told us when we arrived," I tried reasoning again. "He would certainly have warned us about any wolves."

"Who the hell is Craig?" Simon asked, still looking over his shoulder in alarm.

"The camp caretaker, Craig. The guy in the cabin at the first gate, with the safari clothes, the round glasses and bushy moustache," I said.

"I don't remember him," Simon said.

"Well, Craig didn't say anything about dangerous animals roaming the camp." I tried to reassure them, but the growl that followed my statement wasn't as soft or subtle this time around. No way could trees or the wind make that kind of sound.

There was definitely something out there.

It was out to get us.

And it was getting closer.

Chapter Nine
The Last Breath

The moment the second growl came, Mayumi, having already lost every shred of self-control, took off running like a deranged lunatic, flailing her arms in the air and screaming at the top of her lungs. Simon's friends didn't take long to follow her lead and also scrambled through the forest in panic, each one running in a different direction.

"Oh, fucking hell!" I groaned, trying to decide which way to go and who to run after.

Simon stood in a semi-crouched position, wracked with indecision as well.

"Come on, we need to get Mayumi back first!" I quickly made the choice. "She will kill herself out here alone!"

He nodded and darted in the direction where he had seen her disappear. I followed him, thankful that I still had his friend's flashlight in my hands.

Whatever the growling thing was, it had evidently now decided that Simon and I were its next meal and was chasing after us. I could hear it running and snapping its teeth right behind us.

"Run! It's following us!" I shouted, and sped after Simon, vaulting over dark bushes and rocks, trying to avoid hitting the small tree branches, which left stinging slashes all over my face. The growling faded gradually into the background. "Simon! Wait!" I tried to make him slow down so we could get our bearings. We were running blindly in the forest and I could still feel us moving on an incline. That surely meant we were heading further and further away from the main house.

"I saw her running past that tree. She must be right over there!" Simon shouted, grabbing my hand and forcing me onwards.

"Hey, Simon, hold on." I tried to make him stop again. Running blindly was a dangerous thing to do, but I didn't have the chance to explain why that was, because what I feared suddenly happened.

Simon slipped and fell into a ravine that had opened abruptly on the ground in front of us. He plunged down the slope, pulling me along with him. The hill became steeper to the point where we no longer had any chance of breaking our fall.

We were like two rag dolls falling. I couldn't even feel the ground underneath me as we slid past a precipice and into the dark waters of the lake below. The plunge into the cold water knocked all the air from my lungs. It hit me like a punch in the chest, burning and stinging all the places where I had scratched myself in the forest.

I pushed with my arms and legs, propelling myself quickly upwards. I spluttered as I broke the surface of the lake, and looked around, trying to find Simon. He burst through the water a second later, splashing around in complete panic. He looked frantic, trying to understand what the hell had just happened.

"We fell down a slope and into the lake," I gasped. Hot puffs of air shot from our mouths as we tried to catch our breath.

The hulking frame of the boulder from where we had fallen loomed right above us. Climbing back up was going to be impossible. Especially in the dark, with only our bare hands to grip with, and our clothes completely drenched.

"Oh, no, no, no . . ." I heard Simon mumbling to himself.

"Simon, are you okay?"

"NO. No, this can't be happening," he mumbled to himself, clearly still in a panic.

"Calm down. Are you hurt?" I asked, but he was so scared, he wasn't listening. "Simon. Are you all right?" I swam closer to get a better look at him.

"I can't be in the water! I can't be in here!"

"What are you talking about?"

"It's the curse! I can't! I'm cursed! It's coming to get me!" He was looking at the water as if some monster was going to appear at any second. "I can't be in water! My brother did this to me. He cursed me! If I'm in the water, something will come and get me!" he cried out. "It's happened before. I swear to you! Please, please, help me! Get me out of here," he begged, scared out of his mind, thrashing about in the water. His dark hair was plastered over his face and his voice was breaking.

"Listen, you need to calm down," I said slowly, treading water. "There's no such thing as curses, Simon." I paused uncertainly: I had faced so many strange things in my life that there was every possibility that curses did exist. "But even if there *is*," I corrected quickly, "nothing is going to get you, all right? I'm here with you. I'm not letting anything get you."

"Y-you don't understand. This is real! I'm not making this up . . . Please, you gotta believe me. I'm not crazy!" he pleaded with a desperate sob, struggling to keep afloat in all his panic.

"I believe you, okay? But we need to get out of this lake, then, as fast as we can. If I'm not mistaken, the shore should be to our left. I remember seeing this rock formation when I was standing on the shoreline with Luna. We need to swim in that direction." I pointed through the mist.

"H-how d-do you know it's the right way? I can't see anything in this fog!"

"It's that way. Trust me," I told him with the most assertiveness I could muster, and prayed that, this time, just this one time, I could give the right directions. "Come on, let's go. Swim with me, okay?"

We swam as fast as our drenched clothes allowed us. My soaked jeans and shoes were heavier in the water, and it was a struggle to move with all the extra weight. I was now glad that I had forgotten my jacket; it would have dragged me down if I'd been wearing it.

After a few minutes struggling through the cold waters, the mists gave us a break and swiftly dispersed, opening a clear path that showed us the way.

"There! See, it's the lake's shore, I told you I was right!" I cheered victoriously. It was only a few meters away, but I couldn't brag for long because Simon, who had been slightly ahead of me, turned around, his face suddenly a mask of complete horror.

"There's s-something in the water," he whispered, his teeth chattering with the cold. "I f-felt s-something brushing my leg. T-there's something here with us."

I looked worriedly around, trying to peek into the water, but it was too damned dark to see anything. "It's probably a fish, Simon. Lakes have fishes, right?" I tried to reason, but my voice faltered and then I too felt something brushing up against my leg.

Simon was having a full-on panic attack now, splashing around and looking desperately into the water. "It's here! I'm not crazy, it's down there!" he cried out.

"Simon, calm down, it's noth—" I didn't get the chance to finish the sentence before something grabbed Simon and pulled him down.

I didn't think. I reacted immediately and dived after him, pushing my hands in wide arcs through the dark waters until I found him. I grabbed his hand and gave it a hard tug to pull us both back to the surface. As we surfaced, he sputtered and coughed out water.

"What the hell happened, Simon?" I asked, alarmed.

"I t-told you . . . I'm c-cursed! It's coming to get me, drag me down and drown me!"

"Come on, let's go!" I ordered, taking his warning very seriously now. "The shore is right there. We can make it! Swim fast, Simon!"

He didn't need to be told twice and darted forward, splashing furiously in the direction of the shore, as I followed suit. He'd only managed a few strokes ahead when something pulled him down again. I dived after him. As soon as my hands found his, he latched on to me desperately, but the thing holding him wouldn't let him go. I pushed a little deeper into the water and caught a glimpse of the thing: it had a human-shaped silhouette, but its eyes glowed ominously in the dark waters.

That thing clearly wasn't human.

And whatever it was, it was looking right at me.

Goosebumps coursed through my whole body, the water becoming considerably colder. I kicked the thing's arm a couple times before it finally released its grip on Simon, letting us propel ourselves towards the surface again.

As soon our heads were out of the water, I shouted to Simon, "Swim! Go!"

The panic-induced adrenaline kicked into his system, making him shoot towards the shore as fast as a bullet. The shoreline was almost within reach. Only a few meters more and we'd be out of the water and out of danger.

But the thought had crossed my mind too soon. I felt the hard grip of the creature as it grasped firmly on to me. As its fingers constricted around my ankle, digging in the fabric of my jeans, I gasped loudly.

"Simon!" I called out for help. He was so terrified that he had swum faster and was considerably closer to the shore. "Help!" I cried out again, choking in my struggle. My head submerged for a desperate moment, but I thrashed fiercely and managed to pull myself back up again. "Simon!" I called out one more time, and managed to stay afloat for a few more fleeting seconds – enough for me to see Simon standing on the shore, water splashing at his shins, as he watched me, paralyzed, his eyes wide and his body frozen in terror.

"Help me!" I shouted, and for a moment it seemed he was about to take a step back into the water, but then he stopped and remained where he was, unmoving, his arms hanging limply at his sides. I realized I was unable to do

anything more than watch as Simon took a small step back, away from the shoreline, and as I felt another tug at my ankle, stronger this time, pulling me down with a greater force, the water engulfed me again. I realized that he wasn't going to come for me. He wasn't going to help me.

The coward was going to let me drown in his place.

I kicked and thrashed in the water, trying to free myself, but the thing had an iron grip and kept pulling me down towards the dark depths of the lake. I struggled, stretching a hand up, trying to reach the surface where the moonlight shimmered, and I watched helplessly as bubbles of air escaped my mouth and floated up as if in slow motion.

All I could think of in that moment was Simon's image, standing on the shore: the resigned look on his face as he backed away. All I could think of was how much of a coward he was. I felt betrayed.

And with that thought came anger, filling the whole of me and igniting a scorching trail through my veins. It spread like wildfire with each violent thump of my frantic heart. It was pure rage, bursting through my body.

I remembered this feeling. I remembered it happening before, when I had been taken by Vigil's powers. I remembered how the anger had taken over me until there was no space left for it, and it could only burst out of me in a fiery explosion of rage. Then, the flames had reached as high as the sky. I remembered rattling chains, snarls full of violence, a burning desert and fire. So much fire.

Let it burn.

I didn't feel cold any more. The water was bubbling all around me, as if it was boiling. I closed my eyes and let all my anger out. This thing holding me, dragging me to the lake floor, needed to stop.

Let it burn, something whispered in my head.

I unleashed all the fire and rage I felt inside. No flames could burst out of me because I was under water, but nonetheless, the scorching heat I released burned everything in its way all the same.

The creature – whatever it was – was no longer holding me: it was no more. I watched as it screeched a last agonized breath and melted away, dissolving quickly into the black, boiling water.

I swam upwards sluggishly until I reached the surface. My clothes felt too heavy, as if they were made of lead. A thin spray of water was falling on the top of my head, like I had just caught the end of an explosion, and smoke billowed inside a ring of fire all around me, burning at the surface of the lake. I glanced to where Simon stood. If it was possible, his eyes were wider and more scared than before.

I tried to call for help again, but I kept swallowing water and coughing up too much to be able to talk. I swam slowly out of the smoking ring of fire, knowing from past experience that the fire I created couldn't burn me, but I was too exhausted and swimming was becoming extremely hard for me.

I had spent too much energy burning through water, and now I only had a wisp of it left to swim back. The last remaining meters to the shore were an agonizing torture.

I was weak, but I thought I could make it. I needed to focus. But then I saw Tristan bursting from the depths of the forest to the shore so fast I could barely recognize him. He halted next to Simon, who pointed a shaking finger in my direction, and then took off again, running towards the water.

He dived in like a professional lifeguard, and I sighed in relief. I only needed to hang on for a few more seconds and I would be safe; only a few more seconds, and he would reach me. A small wave rolled over me and my head was momentarily submerged. I was so tired; all I wanted to do was close my eyes and go to sleep, but I knew I had to keep fighting for a few more seconds. I gave one more push with my legs and my head was out of the water in time for Tristan's arm to snake under my arms, pulling me up against him.

"Joey! Thank God!" he called out in worry. "Your head disappeared for a second and I almost couldn't see you! Are you okay?" He pulled me closer, making sure my mouth and nose were always clear to breathe.

I didn't have the strength to reply, so I just nodded, spluttering when another small wave hit us. He pulled me along with him, swimming quickly to the shore, and only when we were finally out of that damned lake did I notice Luna standing next to Simon. She also looked worried as she and Simon watched Tristan carrying my limp body in his arms.

"Is she okay?" Simon asked, his face pale and still full of fear.

Tristan halted abruptly, maneuvering me out of Simon's reach. "You stay the fuck away from her," he barked at Simon. "She was right there in front of you, and you did *nothing*. You left her behind. You were going to let her drown, you damned bastard! Don't you fucking dare even look at her now!"

Tristan never cursed. He was always very strict about it. He'd definitely lost his cool and looked mighty angry.

Simon staggered back, frightened by Tristan's rage,

while Luna stepped between them to prevent a fight from breaking out. Not that a fight could happen, since Tristan was still holding me.

"Tris . . . stop." I tugged weakly at his drenched shirt, trying to get his attention.

I wanted to tell him to let it go, to leave Simon alone. It was probably for the best that the boy had left me behind. If he had been with me when I'd flared up, he would've been boiled alive in the water, along with that creature.

"Tris . . ." I wanted to tell Tristan I was tired because I had used too much magic. I was going to be all right; I just needed some rest. I wanted to tell him to take me back to our cabin and as far away from the lake as possible, and to hold me in his arms until I was okay again.

But I didn't get the chance to say any of those things, as I had already slipped into unconsciousness.

Chapter Ten
An Epic Win

I heard voices talking nearby.

"Luna said there was a girl's vision in her Gathering, but she had no idea it was something about to happen."

I recognized Celeste's voice, and stirred.

"The girl saw hands grabbing in the lake, and something about fire . . ."

I blinked sleepily, opening my eyes to see a room full of worried faces.

Josh, Sammy and Seth were sitting in chairs next to me, and Tristan and Celeste were standing close by, talking to each other. I was lying with my head in Harry's lap, but it was Sammy who first noticed I was waking up.

"Hey, guys, she's awake!" he announced. "Joey, are you okay?"

Rocko jumped up and down on the couch, trying to get a good lick at my face.

"Rocko! No! Down, boy!" Sammy chastised, but the dog continued his excited attempt to slobber all over me.

I stared groggily at Harry's face above me, his eyes

glinting with worry. "Uh, I think Harry's the winner, then," I murmured in a slurred voice. The boys looked at me as if I had gone bonkers in the head. "Your wager, remember, guys? Harry's bet was on trouble happening on day one." I swayed slightly as I sat up on what turned out to be the living-room couch. My clothes were still soaked from the lake, and my hair was dripping wet. "Guess he won, then. Congrats, Harry."

Harry's deep frown softened, and he smiled at my joke. "I told you guys she was just sleeping. Pretty heavy sleep, but look, she's fine now." He exhaled in relief and handed me a towel that was beside him so I could dry myself, now mostly from Rocko's slobber.

Tristan, who had been standing with Celeste, was by my side in a second. "Rocko. Down. *Now!*" he ordered firmly, and the dog scurried off the couch, moving aside for Tristan, much to Sammy's chagrin. Rocko obeyed Tristan's every command, even though he wasn't his owner.

"How are you feeling?" Tristan asked, and cupped my face carefully, looking worried. "You have scratches all over you. You blacked out after I got you out of the lake, but you didn't seem hurt, so we brought you back here. I was about to call for help . . ."

"I'm okay. A little worse for wear, but okay. I think I passed out from exhaustion. I'm just tired, not hurt." I leaned in and gave him a tight hug. "Thanks for saving me. How did you even know I was in trouble?"

"You're not gonna believe it, Joey!" Seth jumped into the conversation while Tristan placed another towel around my shoulders, and I scratched Rocko behind his ears, making him waggle his tail in response. "We were all in our cabin, talking about some ideas for the new single and waiting for you to get back from your class, when Tristan stood up, like he'd been struck by lightning, saying something was wrong with you. I didn't know you guys could do this telepathic trick! It was so cool! And then he freaked the hell out and darted outside, heading to the main house to find out what had happened to you, so we all followed him."

"Really? You sensed something was wrong with me?" I asked, more than a little impressed and very surprised.

Tristan shrugged awkwardly. "I don't know how to explain it. I just knew something was wrong. I wasn't hearing you in my head, or anything like that. It was more like a gut instinct. I kept having this feeling of danger and that it was somehow connected to you. When we reached the main house, we found Luna at the front doors all upset, arguing with a group of people about the fact you and someone else had been left behind, and that's when a skinny girl showed up, running and crying for help."

"That must have been Mayumi." I hazarded a guess.

"Yes, it was her," Celeste chipped in, adding her part to the story. "I'd been called down to the lobby by Luna when she realized you two had gotten lost in the woods. I arrived just in time to hear Mayumi crying in hysterics at the front doors, talking nonsense about wolves chasing her."

"There are wolves in this place?" Seth asked, looking alarmed.

"No, of course not! We would never hold a Gathering in a place crawling with wolves, for crying out loud!"

"I don't know about that, Celeste. There was definitely some kind of wild animal chasing after us. I didn't see it, but I heard it, loud and clear."

"Okay, that's final. No one is leaving these cabins any more!" Seth stated. "And you wanted me to go for a walk outside today." He harrumphed at Josh in indignation.

"But how did you know where to find me?" I asked.

"As soon as that Mayumi girl finished telling us what had happened in the forest, Tristan's eyes glazed over for a second and then he said, 'The lake,'" Celeste explained. "Luna offered to go, because she knows her way around the woods better than anyone, and Tristan went after her."

"Luna ordered everybody to stay put at the main house, because she didn't want any more people getting lost, but Tristan didn't listen. I don't think anyone could have stopped him from going after you," Seth mused.

"Well, I'm glad Craig showed up after Luna and Tristan left, and helped me calm everyone down in the lobby. Is it really true there was something in the lake, Joey?" Celeste asked, her tone suddenly urgent. "Simon said there was some creature in the water trying to drown you."

"Yeah, there was something, for sure . . . I don't know what it was, but it was definitely there." I pulled up the hem of my jeans to show some bluish finger marks on my ankle.

"There are deadly things in the lake, too?" Seth squeaked, getting more freaked out. "Well, I guess that's another place we won't be going any more, pals. You can most definitely cut the forest *and* the lake from your sightseeing list."

"I've never seen a boy so terrified in my life as Simon was, when they brought him back," Celeste told me, her voice full of sympathy.

"I don't care if he was bloody terrified or not! He left her alone with a creature to drown in that lake!" Tristan snapped.

"I know what Simon did wasn't very heroic, but—" Celeste began.

"'Very heroic'? You gotta be kidding me, right? The guy is an utter bastard! And a bloody coward, too! You don't leave people behind like that, no matter how scared you are!"

"Tristan, I'm not saying what he did was right. You have every reason to be upset. But you have to understand that the boy was scared witless, there. Not everybody is cut out to be a hero," she reasoned. "He panicked. He's very ashamed of his actions; he couldn't even look me in the eye when he was telling me the story. I'm sure he profoundly regrets what he's done. Joey is the one harmed, here, and she doesn't seem so angry about it. I'm sure you'll be gracious enough to forgive him for his lack of bravery."

Tristan grumbled under his breath, but relented. "Fine. But if I ever see him again, he'll get a good earful from me."

Celeste nodded in agreement. We all knew how soul-crushing Tristan's moral lectures could be. "Well, I'm sure we can talk more about what happened tomorrow, after Joey has had a good night's rest. She looks very tired," she said. "I'll see you tomorrow morning, then, okay, Joey?"

"Yeah, sure," I agreed. I needed time to think before Celeste started asking more questions. I didn't know how much of the story Simon had already let out. I had a gut instinct to keep quiet about my fire-casting ability. First I had to talk to Simon before I decided what, and what not, to reveal.

"I'll go talk to Luna now. Maybe we'll go back to check

the lake and see if there are any clues to this mystery attack. Good night to you all." Celeste bade everybody farewell and left quickly.

"Okay. Now, boys, I have something very important to tell you," I said. "You're not going to like hearing this, Harry, but I have to be fair." The boys huddled closer, ready to listen to what I had to say. Even Rocko had stopped to stare at me, his ears perking up to listen. "I think Josh has actually won your bet," I stated, "because Luna's class went beyond midnight, you see? The whole trouble actually began when the class was over, and technically that makes it day two, right? So congratulations, Joshie. You're the winner." I gave them all a cheeky smile.

"Aaaw, man!" Harry whined, while the rest laughed along with me.

"Yes! The victory is all mine! In your face, bass boy!" Josh boasted. "Oh, boy, that's what I like to call an epic win!"

"Okay," Tristan said with a smile, shaking his head at all our silliness. "This is all very funny, but let's leave Joey to rest now, guys," he ordered firmly.

The boys each came to give me a goodnight hug and kiss before they left Tristan and me alone.

"Okay, now spill. What really happened out at the lake?" Tristan could always tell if I was hiding something.

"You don't have to worry about the creature. Whatever it was, it's been obliterated to ashes," I told him. "The lake is pretty safe now. I'm not so sure about the forest, though. That wolf could still be out there. But Celeste is right about cutting Simon some slack, you know."

Tristan scrunched up his nose, making a face at me.

"Hey, I'm not saying I love the guy for what he did, but in the end I think that staying away was the best thing for everyone, Tris. If he had come back in to help me, we would both have been drowned. Either I wouldn't have been able to blast the thing up, or Simon would have ended up fried, too. Plus, I was so pissed at him for being such a cowardly douche bag, that if he'd come in to save me, I don't think I would have had the fuel needed to fire me up. I toasted that fucker, whatever it was, because of Simon. So, in a strange way, he kinda helped me."

"Okay, I understand," Tristan grumbled half-heartedly. "But don't expect me to go thank him for what he did. That's pushing your luck."

I laughed at his disgruntled, adorable face. "There's no need to thank him. But don't go scolding him endlessly about this, either, okay? Just leave him be."

"Okay. As for you, missy," he said leaning down and taking me in his arms, "let's take these wet clothes off you and get you into bed."

I quirked an eyebrow and hooked my arm around his neck. His drenched white shirt had gone see-through, and the fabric was clinging to all the chiseled muscles of his chest. There were a lot of muscles to see there.

"So you can rest, Joey," he added, with a knowing look, amused that I could even be considering doing anything else at the moment.

"Right. I knew that." I tried to play it cool and snuggled my face into his neck to hide my blushing cheeks.

"I think you've had enough excitement for one day, sweetheart. As great as . . . other stuff . . . would be, you look like you're going to fall asleep any second," he said, carrying me carefully to bed and kissing me lightly on the

lips. "We still have a lot of time to catch up on our interrupted honeymoon. But for now we're going to get some
rest. I have a feeling tomorrow is going to be another day
full of surprises."

Chapter Eleven
Returning Favors

I woke up to the sound of arguing coming from the direction of the front door. I recognized Tristan's angry voice immediately, but it was only after I heard what he was saying that I recognized whom he was talking to.

"You have some nerve showing your face around here, you know?" Tristan snapped.

"I-I understand you're mad, but I only want to talk to her, and . . . I should apologize." Simon's tone was cautious, almost afraid.

I scrambled out of bed, grabbed a robe and headed quickly through the cabin to the front door, before Tristan had a chance to do something he would regret. He never resorted to violence if he could discuss a problem, but I knew that edge in his voice. He was a second away from losing his temper.

"You 'should' apologize? It's a little too late for apologies, pal. You *should* have dragged your skinny ass back into that lake last night, and helped her. That's what you *should* have done."

"Well, hello," I interrupted, maneuvering myself between Tristan and Simon. "Why are you here, Blaine? Has something happened at the main house?"

Simon took a nervous step back and glanced from Tristan to me, choosing his next words carefully because of Tristan's warning glare. There were dark rings under his eyes and weariness behind his gaze. The over-confidence he'd previously exuded was no longer there.

"H-hello. G-good morning," he stammered cautiously. "How a-are you?"

"I'm okay, Simon."

"No thanks to you . . ." Tristan muttered. I elbowed him in the ribs to shut him up.

Simon pretended he hadn't heard Tristan's jibe and continued, "I'm very sorry for disturbing you this early, but Miss Harker said she urgently needs to talk to the both of us about yesterday, so I offered to come and get you. I-I was wondering if maybe I could have a word with you before we talk to Celeste?" he asked politely. "We can talk while we walk to the main house."

"Sure, no problem," I agreed promptly. I also wanted to have a few private words with Simon before we talked to anyone else.

"You're not going anywhere alone with *that* guy," Tristan protested.

I forced a smile and said to Simon, "Excuse us for a sec. I'll go throw on some clothes and be right back, if you could just wait outside for a little bit." I grabbed Tristan by the arm and pulled him firmly back inside with me, shutting the door in Simon's face.

"Tristan," I hissed quietly, so Simon wouldn't hear us. "First, you don't need to worry about me being alone with

Blaine. His problem is that he *doesn't* do things, not the other way around. Second, I thought we'd agreed that you weren't going to give him a hard time about what happened last night. We've talked about this, Tris: stop blaming him! It was best for everyone that he stayed out of it, you know that." I headed for the bedroom and grabbed some clothes.

"Now, listen, this is actually just what we need." While I started to dress, Tristan stood in the doorway, his arms crossed over his bare chest and a stubborn frown on his face. "I have to talk to Simon and find out how much he saw, especially what he *thinks* he saw. The last thing we need right now is people gossiping about my volatile situation, okay? Believe me, if rumor gets out, it will spread like wildfire – pun intended. Witches gossip so much, you have no idea. We can't let this happen. So I *need* to talk to him, all right? Now, you go ahead and take your shower while I talk to Simon, and when you're ready, come down to the main house and we'll have breakfast together, yeah?"

I didn't wait for a reply and was already walking out of the bedroom, through the living room and out of the front door, before Tristan could stop me.

"Okay, sorry for keep you waiting, Simon, I'm ready to go," I announced to a startled Blaine, who was leaning over a tree trunk a few feet away from the cabin.

"N-no, it's fine. That was really fast," he said, avoiding eye contact. "Your boyfriend is very intimidating. I thought he was going to punch me, for sure."

"He's not my boyfriend, he's my husband. I'm Joe Halloway now, remember? Sorry about that, though. You have to excuse Tristan. He can be a tad overprotective, sometimes."

"No, that's okay. I get it. I would probably be the same

if I were in his place," he mumbled, his eyes glued to the ground. It was just like Celeste had said. He was so ashamed he couldn't even look me in the eye.

"How are you, Simon?" I asked, glancing at him. "You don't look so good."

"I-I'm fine. Didn't sleep much last night, is all."

He looked like he'd been through hell and back, by the size of the dark bags under his eyes and the weariness in his voice. If I'd still had a smidgen of resentment about what had happened last night, it was now replaced by pity.

"Shouldn't we be worried to be walking this trail with a supposed wolf running lose?" I glanced around, feeling anxious.

"Miss Harker has already notified that Craig guy. He's been doing the rounds since last night. Anyway, he told us wild animals tend to avoid spots where there are too many people. I think we're safe if we stick to this road."

"So, tell me, what can I do for you?" I asked as we walked.

"Oh, first I-I want to apologize . . . you know, for yesterday," he began, clearly very uncomfortable with the topic. "I know what you must be thinking of me, b-but . . . I want to explain why I didn't do anything. I mean, I *wanted* to. I would have helped you, if it hadn't been for my curse."

"What's this curse about, Blaine? I thought you were just messing with me, but that was seriously scary!"

"No, it's not a joke! The curse is very real – you saw for yourself! Do you remember when I told you about my brother, Cillian, who's in the Top League? Well, he's there because of the things he can do. He can, well, he can curse people."

"Seriously?"

"Yeah, I swear. The first time it happened, we were just kids. I was seven, he was ten, and we were by the pool. He had messed up one of my favorite toys, so, as payback, I decided to embarrass him in front of a girl he liked. He was so mad at me – he really liked that girl, and I'd ruined his chances – so he shoved me into the pool, because he knew I was scared of water. He shouted that he wished there really was a monster in there, and that it would grab me and drag me down to the bottom, forever. He wanted to make me cry. You know how it is, the things kids say when they're mad at each other," he said, playing his fingers nervously over his blue-tipped fringe.

"But then something really did grab me and pull me down, just like it did last night. I almost drowned. That was when I discovered what my brother could do: he could curse people and make the curse come true. We received a visit from the Top League soon afterwards. They took him away to figure out what exactly were his powers and what was the range of his ability. They said they were taking him to tutor him and help him hone his powers, but I don't know what really goes on in that place …"

"I've heard rumors that he has a different ability," I countered.

"About how he puts fear into your head, you mean? Yeah, at first the Top League said Cillian's ability was about that, but how can you explain the thing grabbing me in the pool? They said it was only in my mind, it wasn't real, but then how do you explain the bruises it left on my leg? And then it happened again and Cillian wasn't even there.

"It took me a couple of years to gather up enough courage

to risk going into the water again. It was a river close to a friend's cottage; we had gone there for the holidays. It happened again. Something almost drowned me in that river, and I knew then that this curse was really real, and it was still active. I've never gone back into the water again – no pools, no sea, no lakes. I stay away because I know what will happen. I'm not sure if this curse can be lifted.

"And if it was really some stupid fear Cillian had put inside my head, it wouldn't had affected you. But that thing in the lake, it went after you too! You know I'm not imagining this, right? It was real!"

"Yeah, it was," I agreed, the image of glowing eyes in the water flashing vividly in my head. Simon wasn't imagining things, which meant this curse was really real.

By the time he'd finished his story, he had both hands deep in his pockets and a miserable look on his face.

"I-I'm really sorry about yesterday, Joe. I knew that if I'd gone back into that lake, I would have been in serious trouble, most likely even dead. I know I should've helped you, b-but I was so scared. You were really brave. You saved me, and look how I repaid you!" He shook his head. "I'll be for ever in debt to you. If there's anything I can ever do . . ."

I hadn't saved him with the expectation of a favor in return, but as he made the promise, an idea suddenly struck me. I wouldn't have an opportunity like this again . . .

"Actually, there is one thing you can do for me . . ." I said. He looked at me in surprise. "Do you think you can contact your brother and ask him something for me?"

"Okay," he agreed reluctantly. Clearly talking to his brother wasn't something he liked doing very much. "What do you want to know?"

"It's about someone in the Top League. Can you ask your brother about a member? Last name's Gray. Anything you can dig up about that, you know, anything at all, would be helpful."

"Gray? Is it a relative of yours?"

"Yeah, I'm looking for a long-lost relative, and I heard there was a Gray in the Top League. I know it's a long shot, but I'm running out of places to look. I don't have any connections there myself to ask about it, but if you could help me with this, we can call it quits."

He paused and stared at his feet. "Look, I'm not very close to Cillian. I haven't talked to him in years. He only shows up for Christmas to see our parents, and even then, we hardly interact. But I'll see what I can do. My brother never talks about anything that goes on in that League, though. To be honest, the chances of him telling me anything are close to none."

"I'm sure you can think of something, Simon. Tell him about last night – maybe you can guilt-trick him into telling you. You can put the blame on this curse, and maybe make him think it's his fault? It'd really help me if you could find this out for me."

"I'll see what I can do. I'll try my best," he promised.

We were getting close to the main house when he gathered the courage to say, "Before we go talk to Miss Harker, I wanted to ask you something, Joe. What happened in the lake? You were pulled down and disappeared for a while – I was sure you were gone. But then there was some type of explosion, and water sprayed up in the air like a geyser! When I looked back, there was a ring of fire in the lake and I couldn't see you anywhere! I don't know how your husband found you in the dark . . ."

"I don't know what happened either, Simon," I lied. "All I know is something was grabbing me by the ankle, and then the water started to get really hot and the creature suddenly let go. I thought it was some magic you did, to be honest."

"N-no, I didn't do anything! I could never have done something like that! It takes too much power. And I wouldn't even know how – I'm just an Advanced student." He wasn't totally convinced, though: I could see a glint of doubt lingering in his eyes. "Look," he said, "until we find out exactly what happened, can you not tell this to anyone?"

"Sure. I think you're right," I agreed. "We should figure things out first before we say anything."

I mentally high-fived myself. Things couldn't have gone any better. I had managed to convince Simon that this was somehow his secret to keep, rather than mine. I couldn't believe he was going to keep his mouth shut about last night!

He exhaled, relieved. "Okay, then. That's a deal."

We shook hands on it.

Chapter Twelve

Baby Talk

"Simon! There you are. I've been looking all over for you." Luna Harker ran to meet us as soon as we arrived at the front steps of the main house. "Your mother is on the phone, demanding to talk to you. I've put her on hold. Word about the attacks in the camp has reached her, and she's flipping worried about you. You have to take her call right now!"

"Oh. Okay, I'm on my way. Can you please tell Celeste I had to go take care of this first? She's also waiting to talk to me," he said.

"Yes, I'll find her and tell her." Luna nodded, hurrying up the steps after Simon and not even bothering to say hello to me. Luna wasn't a big fan of niceties and pleasantries when interacting with people, especially when she was busy or had urgent problems to take care of.

"Hey, Joe, wait up!" Tristan was jogging down the trail, his hair in disarray – he had clearly left our cabin in a hurry. He must also have skipped his morning shower: he wouldn't have had time.

"I left a note on the boys' door, explaining we'd be here for breakfast," he said, slightly out of breath from jogging.

"That was impressively fast. What happened to your shower?"

"Wasn't in the mood for showers today." He shrugged nonchalantly.

"Of course not." I shook my head at his blatant lie. "Tris, you don't need to babysit me all day. Blaine is no threat, I swear to you. And I'm not doing anything dangerous, I promise. I'll be careful."

"Oh, I know that. He's def no threat. But he's no bloody help, either! I still want to be with you today, just in case any more dangerous things happen to you."

I rolled my eyes. I couldn't even blame him for worrying; things really did tend to happen to me, whether I was careful or not.

"Plus, I'm supposed to help you when you get into trouble, remember?" he said. "That's my job. This ring says so." He pointed to the white gold wedding band on his left hand to prove his point.

"Oh, all right, then." I didn't want to fight him on this. "Come on, let's have some breakfast before we go talk to Celeste." I interlaced our arms and directed him to the lobby.

"So, what did you and Simon talk about? What did he want?"

"He's confused about the fire bomb at the lake. But don't worry, he feels so guilty about the whole thing that he somehow believes it's his fault. I've left him thinking that way. We've agreed to keep our mouths shut about the whole incident until we figure things out."

Tristan raised an eyebrow. "That was a smart move.

How long do you reckon before he starts putting two and two together?"

"I don't know. But I'll try to keep it on the down-low for as long as I can. I have a feeling I should keep this secret close to the chest, you know?"

As we stepped into the lobby, a few people were ambling around, preparing to head to the cafeteria for their breakfast. I was used to seeing the reaction Tristan provoked whenever he entered a room full of women, but, nonetheless, the scene was always amusing to watch. There were so many loud gasps and hushed whispers when everyone noticed Tristan, you would think they'd never seen someone good-looking before.

Even though Tristan wasn't prepped up in the tidy Fifties style in which he usually liked to go out, he still pulled off the scruffier look: slightly tousled hair, the hint of a beard, worn-out jeans over a blue T-shirt and black leather boots that were perfect for stomping around camps in the woods. I had to confess he resembled our favorite musician Caleb Jones a lot, right now.

Okay, maybe all the loud gasps were justifiable, then. He was rocking the rough look like a true rock star.

Tristan's way to cope with this extreme reaction was to pretend he hadn't noticed it, and act as obliviously as he possibly could. The girls kept their distance, though, and didn't dare approach, because Arice was already coming to greet us – and the Harkers had been very clear on the rules about harassing any of The Lost Boys.

"Oh, hello, Joey. You brought Tristan today. How lovely!"

"Arice Harker, good morning! It is so very nice to see you again," Tristan said, bowing slightly and taking Arice's hand in his, like he'd been brought up to do.

"Oh, my!" Arice was flustered at the charming – though old-fashioned – greeting. "How are you doing, Tristan? I forgot to ask Joey yesterday, but I hope you liked the gift we sent to congratulate you on your wedding. It was such short notice, I'm afraid we didn't have much time to shop . . ."

"Oh, I liked the gift, very much so." Tristan smiled. "I thought I asked Joey to call and thank you for the thoughtful present. Didn't she?"

"She did, don't worry." Arice waved a hand at him. "But I wanted to make sure."

"Of course. We both loved it, Arice, thank you. You didn't have to go to all that trouble, but I appreciated the gesture and the gift very much. It was very lovely of you."

She gazed at him with stars in her eyes. "You're such a gentleman!" She giggled – and was that a swoon? "Why can't we have more men like him in the world, Joey?"

I chuckled. "Sorry, Arice, but I've already called dibs on this one. You have to keep looking for yours."

She pouted a little. "You two are insufferably perfect for each other. And the most gorgeous couple I've ever seen. You're going to make such beautiful babies!" she chirped excitedly. "How many are you planning to have? I'll bet it's a big batch of cutie pies, ain't it?"

"Oh, I wanna have a whole team of them!" Tristan said happily.

"Okay, how about we talk about something else?" I quickly intervened. I didn't want to go into baby plans here, and Tristan's goofy smile was a good indication that this was exactly where the conversation was going to go, if I let it. "Do you have news from Celeste? I hear she wants to talk to me and Simon."

Arice immediately snapped out of her baby-bubble dream, her expression changing quickly to a worried one. "Oh, yeah, she asked me to wait for you here in the lobby. She was called upstairs to take some emergency phone calls. There are a few angry parents demanding to know what's going on. You know how it is . . . Luna is helping out. And I'm taking all groups inside today; there won't be any outside classes until we make sure everything is safe. We don't want anyone turning into a wolf snack, now."

"So you did find signs of a wolf?" Tristan asked, surprised.

"Oh, no! I didn't say that! We want to be careful, though. Better to be safe than sorry, right? Celeste called Craig, and he's been doing the rounds and looking for animal traces out there. We're still waiting for his report," Arice explained. "And Luna went back to the lake, after she was sure Simon's two lost friends had got back safely. She gave them a mighty scolding for running away like they did, mind you . . . But anyway, she went back to the lake to search for any sign of paranormal activities in the water."

"What do you mean, search for signs?" I asked, startled.

"You know, there are ways of detecting if there are supernatural presences around. But Luna didn't find anything. Only a few dead fish floating near the shore. Whatever was in the lake, it ain't there any more."

"So no one has found anything, anywhere?"

"Pretty much, yeah." She sucked at her teeth and stared blankly into the distance.

"Then what do we do now?"

She shrugged. "Like I said, we're gathering everyone in the meeting hall for the day. So we can go have breakfast now and then wait for Celeste. She'll get off the phone, eventually. However, I think that, right at this moment, you're free to focus on your friends."

"What friends?" I asked, puzzled.

"Those four handsome men walking towards us." Arice pointed to the front doors, where four Lost Boys had just waltzed into the lobby.

Chapter Thirteen
Blackout

"There you are!" Sammy exclaimed, and the rest of the boys turned their heads in our direction. They hurried to the front desk to meet us.

"Hey, guys. You're up early," I said.

"Josh woke up at the crack of dawn and kept making all sorts of noises until we were up. He saw Tristan's note, so we decided to come over to meet you," Sam explained, while Harry rubbed his sleepy eyes and gave Josh an accusing look.

"How did you get Seth to come out of the cabin with all the possible wolves ambling around?" I asked, pinching Seth's flushed cheeks and pulling his gray beanie over his eyes.

He huffed and pulled the beanie off his head, leaving a messy crop of blond hair, which stuck out in every direction. "It's safer if we move round in groups. Plus, I figured if a hungry wolf showed up on that trail, these guys would have been snacks first, giving me time to escape." His eyes still flashed with anxiety and worry, in contradiction to his calm demeanor.

"But you're the chubbiest of us all! The wolf would want you first, for sure. Look at that delicious fat belly!" Sam joked, rubbing Seth's stomach and making yummy noises.

"The caretaker has been doing his rounds all over the camp, Sethie. You don't need to worry. We probably got spooked in the dark and imagined stuff, anyway," I said, trying to calm him.

"Really?" He sighed, looking relieved. "That's good to hear."

"I don't think you'll be able to escape this hungry mob here, though," I mused, as I watched the domino effect their arrival had caused inside the building.

People were hurrying into the lobby in excitement, adding numbers to the group that had already been gathering because of Tristan. They moved as one big block of squealing fans, swarming over the boys like a hurricane, asking for autographs, photos and sometimes even hugs and kisses. There were even some camp staff members amongst the mass of euphoric fans. The "harassment rule" was definitely not applicable for the time being, since the boys themselves had come into the building, and people figured they couldn't be in trouble for accidentally being in the same place at the same time.

I wiggled my way out of the screaming tidal wave and hovered near the front doors to watch the commotion from afar. Since there were mostly females in the crowd, the attention was focused only on the boys, so I was left alone to observe the scene in peace.

"Excuse me, Miss Gray?" someone called out. Startled at hearing my maiden name, I turned to see Craig, the caretaker, standing nearby, watching me. "Can I have a word with you, please?" he shouted, raising his voice so as to be heard over the excited yells of the crowd.

"Yeah, sure. What about?"

He frowned disapprovingly at the screaming hoard behind us. "Can we take this outside for a moment? It's kinda difficult to hear in here."

I nodded and followed him outside.

"I understand you were in contact last night with what seems to have been a wolf?" he enquired, as we made our way down the front steps.

"Hmm, I don't really know what it was, to be honest. I didn't actually see anything, but we all heard growling and rustling in the bushes, you know? It could have been anything, though . . ." I tried to explain, but when I looked up to his face, my words failed me: what I saw in his eyes made warning flares explode inside my head.

The last time I had failed to use my empathy-sight on somebody I didn't know very well, I had ended up being stabbed by my own security guard and left to bleed to death in an abandoned warehouse. I had been careless then, and I had vowed never to make that mistake again. Whenever anyone approached me now, I instinctively threw them a quick eye-read scan, just to be sure, and most importantly, to be safe.

Craig the caretaker was definitely trying to hide something. I didn't know exactly what he was trying to hide, because he was working very hard to disguise his emotions, but I could sense it was something important. The dangerous glint in his eyes was enough of a warning for me.

"There was mention of fire breaking out, down by the lake," he continued, eyeing me carefully.

"Really? Who mentioned it?" Only a couple of people

knew about the fire, and the ones that knew weren't telling anyone else. How had Craig known about it? Could there have been scorch marks left on the shore? I'd been so exhausted when Tristan had carried me out of the lake, I didn't remember much about what I might have left that could provide clues for later . . .

"I heard someone talking," was his vague reply.

There was something fishy about Craig. I could see it in his eyes. "I don't know anything about any fire . . ." It was my turn to do a little interrogating. "But, hey, I hear you're new to this camp?"

"Yes, I took the position a week ago. Apparently, the guy before me was too old to handle all the long walks."

How opportune to fill the position just in time to catch the Annual Gathering, I mused to myself. "And how long have you been in the caretaker business, Craig?"

My first question had been innocent enough, and hadn't raised any suspicion, but my second seemed to have caught his full attention. I felt his guard go up in the blink of an eye, like an impenetrable brick wall. He was a damned good blocker.

"A while," he said, his tone clipped.

How vague, I thought. "Right . . . So, anything else you want to ask me?" I took a cautious step back, my posture suddenly defensive. His suspicious manner was making me increasingly paranoid. "Because I need to get on . . ." I took a quick glance back towards the main house. The front doors were only a few feet away. If I could walk that small distance, I would be safe and in Tristan's sight again. I only needed to climb back up those steps and I would be out of harm's way . . .

Craig caught on to my change of stance, and his eyes

became a lot more intense and threatening. "Wait, Gray," he called out, as I climbed the first step. "You have to come with me. We're not done talking."

"I'm s-sorry, but I really have to go." Mental warning sirens were blaring in my head, and flashbacks to a dark, deserted warehouse played on repeat. I was a second away from breaking my cool facade, my heart racing while I tried to act calm on the outside.

I continued climbing the steps – slowly, because I didn't want to trigger Craig into action – but he still advanced towards me, his eyes narrowing menacingly.

In that moment, we both knew that the pretense was over. He knew that I knew he was a threat. His cover was blown.

Still, the hit came unexpectedly. Even though I was on my guard and well aware of the imminent danger, I still wasn't prepared for the blunt force of a full mental attack. Something hit me directly inside my head, overpowering all my thoughts, ramming its presence into my mind like a freaking wrecking ball.

My knees caved and I hit the ground, grabbing my head in pain. I could faintly hear Craig also groaning, only a few feet away from me. He then hit the ground hard in exactly the same way I had done. We locked eyes for a split second.

And then my mind switched off to protect itself, and I blacked out.

I blinked myself awake to find a guy kneeling on the ground next to me, his eyes frantically searching mine as he cradled my head in his lap. He had such strange eyes, which seemed oddly familiar, for some reason, but I couldn't pinpoint why.

"Joey? Are you okay? What happened?" he asked me.

I propped myself up on my elbows, thinking it was kind of odd that this guy's tone of voice sounded so intimate. My head hurt so bad that it made my stomach lurch. I grimaced in a mixture of pain and nausea as I tried to sit up on the grass.

"W-where am I?" I asked groggily, rubbing at my temples. It looked like I was in some sort of park, but I couldn't remember getting here. There was a circle of people standing around me, staring expectantly and waiting for me to say something.

"We're at the main house. A girl saw you collapse and ran inside to call us. She said that one minute you were talking to Craig, the next you were both falling down like something had hit you. What happened?"

"M-main house? Craig?"

"Yeah, he's right over there. He just woke up, too." He pointed to a middle-aged man with glasses and a moustache, dressed in khaki shorts, sitting on the steps. The man looked as confused and bewildered as I felt. "Were you attacked?" the guy continued asking, still holding me to give me support.

"Attacked?" My head spun and I heaved in dizziness.

"Okay, everybody, step away!" the guy supporting me shouted to the crowd. "She needs some space, let her breathe!"

A young woman dressed in a flowery summer dress passed through the crowd and kneeled in front of me, her brown curls falling gently over her round face. "Jeez, Celeste wasn't kidding when she said you attract trouble like honey to bees," she muttered, while checking my pulse. "You were out of our sight for, like, what? Five minutes?"

I frowned at the intrusive poking, and pulled my hand away from her. "I'm fine. A little dizzy, but fine, thank you very much," I grumbled, annoyed. "How did I get here?"

There were four boys also kneeling next to me, watching me, worriedly. They were very handsome, each one in a different way. Nothing like the guy holding me, though: that one was in a whole league of his own, beautiful like a Hollywood movie star.

One of the pretty boys reached out and held my hand, as if we were old friends. He had messy blond hair and the most beautiful, vivid green eyes I'd ever seen.

"Come on, Joey. Stop horsing around. Tell us what happened," he said, squeezing my hand.

I pulled away from him, awkwardly. He seemed so earnest in his concern that I didn't want to hurt his feelings, but I wasn't comfortable with a stranger holding my hand like that.

"Look, this is getting really surreal. I don't know how I got here, or who you people are, but this isn't funny any more! You can stop with the prank now," I protested, scooting away from the movie star guy. He could be as unbelievably handsome as he liked, but I still didn't know him, and he was leaning far too close for comfort. I wasn't used to a guy that good-looking fussing over me in the way he was. Actually, all the boys were too close; it was a little disconcerting.

They all blinked at me, seeming stunned. "She must have hit her head pretty bad when she fell down," Green-Eyed Boy suggested.

"Joey, please, look at me," Movie-Star Guy said, taking my face in his hands and forcing me to face him. The gesture felt strangely comforting and familiar, his eyes coaxing me to trust him, his deep voice soothing. That's when I realized why his eyes seemed so odd and out of place. They didn't have any color.

"What is the last thing you remember?" he asked softly.

I blinked and watched his handsome face. He had a roughly stubbled, square jaw, the most perfect thin nose and mesmerizing gray eyes that twinkled with a mysterious light, as if they were metallic silver rings. So uncanny, yet so beautiful.

"Hmm . . . I-I'm not s-sure . . ." I pulled my face away from his hands, my cheeks heating in embarrassment. Something was tugging inside my head, trying to tell me there was something urgent I should be thinking about, but for the life of me, I couldn't remember what it was. "I remember I was about to move with my mom to a new place . . . Esperanza. Has something happened on the way there? Oh, my God, did the car crash? Where's Mom?" I asked, looking around urgently.

It was the only thing that could explain all this. The car must have crashed on the way to Esperanza, and we were stranded somewhere in the middle of the road, where these people had found us.

"Jesus, man." Gray-Beanie Boy exhaled in shock. "That happened almost four years ago, Joey. Are you saying you don't remember any of us?" he asked, giving me a long, hard stare. His voice sounded so worried, and his hazel eyes looked so honest, I immediately wanted to trust him, even though I hardly knew him at all.

"No, I don't know any of you! How does everybody know my name?" I asked, puzzled. These people weren't making any sense.

Hushed murmurs spread through the circle of people around us, while the boys kneeling next to me all started talking to Movie-Star Guy at the same time. He glanced at me with those mysterious gray eyes and must have seen the confusion and distress I was feeling at that moment, because he called everything to a halt.

"All right, stop talking, everybody!" he shouted to the crowd, his voice full of authority. Everyone stopped at his command. "Arice, you go talk to Craig, find out what happened here, and then get Celeste to meet us at our cabin. I'm taking her back there now. We'll figure things out after she's recovered." He helped me stand up. "Are you okay to walk, Joey?" He held on to my arm and I nodded curtly, feeling slightly flustered.

He looked so incredibly hot when he was shouting orders like that. I wished he would stop touching me, though – maybe then my heart would stop beating so damned fast and I could stop blushing.

"Yeah, I can walk," I mumbled, but I wasn't so certain after I'd taken my first step. My legs felt wobbly, and I wasn't sure if it was because of my throbbing head or the fact that he still hadn't let go of my waist. His arms felt so strong around me. "I'm okay to walk, honestly." I tried wiggling away from him, but he wouldn't let go.

"You still look dizzy. I don't want you falling again and hitting your head," he said calmly, his grip still firm on me. "You really don't remember me, Joe?" His voice had an anxious edge to it.

"I-I'm sorry, no . . ." I was pretty sure I would have remembered him: a guy like that was kind of hard to forget. He was pretty dreamy.

He watched me carefully. "That's okay, you'll get your

memory back soon . . . We just need to figure out what happened to you first," he said, mostly to himself, and gave me a reassuring smile. He urged me to keep walking ahead, while the crowd dispersed up the steps into a big wooden building that I had only just noticed. The other four boys followed us closely.

"Where am I? Where are we going? Is my mom okay?"

"Your mother is fine, don't worry about her, she's safe and sound in her house. You're not moving to Esperanza," he told me with a frown, as he led me up a trail through the middle of a forest. "Your memory seems to have taken a blow and has momentarily lapsed. We are staying in a cabin at the top of this hill, just for this week. But you have pretty much a four-year gap to catch up to."

"You're kidding, right? I've forgotten almost four years of my life? That can't be!"

"When you moved to Esperanza, you had the longest hair. Check your hair now. You had it cut a month ago," he pointed out.

I lifted my hands slowly up to my head and gasped when my fingers touched a very, *very* short, spiked haircut. "Oh, fuck! It's so short! This isn't happening. It can't be true . . ." I muttered, watching Movie-Star Guy wincing as I cursed.

"You *seriously* don't remember us, Joey?" Gray-Beanie Boy asked nervously at my other side. He sounded like a big brother would if his sister were in trouble.

I shook my head. "I'm really sorry."

"What about me? You know me!" Green-Eyed Boy asked, looking expectant. He saw the silent apology in my face, and his body sagged in disappointment. I bit back the urge to hug him and tell him everything was going to be okay. He was a stranger, after all. "What about those two buggers over there?" he tried one more time. "Sammy and Josh? Don't you remember their ugly faces?"

A boy with brown curly hair, wearing a checked flannel shirt, peeked at me with a small goofy smile, and the other guy walking next to him turned to watch me as well. He was very tall and built, with a dark Mohican haircut. He looked kind of intimidating.

"She doesn't even remember her own husband, Harry. She's not going to remember us!" Mohican Guy scoffed.

My brain registered the word "husband". "Wait, what? Husband?" I asked, doing a double take.

"Stop pressuring her to remember, guys. Things will come back to her in due course, don't worry," Movie-Star Guy insisted in a hopeful tone.

"Hold on, stop! This is crazy. A person doesn't forget nearly four years of their life in the blink of an eye!" I protested, maneuvering out of his grasp. "And what's this nonsense about a husband? I'm not married," I squeaked, my voice coming out slightly panicky. My head throbbed violently, and I swayed before he caught me again by the waist.

"Don't be afraid, Joey. You'll be fine," he said. His voice echoed in a distant memory. I could remember him saying the exact same words before in a . . . a dark cemetery. *It was night, the sky was sparkling with colorful fireworks, and he looked so calm and ethereal, like a ghost from the past. I remembered telling him I was not afraid, because he was with me, but then he vanished, engulfed by the dark.*

Was he gone? Dead and gone. *Something whispered in my head, and I blinked, startled by the memories.* He was there, right in front of me, in broad daylight now. He was real, and alive in the present again, his face marked by worry.

"Your name is Tristan," I ventured, and he smiled softly in response, the corners of his beautiful eyes crinkling in warm affection. I reached out, my fingers gently touching the side of his cheek. "I remember this smile," I murmured in a daze.

He was smiling down at me, sitting on a tombstone on a winter's afternoon. The cold wind was blowing past us and I could almost smell the scent of carnations lingering in the air. I remembered how that smile had taken my breath away.

I blinked and swayed again, but this time he had me firmly in his grasp and did not let me falter. "Has anyone ever told you that you have the most strange eyes?" I asked breathlessly, my eyes locked on his.

His smile got bigger. "You may have said something about that once or twice." His tone was light and had a chuckle beneath it.

"You feel really familiar, Tristan . . . but I still don't remember much more about you. Sorry." I gave him an apologetic smile.

"That's all right. The rest will come back to you soon. You're already remembering some things. That's good." He turned his face to the road ahead. "I'm sure you'll feel better after you lie down and rest your head a little. Come on, we're in that cabin over there."

Chapter Fourteen
Blank Page

"Here, take this. It will help with your headache." Green-Eyed Boy – Harry? – handed me a glass of water and a couple of aspirins, and I took them with a hesitant smile. He was still acting like an old friend and leaning too close to me on the couch. I shifted away from him, feeling slightly uncomfortable.

"Man, this is so messed up!" he said, turning to Gray-Beanie Boy, who sat in the armchair in front of us. "Look at her, she's acting like she doesn't know me at all, Seth! How freaky is that?"

Gray-Beanie Boy – apparently named Seth – gave me a weak smile and turned to his friend. "She may have partial amnesia, but she still can hear you, Harry."

Harry glanced embarrassedly at me. "Oh, right. My bad, Joey."

The guy that I recalled being named Tristan was talking urgently to this stern blonde woman that had arrived soon after we got into the cabin. Their conversation sounded serious and intense, but most of their words were too cryptic for me to understand. The woman noticed my puzzled stare and came to sit next to me.

"Okay, Joey, by the look on your face I assume you don't remember me, either," she didn't so much ask as affirm. "So I'm going to try something, here, to see if I can jog your memory back to normal, all right?"

I leaned away, suddenly alarmed. "Are you a doctor? What are you planning to do to me?"

"I'm a kind of doctor, yes, you might say so. For these sorts of affairs, at least," she concurred. "I'm just trying to help and maybe get a glimpse of what happened to you. Please close your eyes and relax."

I eyed her suspiciously for a moment. With a silent nod, Tristan urged me to do as I was told, and somehow I knew I could trust him. Even if I didn't understand what was happening or who he really was, I was certain he would do everything to keep me safe. Where this certainty came from, though, I had no idea.

I closed my eyes and let her touch my temples. I felt a faint pressure, which initiated at the base of my skull, and, suddenly, an intense pain exploded in my head and a jumble of images rushed back to me, all at once, like a flooding river.

I remembered her, then – the blonde woman. Her name was Celeste Harker. A flickering stream of images came into focus: *Her house filled with magic amulets and dusty old scrolls, the two of us arguing relentlessly over something in her study, her sisters Arice and Luna in her house, and an androgynous dark-haired man dressed all in gray, sitting by her side on the couch.* I remembered knowing her, her temperament, and the tone of her voice when she was upset, how she frowned when she was concentrating.

I just couldn't connect the rest of her story to my life. When had we met? What was she to me? What was she doing here now? A lot of memories were coming back, but they were jumbled and disconnected and I couldn't make any sense of them. It was like watching random fragments and small scenes of a very long, complicated movie.

I lurched forward and dry-heaved as if I had been punched in the stomach. The headache, which had dulled since I'd arrived in the cabin, returned tenfold, throbbing violently in my skull.

Retrieving my memories was turning out to be as traumatic and painful as losing them. I recovered from the mental blow to see Celeste beside me, slightly dizzy too. "Whoa. Take it easy, there, Celeste. You are going to make me throw up!" I groaned in protest.

"You remember her name?" Tristan asked happily. "Did you get your memory back?"

"No. I remembered a few moments I had with Celeste. It's all a jumble of images clashing inside my head right now. It's quite chaotic, but I can't see the bigger picture yet . . . I'm sorry. It's such a mess."

"What's the last thing you remember, Joey?" Celeste pressed on. "Do you recall what happened to you before you passed out?"

"I-I remember talking to your sister Arice in the lobby . . . then I was talking to some guy outside the building . . . I remember he looked alarmed about me leaving, but I don't know why. Something happened then, but everything is a blur or a blank. I'm sorry," I said to their disappointed faces. "I do have this feeling that there's something really important I should be worrying about, but I don't know what it is. It's like a nagging splinter at the back of my head." I winced, holding my temple in pain.

Every time I tried to recapture a lost memory, my head throbbed violently in retaliation. "God, my head is hurting so bad. What did you do to me, Celeste?"

"I tried to search for your memories, to see what happened to you," she explained. "But they are locked inside your head. You've gone into some sort of lockdown: you've blocked your mind from outside intrusion. I tried prodding, and you lashed out pretty hard at me. I think you're instinctively protecting yourself."

"Protecting myself from what?" I asked, startled.

"That's what I was trying to find out."

"Have you asked Craig what happened?" Tristan asked. "Maybe he can shed light on what's going on here."

"Craig doesn't remember anything, either. He's very disoriented and confused. We took him to his cabin to recover; he was barely conscious when we left. He must have been talking to Joey about last night. He was really worried about wild animals attacking the camp. Whatever hit Joey and caused her amnesia must have got him, too."

"Wait, there are wild animals attacking?" I asked in surprise, but they paid no attention to me and continued their discussion.

"Do you think there could be someone trying to keep us from finding out who's behind all these attacks? Maybe it's erasing memories to keep it a secret?" Tristan asked.

"I think maybe the girl who found them unconscious by the steps could have something relevant to say – or perhaps even be responsible, somehow. Joey gave the girl's ego a bit of a hit the first time they met," Celeste said. "She could have some kind of grudge . . ."

"Oh, Joe told me about that. It's a girl named Alicia, right? You think she can be behind all this?"

"I don't know. She could be trying to retaliate. Maybe this is her way of getting back at Joey. Although it could be a coincidence that she found them outside . . . But don't worry, Halloway. I will get to the bottom of this right away. I'm going back to the main house and I'll talk to Alicia. If she's hiding anything, I will find out. You have my word."

"And what about Joey's memory? There's still a lot missing."

"Well, my best guess is that it will gradually come back to her, as soon as she stops feeling threatened . . . If not, we can always try another memory-retrieving session later."

"Oh, no, please, don't," I pleaded. "I can't stand another round of this blasted headache."

"Well, we can wait and see how it goes," she said, patting me reassuringly on the back.

"Okay. Thank you so much, Celeste," Tristan said, as he accompanied her to the front door of the cabin. "Please, keep us posted on anything new you discover, yeah?" Once she'd left, he turned to face the others. "I think it's best if we let Joey rest now, guys. It's still very early in the morning. Maybe some sleep will help get the rest of her memories back."

"All right, let's go, guys." The blond named Seth stood up and urged his other friends to follow.

"Yeah, okay," the boy with brown curly hair – Samuel, I think – agreed, standing up. "I have to check on the dog, anyway. I bet he's been chewing on every piece of furniture in that cabin."

"Oh, that's right," I mumbled. "Rocko."

Everybody turned to stare at me.

"You don't remember *us*, but you remember the dog's name?" the curly-haired boy, Samuel, complained with a mighty pout.

"I'm so sorry! The name kinda popped into my head." I gave him a weak smile.

"She'll remember us all soon enough," Tristan said. "This is actually good news, bits of information are gradually coming back to her already."

"Yeah, and at least she doesn't remember *any* of us. Can you imagine if she remembered everyone *but* you, Sammy?" Seth mused with a light chuckle.

"Do you think I hurt his feelings?" I asked Tristan, after the boys had left.

"He'll be all right. Sammy was just goofing around, don't worry about it," he assured me with an honest smile. "Come on, let's go get you some rest." He extended his hand and I took it hesitantly. "You don't need to look so scared. I'm not gonna bite."

"I know that." I tried to cover my blush while he led me through a door into the bedroom. The sheets were crumpled on the unmade bed, and there were clothes tossed everywhere. "So, is this my room?" I asked.

"*Our* room," he corrected.

"Oh, y-you mean . . ." and I trailed off, my cheeks tinting red again.

"We are sharing the room, yes." He smiled. "Married couples tend to do that, you know."

"Are you serious . . . about us being married?" I gasped, feeling shellshocked. "That husband talk wasn't just nonsense, then? I really have a husband . . . and it's you? How can this be possible? I don't remember that *at all*."

"I'm afraid it's true. I am really your husband, Joey,"
he said, and when he noticed the enormity of my discomfort, he added, "I understand that you're feeling uncomfortable with me sharing the room, so I'll leave you alone to
rest, okay?" His voice was calm and collected, but I still
could sense a lingering tension, as if the notion of being
cast out of his own room was not very pleasant for him.

"You're mad that I'm making you leave. I'm sorry. It's
your room, too."

He stopped and regarded me in silence for a moment
before he spoke again. "I'm not mad, I'm just a little
frustrated. But I know it's only temporary. I can give you
some space now, until you're back to yourself again."

I felt light-headed. How could I have managed to score
this *incredible* guy for a husband? Had I won the jackpot,
or what?

"Thanks. Y-you seem to be handling the situation well.
I mean, your supposed wife has gone bonkers in the head
and doesn't remember you . . . I'd be flipping out like
there's no tomorrow, if I were in your position."

His voice was warm and caring when he turned to me
and answered, "I'm not worried. You remember my name;
you know my face. The rest will come back to you soon.
And even if your head doesn't know me right now, Joey,
I know your heart does," he said, brushing a hand over my
cheek. "When in doubt, trust your heart."

"I do. I-I feel safe when I'm with you," I confessed
shyly.

I also felt loved. I trusted my heart, and right now it
was telling me this strange man truly loved me. Even
though my head couldn't remember him, I still could
remember the feelings he had for me. That piece of the

puzzle was already there. Now I needed the rest of my memories to make the picture whole.

He dipped his head slowly, about to kiss me, but I reeled back, uncomfortable with the intimacy. I trusted him, but he still felt like a stranger to me, and the idea of kissing him – even though it was very alluring – was also still too sudden.

"I feel like you're messing with me!" I laughed nervously, shifting back on the bed. "I mean, are you absolutely sure we really are married? I don't have a ring . . ." I glanced down at my bare hands.

"Look at your necklace. Sometimes you take the ring off your finger because it gets in the way when you're playing the guitar."

"I-I play the guitar?"

"Yes, you do, Buttons."

I widened my eyes as a memory lodged itself back into my head, clicking into place. "I remember that nickname!" I whispered in surprise. "What does it mean?"

He sat on the bed and took my hand, kissing the back of it in a gentlemanly manner. "It means you're cute as a button. Which is very true."

"Oh, that's . . . erm, nice."

It wasn't "nice", that was a lie. It was the most adorable friggin' thing I'd ever heard in my whole life. He was so lovely!

"Do I have a nickname for you?"

His lips twitched at the corners and he turned his face away so as not to face me. "No."

"You liar!" I exclaimed, seeing the proof flashing in his gray eyes.

"Well, I see your sight is working better than ever," he

muttered, standing up. "I'm not telling you my nickname, Buttons. You'll have to remember that one by yourself," he told me, with an amused smile.

"Aw, no fair!"

"Life isn't fair, sweetheart. Now get some rest. I'll be right outside. I'm leaving the door open in case you need me, okay?" Then he stepped out, leaving me alone in the bedroom.

I pulled at the silver chain around my neck to look at the silver-colored ring hanging there. A small diamond was set inside the ring, which made no sense. What was the point of putting a diamond on the inside of a ring so no one could see it? There was also a small inscription engraved in the metal:

T.J. Until the End & From the Start.

What a strange line, I thought to myself, frowning with the effort of trying to remember, but my head throbbed painfully in protest.

A crumpled letter came back to my memory. I was crying while I was reading it. Why? What had happened? *I was so, so sad, as if I had just lost someone I loved.* I couldn't remember anything more about it.

"Darn it," I huffed, frustrated, resting my head on the pillow and shutting my eyes.

I guessed I should try to rest for a while. And maybe when I woke up, this whole mess would be gone and my memories would be back again . . .

Chapter Fifteen
Best Friends For Ever

"Don't be afraid," Tristan whispered close to me, his lips brushing against my ear. "Even if you cannot see me, I'll always be right here, by your side. I feel like I've always been by your side, and I will always be. Does that make any sense?"

It sounded crazy, but I knew what he meant, because I felt the same way. Like I'd known him for as long as I could remember, beyond time, even.

"Can you feel this?" he whispered in the dark, and I sensed his lips touching mine, light as a feather, and then fireworks exploded loudly up in the night sky.

The deafening sound faded to muffled bangs, making me blink awake to find myself in a strange bed in a strange room.

The ghostly dream faded quickly, while the banging continued, and I realized someone was knocking on the door. I shuffled slowly out of the bedroom and took a curious peek outside. Tristan was already at the front door, talking to a guy with dark hair and a fringe colored blue at the ends.

"I've heard she wasn't well, and I thought I should come

by, see if everything was all right . . ." the guy was saying, but I couldn't see his face because Tristan's bulky form blocked almost all of the view.

"She's resting now," was Tristan's clipped reply.

"Oh, I see. Well, when she wakes up, if you could please tell her I came over."

"I'll tell her."

It didn't take a genius to figure out that Blue-Fringe Guy's presence wasn't welcomed by Tristan; his whole back was tense and stiff as they talked.

"O-okay . . ." Blue-Fringe Guy sounded completely intimidated.

"Is there anything else I can do for you, Mr. Blaine?"

"Hmm, a-actually, yeah. There was something she asked me to find out . . ."

"Yes? What is it?"

"Well, erm, it's kinda complicated, and I think she should really hear it from me, so . . . if you could let her know that we have things to talk about . . . By the way, the Gathering has been suspended until things have been clarified by the Harkers, so whenever she can meet me, I'll be at my cabin."

"Yes, I'll let her know," Tristan said. Then, suspiciously: "Did you come here alone? Aren't you worried about new attacks?"

"I came with two friends. They're over there, down by the trail. Not that they'd be of any help, anyway; last time there was trouble with the wolves, they bailed pretty fast and left me . . ."

"Well, at least you know how that feels."

There was a ring of dead silence before the guy cleared his throat uncomfortably and excused himself.

"Who was it?" I asked, walking out of the bedroom.

Tristan turned round, slightly surprised to see me up and about. "Oh, hey. It was nothing important. How are you feeling?"

"I'm feeling a lot better, thank you. My head isn't killing me any more; that's pretty great."

"Good. That's good. Has your memory sparked up again?"

"No, I'm sorry. It's still the same: bits of things here and there, most of it not making make much sense. How long have I been sleeping?" I asked, yawning.

"It's already noon. Do you wanna go over to the boys' cabin and have some lunch? You haven't eaten anything since last night."

"Oh, yes, please, that'd be wonderful. Thank you so much."

He gave me an odd look.

"What? Did I say something wrong?"

"No . . . it's just very weird seeing you act so polite. Even when we first met, you weren't this reserved around me."

"Oh. I'm sorry."

He shook his head and smiled. "Stop apologizing all the time. It's not really your fault, is it? Come on, let's go grab us some grub."

Lunch at the neighboring cabin with Tristan and his friends was pretty interesting. Seth Fletcher (Gray-Beanie Boy), Harry Ledger (Green-Eyed Boy), Josh Hart (Mohican Guy, who turned out to be not so intimidating after all) and Sammy Hunt (Curly-Haired Guy – the goofiest and funniest boy) were very loud and constantly bustling around the

table, making jokes, talking about music and sometimes even tossing food at each other playfully. They were hectic and crazy and very weird. But in a good kind of way.

They also kept retelling old stories from their past in a subtle attempt to make me remember things.

After lunch they decided to get out some instruments and play me some songs, certain that the music would jog my memory.

"Who are 'The Lost Boys'?" I had asked, seeing the name on the logo on every instrument around. They had all looked so incredibly sad and crestfallen at that question that I decided to keep any more to myself.

But as soon as they started playing their first song, the lyrics started coming back to me and I could suddenly remember images of shows and concerts that we'd played together. In the same way as the other memories had returned to me, these images were also random and disconnected from the rest. I still couldn't remember the boys and who they were, even though I could remember playing with them.

I still couldn't see the bigger picture, either, which was very frustrating. Why couldn't I get all the pieces back in my head, already?

The boys seemed very happy with this small victory, though. I had remembered the songs and, to them, it was like hitting a home run. Tristan was the happiest of them all, the smile on his face wide and full of affection.

I was in awe at that smile. I wished he could keep smiling at me like that all the time, that he would never stop smiling, ever! I wanted Sam to keep telling jokes, just so I could hear Tristan's laughter ringing in the room. It was like it had an invisible string linked directly to my heart, making it vibrate with happiness. I loved hearing his laugh; I loved seeing his smile. I never imagined I could fall for a guy so quickly like that, but here I was: falling as fast as a bullet.

After playing a lot of songs to me, the boys took a break and Tristan went to get some water from the kitchen. My eyes followed him with a deep longing – love-sick fool that I was.

"That is the darnest, cutest thing ever!" Harry's laughter from beside me on the couch made me snap out of my reverie.

"What?" I asked awkwardly. "I wasn't doing anything."

"You, with your starry eyes gazing at Tristan! You're non-stop swooning over him. It's kinda funny seeing you flirt with your own husband like that."

I looked around, alarmed, to see if anyone had overheard him, but the rest of the boys were goofing at each other in the background and weren't paying attention to us.

"Shhh, Harry! People can hear you!"

"So? They don't care if you're carrying a torch for your hubby. Plus, you really think they haven't noticed it?"

"No, they haven't! And if you keep your mouth shut, no one else needs to know about it. So shut up! God, this is so embarrassing . . ." I buried my face in my hands to try to hide the massive blush creeping up my neck.

"What are you so embarrassed about, anyway?"

"You're making me sound like I'm some sort of floozy, flirting with a guy I just met!"

"*Just met?* You've known him for almost four years! You do know that you guys are married, right? You *are* aware of that."

"Yeah, but I don't remember any of it. To me, we've

just met," I huffed, mortified. That only made him laugh even harder. You've heard the "roll on the floor laughing" expression? Well, he was rofling his ass off over there.

"Oh, boy. Talk about priceless . . ." he wheezed out between chuckles.

"What's priceless?" Tristan asked, looking curiously at Harry, coming to sit down by his side, water bottle in hand.

"Halloway, you won't believe wha—" Harry started saying, but I slapped a hand over his mouth just in time to stop him from blabbering.

"What is it? Why is her face like that?" Tristan asked, the curiosity rising in his silver eyes.

"It's nothing! My face is fine!" I squeaked in utter embarrassment.

Harry wriggled out of my grasp. "She's just trying to hide that she's got the hots for you, is all!" He'd ratted me out, the utter bastard.

"Oh, that's what this is about?" Tristan smiled, taking a sip from his bottle. It was as if that tidbit of information wasn't the most embarrassing thing ever for me. "This is actually kind of lovely. It's been a long time since she last blushed like that because of me . . . But you don't need to hide that, Joey. I've got the hots for you, too. Always have, always will." And he shot me a charming wink, which only made my blooming face even redder.

"What always will?" Josh asked, directing the attention of the whole room towards us. I felt like I was on the verge of passing out from embarrassment right there.

Harry jumped up from his seat, ready to spill the beans, when Tristan interrupted him. "It's nothing. We were just saying I'm taking Joey back to our cabin so she can rest now. It's almost dark and we've forced her memory far too much for one day as it is. I'm sure tomorrow she'll wake up with a refreshed head on her shoulders, right?" he proposed, politely extending his hand towards me.

I took it and we stood up. Tristan squeezed my hand reassuringly. After we had said our goodbyes to the boys, he pulled me to the door. I could barely look Harry in the eye when I said goodbye. I knew he was going to tell everyone about my ridiculous crush after we'd left.

"Joey, wait up!" Harry called out, following us outside. I turned round and looked at my feet, feeling dejected as they'd all be making fun of me soon enough.

Harry closed the distance between us and wrapped his arms around me, giving me a tight hug. "I'm sorry I laughed so much back there. I wasn't laughing at you, I was just laughing at the situation. It's pretty surreal. I would never make fun of you. I won't tell anyone, if that's what you're worried about. I promise."

"Really?" I asked quietly.

"Of course. You may not remember now, but I'm your best friend in the whole wide world!"

"You are?" I asked, surprised, and looked into his eyes. They sparkled the most intense green with complete honesty.

"Yep," he said, popping the "p". "I've got your back, Jo-Jo. We all do, actually. You don't need to be ashamed around any of us, ever. We are your friends. What would we do without you?" He gave me another hug. It made me feel all fuzzy and warm inside, as if it had magical powers of some kind.

"Thanks, Harry Bear," I murmured in his ear. A thread of flickering images flooded into my head then. *Harry running through the school's hallway laughing, his spiked red hair bouncing all over the place; Harry holding me in his arms because I was feeling upset; us all piling on top of him in the practice room while he screamed and laughed; him crying beside me while I was in a hospital bed; dancing with me in a small Italian plaza, a sparkling ocean in the background, as bright and intense as his beautiful emerald eyes.*

He stepped back, eyebrows arched in surprise. "You remembered my nickname!" he gasped with a happy smile.

"Yeah . . . it kinda popped into my head," I murmured, slightly dizzy from the rush of memories, but I didn't say anything more. Tristan was right behind me and he might feel hurt or offended that I had remembered Harry's nickname before his.

"Come on. Let's get you inside," Tristan urged, holding me by the waist again as he noticed my dizziness. "We'll meet up for breakfast tomorrow, okay, Harry?"

"I hear you, Captain! See ya tomorrow, then." He saluted, beaming broadly as he waved us goodbye.

Chapter Sixteen

Fired Up

"Well, what do we do now?" I asked, fidgeting on the couch.

I had insisted on making a call to my mother, so I could confirm this whole story about the best part of four years of my life being blanked from my head, and after a few confused replies from her, everything was duly verified. Tristan talked to her afterwards, reassuring her everything was fine and that he was taking good care of me, as always.

"What do you mean?" Tristan looked curiously at me, leaning against the kitchen doorframe, legs crossed at the ankles in a laidback stance.

The truth was that I didn't feel prepared to be with Tristan in a private place like we were right now. I didn't know how to act or how to hide the massive blushes I knew were about to bloom red all over my embarrassed face. It was only a matter of time before it happened, and I was desperately trying to find something, *anything*, to do that would take my mind off the fact that a gorgeous man was standing only a few feet away, looking as enticing and alluring as a man could look.

"I mean, w-we should be doing *something* . . ." I tried to explain, but the words failed me.

He raised a pleased eyebrow, a tiny smirk playing at the corners of his incredibly tasty-looking lips. "Should we, now?" he mused, suggestively.

"Oh! N-no! That's n-not what I meant." Curses. I could feel the heat creeping up to my ears already. "What I meant was that we should try to find a way to get my memory back, you know, like, like . . ." I stalled in panic, trying to find any distraction from what he was insinuating, even though he was only taking his cue from me and my big stupid mouth. "Like, hmm, that guy that showed up before lunch – Blaine, wasn't it? He said he had things we needed to talk about. What if he's discovered something? We could see what he has to say, right?" I suggested, gulping dry.

Tristan's amusement quickly switched to worry. "Well, we are kind of stuck. I thought you would get your memories back after your nap, but you woke up and things are still the same. Maybe Simon does have something to say about this . . ." he said pensively. "But I don't know, Joey. It'll be dark pretty soon. I don't want us roaming around after sunset. It could be dangerous."

"The sun hasn't even set yet. Come on, there's plenty of time for us to go ask him before it gets dark."

He sucked his teeth and stood thinking quietly for a moment. When we heard a knocking, he glanced at the front door and then back at me. "It's probably Harry wanting to apologize again. He doesn't like it when you're mad at him . . ." He went to open the door.

"Oh, hello, there!" a girl's syrupy voice greeted at the

other side. "I didn't know Joe had company. And, *oh my*, what company it is," the girl purred seductively, making me rise from the couch pretty fast to check out the owner of the voice. "I'm Alicia Collins, by the way. It is so very nice to meet you . . ."

"Hello, Miss Collins. I'm Joey's husband, Tristan. Nice meeting you, too," he replied politely, but I noticed the assertive way he pronounced the word "husband", making it very clear that he was a taken man. Brownie points to him for that, I thought to myself. It was good to know I hadn't married a womanizer. A guy that gorgeous should by rights be all kinds of trouble for a wife to keep track of.

"Oh, is that you in there, Joe?" she asked, pushing past Tristan and already walking inside. "I thought I saw you. How are you? Are you still having trouble remembering things, darling?" she asked me in the same over-sweetened tone.

"Huh, y-yeah, sort of," I responded. "I'm sorry if we've met before, but – who are you?"

She clasped a hand over her heart, giving me a look filled with pity. "Oh, gosh, that's so sad! You really don't remember me at all?" Her face portrayed the epitome of good-heartedness, but her eyes twinkled with an evil glint, betraying her real intentions. I may not have remembered her, but I knew she was up to no good.

"Her memory isn't quite back yet, but she's getting there," Tristan intervened, closing the door. "She mentioned what happened between you two yesterday morning, Miss Collins. Before she lost her memory, of course."

Alicia seemed to falter for a moment, but recovered fast, quickly pasting on a fake smile. "Oh, that? That was such a silly argument!" she cooed, wrapping an arm around my shoulder to show Tristan how friendly she was. "It was just a big misunderstanding. We've put all that behind us. We're friends now, Joe and I. She'll tell you all about it when her memory recovers. In fact, I was so worried about her that I had to come up to see how she was doing. I felt so frightened when I found her collapsed at the bottom of the steps. Boy, what a scare! I start shaking just thinking about it. Look!" She showed us her trembling hands.

"Well, thanks for your concern, Miss Collins, but Joey's fine now."

"I'm so glad to hear that! I was so worried, you know."

"She so wasn't," I muttered, so low only Tristan could hear.

"Miss Collins, can you please tell us why you're really here?" Tristan asked, his patience finally starting to wear thin. Her concerned act didn't seem to be fooling him, the same way it wasn't fooling me.

"W-what?" she stammered, feigning bafflement.

"What do you want? Why have you really come here?"

She flicked her gaze from me to him a couple of times before finally giving up on her charade. "Fine. I came here to see for myself if she really can't remember anything."

"Why do you want to know?" I asked, curiously.

"Because I think you're faking it!"

"Why would I fake this? What could I possibly gain from faking this?"

"Because you're trying to put the blame on me, that's why!" she snapped. "Celeste came to interrogate me, as if I was some petty criminal. Me! The insult!" she scoffed. "She's been asking all kinds of suspicious questions all day about what I've been doing – when, where, with whom.

I didn't understand it at first, but then I got it. She was trying to find out if I was the one behind the wolf attack, whatever happened at the lake and now your blackout! She thinks I did all those things. Me!"

"Why would she think that?" I asked, confused.

She gave me a long, hard stare, her lips pursed. "Oh, you're good. I can almost believe you really don't remember anything."

"I don't!" I snapped, feeling just as irritated as she looked.

"Right. Fine, whatever. I'll play along. Celeste thinks I'm doing this to get back at you because of that stupid little scene in the meeting hall. Like I care about that."

"It was a pretty good burn she gave you," Tristan pointed out. "You might be wanting revenge now."

"Oh, please. So what, she pranked me. That potion was crap, anyway. It had no effect. It can hardly count as a burn if it didn't even work," she grumbled, picking at her nails distractedly. "Serves me right for buying things from filthy gypsies. Everybody knows they only cheat and steal, the bastards. I'll bet that crystal pendant is crap, too. I can't wait to graduate. Then I'll learn how to make spells myself and won't need to beg other witches for things, or buy from them tramps."

"So, you're really not trying to get back at Joey?" he asked cautiously.

"No! How many times do I have to spell it out for you people?" She rubbed her temples, looking annoyed. "And now Luna thinks I'm trying to get back at Joe out of envy, too. So what that she was the only one who didn't fall for the prank at the lake? Big whoop dee doo. I'm not going to fake wolf sounds in the middle of the woods just because of that. I've got more important things to do with my life, you know? And how could I possibly be behind that thing at the lake? Tell me that! I don't even know what happened there. No one is telling us anything!" she wailed in protest.

"Look, I'm not taking the blame for all this stuff, you hear?" she continued when Tristan and I said nothing but continued to regard her suspiciously. "You wanna know what I think is really going on? I think this amnesia story is bull. As soon as people started asking too many questions – bam! – she can't remember anything. How very convenient. I think you're the one behind all these creepy attacks, Joe Gray. You're doing it all and now you're trying to put the blame on me. Well, think again, sister. I'm not taking the fall for you. Nuh-uh."

"Hey! I don't know what you're talking about. I don't remember any of those crazy things you said are happening! This is nuts. I would never attack people. I would never hurt anyone!" I snapped, my temper rising from all the accusations.

"Miss Collins, you have my word on this: Joey is not responsible for any of those attacks. We want to find out who's behind this, too. I swear to you," Tristan said.

She watched him in silence for a moment and then let out a deep sigh of resignation. "Okay. I believe you. I swear I'm not behind any of it, either." She uncrossed her arms and stopped pouting childishly. "Can you please ask Miss Harker to lay off me? I can't take her long-suffering interrogations any more."

"I can try," Tristan said, in an attempt to appease her temper. "But we can't really tell Celeste what to do. I promise I'll ask her, though."

"Thanks. That'd be marvelous. Say, can I get a glass of

water, Joe? The hike up the hill and all this talk has left me parched," she said, her attitude changing abruptly; her mood had gone from sour to sweet again in the blink of an eye.

"O-okay," I muttered, giving Tristan a quizzical look as if to say, *What the hell was that about?* – to which he responded with a puzzled shrug. I went into the kitchen to get her a drink.

"So, you two are really in a band?" I heard her ask Tristan.

"Yes, we are."

"That must be so exciting!" she exclaimed. "My little sister is a big fan of yours."

I grabbed a glass from inside the cabinet and when I turned round again, I could see her leaning too close for comfort towards Tristan.

"I haven't met the other members of your band, but I have to confess, Tristan, you are already my favorite!" She giggled – flirting shamelessly – and pressed a hand lightly against his chest.

I frowned and balled my hands into fists. Had that girl no shame, trying to seduce a married man? He'd just told her he was my husband! The nerve of the girl!

And then images started to flash in my head: *A red-haired woman in a tight red dress pressing herself up against Tristan in a narrow hotel corridor. She was a breath away from kissing him. Glass shattering everywhere, the tinkling, crackling noise filling my ears along with sinister, angry whispers and loud rattling chains. I remember the anger: fiery, searing anger taking over my whole mind.*

Heat rushed through my veins. The room suddenly felt

stuffy and too hot. When I glanced down, I realized the heat was emanating from my very own hands.

My hands were actually sprouting real, burning flames!

"Oh, God!" I gasped when the fire licked at the towel hanging off the bar close to me. I waved my arms, trying to put the fire out, but that only made it spread faster. I looked around frantically, grabbing at the burning towel, tossing it into the sink and turning on the tap in panic.

Tristan had noticed that something strange was happening before Alicia had figured out what was going on. He must have seen the smoke coming out of the sink, and his eyes widened in realization. I thought he was about to cry out, and draw attention to what I was doing, but he grabbed Alicia's arms and turned her around so she had her back to the kitchen — and to me.

"As I was saying, Miss Collins, thank you very much for being honest about the reason for your visit, but I think it's time you got going . . ." He kept taking surreptitious peeks over her shoulder while he spoke.

I watched in relief as the flames on my hands and the towel extinguished under the cold water. "What's that smell?" Alicia asked, wrinkling her nose and sniffing the air.

"What smell? I don't smell anything," Tristan lied, but Alicia wriggled out of his hold and came towards me in the kitchen.

"Oh, it's the cookies, that we were, erm . . . baking, honey," I improvised. "I'm afraid I forgot about them. They're all burned, sorry." I gave Tristan a weak smile and turned off the tap, stepping away from the sink as fast as I could.

"It's okay. Baking is not for everyone," he said nervously.

I could hear the relief in his voice as he forced a playful laugh.

"Oh, I know how to make the most delicious chocolate chip cookies ever," Alicia chipped in, clearly trying to impress him.

"I'm sure you do, Miss Collins, but again, if you wouldn't mind, it's really time for you to leave." He pushed her gently towards the front door.

She made a Eureka! face then, suddenly remembering she had one more card up her sleazy sleeve. "Oh, I can't believe this, I'm such a silly airhead! I can't walk back to my cabin alone, not with all these dangerous creatures attacking the camp! If it's really not Joe doing this, then it's very dangerous for me out there. What am I going to do?" Her lips trembled, as if she was ready to cry.

"Oh, I'm sure you'll manage to get back in one piece. Nothing happened on the way here, and I'm positive nothing will on the way back," I countered swiftly.

"I can't keep counting on sheer luck all the time, Joey!" she admonished. "What if my luck runs out? Would you be so kind as to accompany me, Tristan? If I had a strong, valiant man like you by my side, I wouldn't be so scared."

Tristan hesitated, looking conflicted and unsure what to do, but then he sighed and nodded in agreement. "Of course, I can't let you walk back alone."

Alicia gave a victorious smile, her eyes glinting with a predatory glow.

"Okay. Can you excuse us for just one sec?" I said, grabbing Tristan by the arm and pulling him to the bedroom, where we could whisper in privacy. "What the hell do you think you're doing? I'm not letting you go with her!" I said, crossing my arms stubbornly. "I may not remember that you're my husband right now, but the fact remains that you are, so you can't go."

"Joey—" he began to argue, but I cut in.

"She's not even scared! I can see it in her eyes. She just wants you alone so she can make a move on you."

He tried to swipe the pleased, amused grin from his face, but made a half-assed job out of it, the cheeky smirk still there. "Joey, sweetheart, it makes me very happy to know that even with your amnesia, you still care, but if you could remember things properly right now, you'd also know I was brought up to always do the right thing. I can't let that girl go back all by herself. It really is dangerous outside: something might happen to her, and I wouldn't be able to live with myself, knowing that I could have prevented it. I know you would feel guilty too if something were to happen. Wouldn't you?" he reasoned.

I stared at him, pouting, before I groaned in agreement.

"You don't need to worry. I'll be back before you know it," he said, smiling, and then his voice suddenly softened. "What happened when you were by the sink? Are you all right?" He took my hands in his. "I didn't think you'd be able to fire up if you didn't remember how to do it."

I widened my eyes in shock. "You knew I could do this? What the hell was it? *My hands were on friggin' fire, Tris!*"

"Yes, hmm, this is a long story . . . and kind of compli- cated. I was hoping you'd remember things before any 'fire' happened, but listen, don't freak out, okay? I'll explain everything to you later when I get back. This sometimes happens when you're angry."

"For real? This happens every time I get mad?"

"Yeah. Or when things get, erm . . . too heated . . . with

kissing and stuff, if you know what I mean . . ." He trailed off, a faint blush tinting his adorable cheeks.

"Shut. Up. You're joking!" I exclaimed.

He gave me a sheepish smile, but his gray eyes twinkled with mischief. "I'm really not. You literally fire up when you're too excited. I can prove it to you later, if you want."

I had no reply to that. I was too busy blushing like crazy.

"Fire isn't the only thing you can do. We have to have a long talk about magic in your life, when I come back," he added.

"Magic? Are you serious?"

"Huh, guys? He-llo-oo? What's going on in there?" Alicia bellowed from the living room.

Tristan straightened up and patted his T-shirt, arranging his face in a stern expression. "I have to walk her back now, Joey. It will be dark soon. Wait for me, okay?" he said, leaving the bedroom.

"Oh, hell no! I'm coming too," I shouted after him.

If that girl thought she could put her claws all over him, she'd better think twice. I wasn't going to leave him all by himself with the likes of *her*.

If he was going, I was going with him!

Chapter Seventeen
Haunted

The walk down the trail would have been a very lovely end-of-afternoon stroll if weren't for the presence of that obnoxious little home-wrecker, who kept hanging on to Tristan's arm like a leech the entire time. I was silently fuming in righteous jealousy at his other side.

She also tried to strike up a conversation with him every five seconds, but Tristan kept his answers to monosyllables, while still trying his best not to sound rude. I was deeply relieved when we finally left Alicia at her cabin's front door. I had to yank her bony, greedy fingers away from Tristan's arm so she'd let him go, though.

We were about to turn round and head back to our cabin, when I remembered my initial plan to question that Blaine guy, but Tristan was reluctant to go and see him.

"I don't know, Joe. It will be dark very soon. We should head back now," he immediately argued when I reminded him of my request.

"Well, it wasn't a problem to go out a minute ago when you had to escort Miss Scaredy Pants over there, but all of a sudden it's a big deal to stay a little bit longer for me?" I sniffed indignantly. "I see how it is."

He rolled his eyes. "You're being childish, Joey."

"Come on, Tristan. We're already here at the cabins! It will only take a few more minutes of your time to find Simon's and speak with him," I insisted. I was dying to get my memories back and to know more about these fire abilities I had. And Simon could be the key to unlock those memories. I had to talk to this guy.

"We don't even know which cabin he's staying in," he pointed out.

"We can find out. Isn't that big hotel building where I woke up right over there? There must be a reception desk where we can ask."

"Yeah, that's the camp's main house." He nodded, looking over at the building.

"Come on, don't you want me to get my memories back?" I asked eagerly.

He let out a deep sigh. "Okay, we can ask."

It wasn't really that hard to coax the information we wanted out of the receptionist, let me tell you. The girl handed over Simon's cabin number along with a little map. I couldn't help but notice her phone number swiftly scribbled at the bottom.

Simon's cabin wasn't very far from the main house – about the same distance as Alicia's, if I had to hazard a guess. We were about to knock on the door when a tall, skinny guy with dark hair dyed blue at the tips walked out, bumping awkwardly against me.

"Oh, hello, there. Sorry, didn't see you coming," he apologized, eyeing Tristan with a nervous glance.

"Hello, Blaine. We thought we should come over so

you can talk to Joey about whatever you wanted to discuss."

"Oh. I-I was actually heading to the main house for dinner, you know? Before it gets too dark. Maybe we can talk some other time . . ."

Tristan crossed his arms, a deep frown marking his face. He did not look pleased with that answer.

"Or maybe we can do it now. Dinner can wait, I guess. Your thing is more important," Blaine grumbled under his breath. "It's not like it's *incredibly* dangerous around this place after dark, anyway . . ." He motioned for us to follow him inside his cabin. "My room-mates have already left for the main house. We can talk in private; we're alone in here."

"I guess we could come back another time . . ." I whispered to Tristan.

"You were the one insisting we come here in the first place. I don't care if he's scared of the dark. We're going to talk. *Now,*" he said, and stomped inside.

Simon's cabin was very modest compared to the one I was sharing with Tristan, and significantly smaller as well.

I sensed Tristan's anger wasn't aimed at me. I'd noticed his eyes hardening every time Blaine was mentioned in a conversation. Why was Tristan so pissed at this guy, anyway?

Then a memory of a dark lake drifted back to me: *Blaine was standing still on a gray shore, facing me. I was in the lake, drowning, and he just stood there, unmoving, watching me with wide, scared eyes. I shouted for help and was angry . . . so very angry . . . that he did nothing . . .*

"Hey. You look like you're about to faint. Are you okay?" Blaine asked, and I blinked, startled, realizing I was already inside the cabin, standing next to Tristan.

I swayed a little as I returned to the present, images of the lake swiftly disappearing into the recesses of my mind.

"Y-yes, I'm fine," I mumbled.

Tristan gave me a concerned look.

"Look, I know you don't want to miss your dinner, so we'll try to be really quick, all right? Tristan told me you had something you wanted to talk to me about?"

"Yeah, it's nothing urgent, though. It's about that thing you asked me to look up, about that lost relative of yours that might be in the Top League?"

Since I had no idea what he was talking about, I just nodded and went along with it. I hoped Tristan and I had a close enough relationship that he'd know what was going on in my life, and could figure things out on my behalf.

"What did you find out?" Tristan asked.

Simon sat down on a bed nearby and continued. "So, I rang my brother Cillian to ask. It wasn't easy getting him to talk about the Top League. Like I said before, he's very secretive about his job. And I never call him, like, ever. So that made him even more suspicious and closed off . . . But in the end, I played the guilt card, like you suggested, Joe, and it kinda worked!"

He looked expectantly at me, hoping for an "atta boy", or something, but I just blinked back at him in complete ignorance as to what he was talking about.

He cleared his throat, mildly disappointed by my reaction, but continued with his story. "So, anyway, it turns out there was an old member in the Top League with the surname Gray, called Jonathan. My brother remembered hearing the name mentioned once at the headmaster's. From what I could squeeze out of Cillian, this guy quit the League a long time ago, like, twenty years or so. Cillian said they tend to keep track of all members – old, new, attending or not – but this dude went a hundred per cent off the grid. He disappeared completely: nobody ever heard from him after he left. That was why my brother recalled the guy: it's quite hard to disappear the way he did. And that's it, that's all I could find out."

"Hey, that's my fa—" I was about to mention the coincidence of this Top League dude having the exact same name as my father, but Tristan quickly cut in.

"Okay, Blaine, thanks."

I frowned at him, upset that he had been so rude interrupting me, but his eyes flicked quickly to me, flaring in alarm and silently warning me to be quiet. Hey, message received. I clamped my mouth shut immediately.

"We've been trying to locate this long-lost relative of Joey's for a while now, a great-great-uncle of her cousin," Tristan continued, but I could see the lie in his eyes. Why would he lie about this? "I don't think this guy has anything to do with it, though – the relative's name isn't Jonathan. But, hey, it was worth a shot, eh? We knew it was a stretch. But thanks anyway, Blaine."

Why was Tristan acting so strangely? Why was he lying to Simon? And what was this Top League they were talking about? Boy, I'd never wanted my memories back so badly as I did right now!

A memory flared in my head again: *I was very little and I was crying in my crib. Something had spooked me and I felt so scared. A man walked into the dark room, eyes heavy with sleep and black hair in disarray. "Hey, baby girl. Why are you crying?" he asked tiredly, leaning over the crib. "Come on, now, you don't wanna wake your mommy with all that wailing, do ya?" He picked me up and cradled me in his arms, trying to make me go back to sleep, but I was still scared and kept crying.* "Hey, want to see something pretty?" *he murmured softly, trying to bribe me into silence. He waved his fingers in front of my face and my weeping subdued into soft sobs, until tiny sparks sprouted from his hand and a small flame appeared, dancing on his fingertips.* "Look! Look, how pretty is the dancing flame?" *he cooed at me.* "Makes you want to stop crying, doesn't it, chubby cheeks?" *I immediately stopped sobbing, enchanted by the fire, and giggled, reaching out my hands to grab the flame.* "Look at that. My fire doesn't hurt you." It was the last thing I remembered him saying before Simon's voice jolted me awake.

"You okay? You look like you've just seen a ghost."

"W-what?" I stammered, confused. "A ghost?"

Another memory lodged itself back – forcefully, this time, like a punch in the head. I felt as if someone had grabbed me and plunged me under cold water, goosebumps rising all over my skin . . . .

It was night-time, and Tristan was standing on the grass. He was looking pleadingly at me. I was angry so I punched him, but my hand passed right through his chest, as if he was made of thin air.

"Joey, please, I'm so sorry . . . I was going to tell you. I lied so you wouldn't be scared of me . . ."

"Oh, God, it can't be true," I mumbled to myself. Was he . . . a ghost? How was that possible? "I remember . . . m-my hand passed right through his chest." I gasped and swayed a little, still immersed in my memories.

"What? You mean you've actually seen a ghost?" Simon asked, oblivious to my mental flashback. "That's nonsense. Everybody knows we can only contact spirits in séances or through Ouija boards. Are you honestly saying you've just seen one?"

"I could see . . . it felt so real. My hand . . . it passed right through . . ." I whispered, my eyes glazed and my fingers extending to touch Tristan's chest, as if I was still in a dream state.

"Joey, calm down. This is just your memories flaring back." Tristan's soothing voice washed over me, making me slowly detach from my memories.

"G-ghosts are real . . ." I mumbled dizzily.

"Pft, yeah, right!" Simon scoffed. "I bet you're making this up. You're so full of it. The fantastical tales of Joe Gray. You keep fabricating these crazy rumors just to make yourself look important. I bet you don't even believe in them. I bet you don't even think ghosts exist!"

"Oh, they're real, all right," Tristan said.

"Oh, now you can see them, too?" Simon jeered, his tone dripping with sarcasm.

"Trust me, pal. I've seen more ghosts than you'll ever be able to see in all the séances of your life." Tristan's voice had an eerie quality and was filled with so much vehemence that it made Simon's certainty falter.

"Y-you're just t-trying to scare me . . . so you can make fun of me."

Tristan gave him a cold shrug. "It's the truth."

"I-I d-don't believe you." The ceiling light fuzzed and sparked, almost going out. We all looked up, startled. "Are you doing this? Did you plan this to scare me?" Simon whimpered, looking around fearfully.

"We're not doing anything," Tristan stated, trying to calm everybody in the room. He wrapped an arm around me protectively.

The walls of the cabin started to tremble, making a few picture frames shake. The light blinked on and off again, and the temperature in the air decreased dramatically until it was freezing cold inside the cabin.

"P-please stop it!" Simon shouted, his breath forming warm puffs of condensation in the air. "This isn't funny, all right? Stop!"

"Simon, we swear we're not doing this," Tristan snapped, tightening his hold on me.

"T-Tristan? What's going on?" I asked, scared, looking around the room for clues. "What's happening in here?"

"I don't know. But something is definitely not right." He had just finished speaking when the objects that had been on the night-stand started to fly around, flung all over the room.

I ducked my head as a hairbrush missile approached my face, while Tristan tried to swerve away from a deodorant can and a flashlight flying in his direction. Simon was crouched on the floor, trying to escape the onslaught of domestic utensils.

"It's a ghost!" Simon shouted, frightened out of his mind.

"A very angry one," Tristan hissed, as a pack of batteries hit him squarely on the forehead.

"An angry ghost? Like a poltergeist? Why is it angry with us?" I shouted over the noise of clunking objects smashing against the walls.

"I don't know." Tristan turned to look at me.

"What are we going to do?" I asked in panic, as the windows started to fog and crack from the cold air. The light bulb finally gave up and burst in hot shards over our heads, leaving us in complete darkness.

"Don't be scared. I won't ever let any ghost hurt you," Tristan promised me, grabbing my hand. "We need to get the hell outta here. Now!" he commanded, pushing his way towards the front door without a care for the objects that were still flying around us.

He made a quick stop close to where Simon was, crouched on the floor with his hands over his head, and pulled him up. He grabbed Simon's arm in a tight grip.

"Simon, listen up. You're coming with us. I don't want you doing anything stupid like running off into the woods like a crazy lunatic, okay? The last thing we need now is for you to get lost in the dark. Come on!"

He pulled Simon's arm sharply and dragged him outside, taking long purposeful strides, while I held fast to his hand on his other side.

Chapter Eighteen
Perks of a Husband

"Don't worry, nothing bad is going to happen," Tristan said, as we hurried down the graveled road towards the main house. "If you count out the huff and puff and the occasional flying toothbrush, it seemed there was nothing more that ghost could do to us, anyway."

The sun had already set, and walking on a deserted trail in the dark, surrounded by a very ominous forest, wasn't exactly calming for my nerves, especially after the scare in Simon's cabin. Every rustle of leaves made me jump nervously, but nothing seemed to have followed us, and whatever it was that had attacked us, it looked like it had stayed behind in the cabin.

"How do you know what it can or can't do to us?" Simon asked, wheezing as he tried to keep up with Tristan's long strides.

"I know a thing or two about ghosts."

I took a sideways peek at him, understanding his cryptic answer. Of course he knew a thing or two about ghosts: he was one! I knew I should be scared – the last memory

I had of him was of my hands passing right through his chest – but something in my gut told me I didn't need to worry. I knew I could trust him completely; that certainty was etched in every fiber of my being. I may not have remembered much of our story yet, but I knew the trust I had in him. Tristan would never hurt me, not in a million years.

"Where did you learn all this stuff about ghosts, anyway?" Simon asked, stumbling as he looked anxiously over his shoulder.

"It doesn't matter how I know, I just know," Tristan replied curtly.

"You can let go of me now. I can walk by myself," Simon snapped, pulling his arm away, but Tristan's grip tightened, not letting him go.

"I don't think so. I'm not in the mood to play tag in the middle of these woods to save your sorry ass." Tristan pulled him back with a sharp tug.

"Who says I'm going to run into the woods? I'm not stupid!"

"But you are scared. People do stupid things when they're scared."

"Who's asking you to rescue me, anyway? Just leave me the hell alone!" Simon protested again, his pride wounded.

Tristan stopped abruptly and turned to face Simon straight on. "Listen closely, Blaine, cos I'm not gonna say this again. I'm not letting go so you can run away in panic. If you run off, I will have to go after you. Even though I don't want to, I'll have to. Wanna know why? Because *I don't leave people behind*. I help people when they need it, *even* if I don't like it. Because that's the right thing to do. So I'm not letting you go. *Period.* Suck it up and stop delaying us. Let's go!" He glared hard at Simon for a second, before turning round and continuing along the trail.

Simon let himself be dragged by Tristan, sulking like an angry child the entire way to the main house. The Harker sisters were quickly summoned as we arrived in the main lobby, and a nervous debate then ensued in which every one of us had to give repeated testimonies of what we had witnessed in Simon's living room.

Tristan even went back to the cabin with Celeste and Luna to try to track down the poltergeist.

He had firmly requested that I stay at the main house with Arice, for my safety, and that I should wait there for him to return. I had to bite down the urge to start a fight right then and there. That seemed an awful lot like an order to me. I didn't like being bossed around like that by anyone, husband or not. He had no right to tell me what to do.

I also didn't like the idea of staying behind like a helpless little girl. Something in the back of my head gnawed at me, protesting in indignant offense at the thought. I knew, deep down, that I was more than capable of defending myself, and even defending Tristan if necessary. Why couldn't I go with them? What if something happened to him? Who was going to come to his rescue then?

But he was gone before I could even have a say in the matter, leaving me behind, silently seething.

Arice saw how dejected I was and tried to distract me by making small talk.

"So, yeah, things have been pretty hectic around here, huh?"

I shrugged and kept on sulking in silence. How dared

Tristan leave me behind with the flowery lady while he went on a rocking search party with the tough girls?

Arice sucked at her teeth and tried again. "And with Craig still out of service, I had to do the camp rounds all by myself, can you believe it? He's still not feeling well after his blackout, so I had to do it for him. You seem to be recovering pretty quickly, though. Well, men always make such a fuss when they are sick, right?"

She glanced at me but I continued, unmoved, with my sulk. "Anyway, like I was saying, I had to do the rounds and try to find some clue for this craziness here. Funnily enough, I did find wolf tracks near by the lake, you know?"

That snapped me out of my sulking, fast. "You did?"

"Yeah!" she exclaimed, happy that she'd finally got me out of my funk. "I'm no expert, but I was a member of the Girl Scouts when I was a teen, and we had to learn to recognize all kinds of animal tracks. Wolf was actually number one on the list, so I remembered it pretty well. It was definitely a wolf paw print there. It was bigger than is typical, but it could have been a big wolf. That's why we're ordering everyone to stay indoors now."

"But Tristan, Celeste and Luna are out there right now!"

"It's okay, calm down. Luna and Celeste can deal with any wildlife, trust me. They are completely safe and they went prepared. You don't need to worry."

"What is going on in this place, Arice? I'm losing chunks of my memory and nobody knows why. You are finding wolf paw prints all over the place, and now there's a frigging poltergeist attacking?"

"Well, at least you don't have to bring any more ghosts back to life, fight Vigil or Death, or wrestle with evil intergalactic sneaky creatures and their weird magic ball powers . . ."

"*What?*"

"Oh, you still don't remember those things? Never mind, then . . ."

"I swear, you lot are all insane . . ." I muttered under my breath.

Tristan, Celeste and Luna soon returned empty-handed and as clueless as they had left. They hadn't found anything lingering in the cabin that could serve as evidence of any occult activity. Tristan said there was nothing there any more, only the remains of a few objects scattered all over the floor.

Simon and his room-mates were skeptical and refused to return to their cabin, preferring to stay in vacant rooms at the main house for the time being.

After things had been thoroughly discussed and nothing was either concluded or resolved, Tristan and I were finally excused for the night. I was still fuming at being excluded from their special search party as we walked back up the trail to our cabin.

Only when we were halfway there did I remember Arice's news about real wolf paw prints in the camp. I realized we didn't have the Harkers' protection now, and we should be worried about walking up the trail in the middle of the night by ourselves.

"Hmm, I think I should've told you this sooner, but there is some real evidence now of a wolf roaming around these parts . . ." I said, looking cautiously at the dark forest surrounding us.

"Yeah, I know. Celeste told me," he said, undisturbed, pointing the flashlight onward to illuminate the path for us. "She asked me if I'd like us to stay in the main house for the night, but I want to get back to our cabin. I need to tell the news to the boys. Don't worry, I've got a flare and some pepper spray with me. I don't think we'll need them, though. Animals usually get spooked around me and tend to stay away."

"Why do animals get spooked around you?"

He glanced quickly at me, unsure if he should explain this right now.

"Is it because you're a ghost?" I risked.

"I'm *not* a ghost. Not any more." His tone was clipped. The topic seemed to bother him somehow.

"But that was why you weren't scared at Simon's cabin, wasn't it?"

Since we'd walked out of Simon's cabin, he had looked like the possibility of new ghost attacks didn't worry him in the least.

"The day I'm scared of ghosts is the day when pigs fly, Joe." Then he bit the inside of his cheek, looking hesitant. "But to be honest, I don't even know if '*that*' was really a ghost . . ."

"What do you mean?"

"It just didn't feel like it, you know?" he said, as we reached our cabin and I could finally breathe in relief. "See? We're here, safe and sound." He unlocked and opened the door. "There's something more to this, Joe. I don't know what, but . . . all I know is that it didn't feel like a ghost to me."

"And what did it feel like, then? Do you have a guess as to what it could be?"

"That's the thing . . . I've been thinking hard about everything that has happened to you since we arrived at this camp . . ." He tossed the keys on to the counter as he entered the kitchen. "I mean, first it's the wolf attack that turns out to be from a real wolf. Then it's a swamp creature nobody saw but you, trying to drown you, then your sudden mysterious amnesia, and now, out of the blue, some angry poltergeists? There's no connection between any of it: nothing adds up!"

I laughed nervously but stopped when I saw how serious he looked. "I'm sorry, but when you list everything that's happened all in a roll, it all sounds so unreal."

He sighed, shaking his head. "I wish you had your memories back already . . . this would be so much easier . . ." he murmured to himself. "Look, Joe, I know this is all a bit too much to take in, but trust me on this. I mean, you know now that you can create fire out of your bare hands. Take a leap of faith here and say you believe me about all of the rest, yeah?"

I gave a small nod and sat on the kitchen stool while he sat the other side of the counter, facing me. "So, what you need to know first is that magic is very present in your life, and has been for most of the past four years, okay?" he began explaining. "I know it sounds crazy and not real, but indulge me for a sec. Say you believe magic and supernatural things are real," he proposed, and when I nodded again, he continued.

"Good. Then hear me out. At first I thought it was something to do with that Alicia girl, the one who came by this afternoon to check on you. Luna told me she was in your group that night by the lake: she could have lagged behind and made some noises to scare you guys. I mean, everybody said you only heard growls, but none of you actually saw anything, right? Then, the lake creature happened, and that one was definitely real – you have finger-mark bruises on your ankle to prove it. But there was no way Alicia could have done that, so I thought, maybe it's Simon, then. He was with you when that lake creature showed up." He gesticulated while explaining his line of thought. "But that doesn't make sense, either, because he was attacked too, right? That thing was after him! Why would he conjure up some water creature that could end up killing him, too? So I reckon it wasn't him. He wasn't anywhere near when you lost your memory . . . but then again, Alicia was. She was the one who found you unconscious.

"But then there's Craig. Luna mentioned you guys bumped into Craig on the way to the lake that night, but he was also attacked at the main house. Nothing adds up and no one person fits the part on all occasions. And now there's this ghost that doesn't feel like a real ghost to me, showing up out of the blue. I'm wracking my brains, trying to think of an explanation, but I can't make sense of anything!" he said, passing a hand through his hair.

"I'm not smart as you are, Joey. If you had your memories back, you'd be solving this mystery in no time. Usually, it's you who solves all the problems, you know. You're stubborn as hell, and you never quit, even if it's bloody dangerous and even if I try to stop you: you never give up and you always fix things in the end. I wish I had you back to normal. You'd crack this one in a second . . ."

"Really? I do all those things?" I asked, surprised.

"Yeah." He smiled proudly. "You're incredible."

"You were very brave back at the cabin, you know," I said, shyly. "I was really impressed; you didn't seem scared at all!"

"Yeah, well, I've learned from the best," he told me, with a sideways smile.

I glanced down and fumbled with the hem of my tank-top, blushing hard. "I can't believe I don't remember any of this stuff. It's so frustrating!" I said, aggravated. "Ghosts, magic, fire . . . everything sounds so crazy, but . . . at the same time, it doesn't. And the worse thing is that I know I should be freaking out about these crazy things, but something tells me it's all very normal – and then I just accept it, just like that. And that's freaking me out even more! Plus, I keep remembering all these silly, unimportant things, yet all the serious life-changing memories are still a blank. Why? Why do I remember the sound of your voice, and your smell, but I can't remember who you are? Why? It's ridiculous." I tugged at my hair, as if I could dislodge memories by yanking them out by force.

"So, let me get this straight," he said. He was clearly trying to stop himself laughing, but his lips twitched and gave him away. "You're freaking out that you're not freaking out when you know you should be freaking out."

"Yes! That's exactly it! How come you always know exactly what I'm thinking and how I'm feeling? It's so spooky!" I exclaimed.

"Perks of being your husband, buttercup," he stated, looking smug, and leaned over the counter, tugging a lock of hair under my ear. "Don't worry, Joey. You'll get your memories back. But for now we shall try to make the best of things, all right?"

"Okay," I mumbled, half-heartedly.

"Are you hungry? I can make us some sandwiches . . . or do you want a real meal for dinner? I can cook something, if you want, but it will take longer to be ready." He stood up.

"You know how to cook?"

"Let's just say that if I didn't, we'd both have starved to death by now. So, what's it gonna be?"

"A sandwich would be great, please. Thank you."

"Swell! Coming right up, buttercup." He gave me a quick wink and went to prepare what was about to become the best ham sandwich I'd ever eaten in my whole life.

Chapter Nineteen
Dinner for Two

"So, tell me, Tristan, how's life been for us over the past four or so years?" I asked, as he placed two plates with two delicious-looking sandwiches on the counter between us. I was dying to find out more about our life together, and this was the perfect time to ask, while we dived into our late-night dinner snack.

He gave me a quizzical look for a moment before sitting back down in his seat opposite me, leaning his elbows on the counter and crossing his fingers under his chin.

"It's been a good life so far," he told me. "Right now, we're having a lot of fun finding things for our apartment. We shared a house with the rest of the guys for about three years, but we decided it was time to move into our own place after we got married a month ago. Now we are picking out furniture and décor for the apartment. You are very excited about that."

"Oh, I am?" It didn't sound like me at all, to be honest. I'd always hated shopping for anything. Furniture shopping must be boring as hell.

He chuckled at the face I was pulling. "Yes, you are. You hate shopping, but you're really excited about decorating our home. You choose the most random, weird things, but when we put them all in the room, it all comes together, somehow. It's like having your place filled with bits and pieces of memories and things we both love. It's a shame we're not there now. I'm sure it would help spark some memories. Our home is warm and cozy, like a good home should be."

"When you say it like that, it sounds kind of fun," I mused, grabbing my sandwich and taking a bite. "Oh, my God!" I moaned in surprise after taking the first bite.

"Is it good?" he asked, smiling, then taking a bite of his own.

"Good? This is amazing! How can you make a lame ham sandwich taste as incredible as this?"

His grin widened. He looked pleased that I was enjoying the meal. "It's an old recipe my mom taught me. The key is in the condiments. It's actually your favorite; that's why I made it now for you."

"No wonder it's my favorite. This thing is off the charts! You should be a professional ham-sandwich chef," I mumbled, with a mouth full of food.

"Nah. I'm quite happy with my current profession."

I frowned, trying to grasp at any recollection of the band we were supposed to have been in for more or less the last four years of my life.

He paused, waiting to see if my memory sparked at that tidbit of information. "I'm sorry, I can't remember much about the band at all. Man, this amnesia sucks, big time!"

"You remembered the songs, though. That's a good thing. The rest will come back to you in time, don't worry."

He resumed munching on his sandwich, his expression relaxed. "It's returning slowly, but you're getting there."

"How do you manage to be so calm about it?"

He gave a small shrug. "Would it help if I was freaking out?"

"No, but it's normal to react that way, I guess."

"'Normal' has never been very present in our lives, sweetheart. I don't think it's wise to start now."

"You don't need to tell me. I'm beginning to realize my life revolves around all kinds of weird . . ."

"Weird can be a good thing," he said. "That's what you always used to say when you were trying to cheer me up. I'm all kinds of weird, too. But you love me anyway." He gave me a small, shy smile.

"Yeah, about that . . . I'm trying to figure out a gentle way to ask you this, but I'll just go ahead and ask. I know this sounds completely insane, but I remembered a scene with you. There were fireworks in the sky and you . . . my hand passed right through you! I wasn't imagining that, was I? That really happened, right? You are a ghost?"

"Yes, I *was* a ghost." He put the sandwich slowly back on his plate and raised his head to look at me. "But I'm not one any more. Look, it's—"

"You're going to say it's a long story and kind of complicated, aren't you?"

"Please, don't freak out. I know it all sounds crazy . . ."

"Oh, we passed crazy a long time ago, buddy. This is beyond crazy. We're light years past crazy here. I mean, I'm a real life matchstick, you're an ex-ghost . . . it cannot get any weirder than this!"

"Oh, believe me, it can. And it has," he said, amused. "But, hey, I've had years to get used to it. You've only had a day. It's normal for you to be freaking out, right? You have to trust me on this. We have a good life together, even with all the weird."

I bit my lip, my brows furrowing in agitation. I wished I had my memories back already. These blank holes in my head were infuriating.

"Joey, look at me," he said, and I looked up from my plate, startled by his tone. He put a hand gently over mine. "You *will* remember us. I promise you. Okay?"

I gave a small nod. "Okay."

"Good. Can I have that okay again with a smile this time, please?" he asked. The smile was there before he could even finish the sentence. "That's better," he said, squeezing my hand. "So, what else do you wanna know? Hit me with your best shot."

"Hmm, okay . . . What's our favorite pastime?"

He stared at the ceiling, chewing silently for a while as he reached for an answer. "There are a lot of things . . . let me think. We watch a lot of movies. You like to show me the ones with special effects, which are awesome, by the way. I still can't get over how realistic those things can get. And I make you watch the old classics that I like. It's a lot of fun. We do the same thing with our favorite music, too." A smile played on his lips as he thought about the memories, completely oblivious of me silently pining for him from the other side of the counter.

I was glad he hadn't noticed how blatantly obvious it was that I was staring, because I couldn't stop myself – even if I tried. He was mesmerizing; I could listen to him talk for ever.

"I like to cook for you, test new recipes, and then you give me grades for your favorites. That sandwich got a big score for me." He shot me a wink and I chuckled shyly.

"But I think our favorite thing is to play our songs on stage together. You look the happiest and shine the brightest when you're doing that . . ." he mused, his eyes focused intently on me.

"I can't believe I'm in a real band! Did you know my father—"

". . . was a musician too," he completed for me. "Yeah, I know."

"Of course. I keep forgetting you know me already . . . sorry." I glanced down, embarrassed. "I never talk about my father to anyone. It's weird that you know . . ."

"Joey " – he reached out again and placed my hand gently in his – "you trusted me enough to tell me once. You can trust me again."

"I do." I held his hand tightly and smiled, silently telling him that I truly did, with all my heart.

The look he gave me was filled with an emotion so strong that his gray eyes glinted with a silver ring around the edges.

"I love to see you smile. You light up the room when you smile," he said quietly, making me blush under the heat of his sterling gaze.

"But I have to say," he continued, his tone lighter now, "my most favorite thing right now is to be able to make you blush again this easily. I've missed your blushes."

The playful smirk on his lips was enough to make my cheeks flame fiercely red again. He laughed, satisfied and all pleased with himself, for having done it again.

Chapter Twenty
Just a Little Patience

"Here's your bag. If you need anything, dig in here." Tristan hung a bag over the chair by the side of the bed. "You usually sleep in one of my old T-shirts, like this one." He fumbled inside the bag and handed me a large worn blue T-shirt. "I'll go finish up the dishes. Howl if you need anything."

I snuck into the bathroom and paused in front of the mirror. There were small cuts on my face, but I couldn't remember how they'd got there. And I still couldn't get used to my short haircut. It looked so different and modern.

As I settled into bed and prepared to go to sleep, Tristan came into the room and made a beeline for the bathroom, not paying much attention to my startled face.

Was he planning on sleeping next to me? In the same room? In the same bed? We were married, after all, so sleeping together should be expected, but my frantic heart couldn't get used to it.

I sat up in the bed, listening intently to his movements in the bathroom. When I heard him turn the tap off, I quickly sank back under the safety of the covers, like a jittery rabbit. As he came back into the bedroom, I noticed he'd changed into black sweatpants and nothing much else. I have to say, I wasn't prepared for a half-naked and incredibly fit Tristan – I was gawking like a teenage girl at the sight. He should have warned me he was going to do that! When I managed to snap out of it, he was already sitting on the bed beside me, patting the pillow as if he were getting ready to climb in.

"We're not going to sleep in the same bed, are we?" I squeaked, pulling the sheets up to my chin.

He stopped what he was doing and turned to face me, one eyebrow raised, half in amusement, half curiosity. "Well, yeah. There isn't another bed in the cabin. You don't expect me to sleep on the couch, do you?"

"Hmmm . . ." I stalled, trying to think of an excuse that would convince him to go to sleep on the uncomfortable couch. "You know . . . hard, flat cushions are very good for your spine. You'll thank me in the morning."

He stared at me for a moment before letting out a resigned sigh. "All right. I suppose it's the courteous thing to do. I'll take the couch," he muttered, grabbing his pillow and walking into the living room.

"Thank you. Sorry. Thank you," I squeaked, full of guilt for forcing him out of his own bed.

I woke up next morning to the sound of pans and cutlery clanging in the kitchen. Tristan was finishing cooking breakfast when I leaned sleepily over the counter top, trying to take a peek at the contents of his steaming pan. Whatever it was he was making, it smelled delicious.

"Morning, buttercup," he greeted me, with a tired smile.

"Morning. You look tired. Was the couch that bad?" I asked, full of guilt again.

He hesitated. "It takes some time getting used to it," he replied, in the politest way he could find. "How about you? Any new memory spark when you woke up?"

"Not when I woke up, but I had a dream last night about a cemetery . . ."

"Really? What cemetery?" he interrupted, his tone eager.

"I don't know. It had graves and the usual cemetery stuff." I gave him an odd look. I'd never seen someone so excited about a cemetery before. "In the dream, I was walking down the lanes and it was a sunny afternoon. It was so nice there, I felt so happy. And no matter where I walked, I kept stumbling upon this angel statue with a broken wing all the time."

"It was the cemetery where we used to hang out in the first weeks we knew each other. The angel statue was next to my tomb. It was our meeting point," he explained.

"Really? That's so weird. Wasn't I scared of you? It's not every day you get to see and talk to a ghost . . ."

He gave me a cryptic smile. "You didn't know I was a ghost at first. You thought I was a regular kid. Well, not so much regular but more like a kind of weird kid. I'm thankful that you're not a judgmental person, or you wouldn't have come to see me again. I was so happy when you came back, you had no idea."

"How did you stop, you know, being a ghost?" I'd been meaning to ask him this since last night. I remembered Arice saying something about how I kept bringing ghosts back to life. "It was something I did, wasn't it?"

"Yes, it was. I was your first bump into magic."

"First? You mean there were other bumps?"

"Let's just say it has been a bumpy road," he said, with a chuckle. "But this was another memory, Joey. They are coming back to you in your dreams. That's good."

"Well, I don't know about good. The dream ended pretty badly. While I was walking, the afternoon all of a sudden turned into night and snow started to fall. At the beginning, it was gentle, but then it turned into a scary blizzard and then snow started piling up, covering me until I was buried and I couldn't breathe and felt so cold. I woke up shaking and gasping for air. Weird, right?"

"Well, no actually. Something like that happened to you. The dream showed it in a weird way, but it does reveal a memory. You fell asleep one night in the cemetery during winter, and it was snowing pretty badly. Josh rescued you before you froze to death."

"Oh. That's horrible. Why I would sleep in a cemetery? Was I crazy?"

"You were waiting for me. I couldn't come see you that night. I tried to, but I couldn't." He sounded so sad that I decided to change the subject.

"Okay. So, hmm, what are our plans for today?"

"Well, we should keep trying to jog your memories. There's still a lot for you to catch up on," he said. "But first, let's eat. There's nothing like a good breakfast to start the day."

We spent the rest of the day in the boys' cabin, talking and trying to make me remember things, but this time, no matter how hard they all tried, nothing seemed to work. My mind had ground to a stagnant halt, and nothing they did, no songs or old tales they shared, were getting any spark of recognition from me.

As the day ended, I could see the worry in the boys' faces. They didn't know why I had stopped remembering things, and they were worried. But it was only after I woke up the next morning, with not even memory dreams to relay, that Tristan decided to call Celeste in for a meeting.

They talked in hushed voices for a while, until they finally reached a decision.

"Fine. We'll try to contact him, then," Tristan conceded, although somewhat reluctantly. "He might know a way to help."

"I'll get the ingredients for the incantation ready, then. Meet me in my room by the end of afternoon—"

"You need all that time to get things ready?" Tristan complained impatiently.

"Miss Violet is a much better witch than I am, and if I'm not mistaken, she took even longer than this, Halloway. 'Patience is bitter, but its fruit is sweet.'"

"All right. I'm sorry for trying to rush you. I'll see you later, then, Celeste."

"Who are we contacting?" I asked, after Celeste had left.

"An old friend. You usually have a faster way to call him, but I think you won't be able to, since you don't remember how to do it."

"Don't tell me, it's a magic way to call this person, isn't it?" I grumbled, frustrated. Everything in my life revolved around magic, even calling a friend.

"Yes. The mark on your wrist connects you to him. You use it to call him when you need him."

I glanced at my arm. A tattoo-like pattern with black lines spread over my wrist like a circulatory system map. "Oh, I thought this was just a tattoo I'd had done. Always wanted one, but my mom was dead against it. I figured I must have had the guts to do one after I left home."

"It's not a tattoo. It's a counter effect of a spell you did once."

I rubbed the mark. "Really? How do I make it work?"

"You concentrate on the mark and call him. I think."

"It's not working, though."

"You don't remember him. I think that's why. You don't know whom to call. That's why we need Celeste to invoke a spell to bring him to us. We did this once, a long time ago."

"And this person can help bring my memories back, is that it?"

"We will ask and see if he can. He'll do anything to help you, I know that much."

"All right, then. Let's do this."

Chapter Twenty-One
Old Friend Return

Tristan and I had been waiting for Celeste to get everything in position to cast her spell for about half an hour. The afternoon was almost at an end as she walked around her room, positioning odd-looking objects on the floor and muttering to herself while she rehearsed all the steps for the incantation, over and over, in a low mumble.

"All right, I think I have everything in order. I think we can start now," she finally said, after lighting a circle of weird candles around the room. The smell of incense was suffocating, but Tristan wasn't complaining so I kept my mouth shut.

Celeste looked up and, at Tristan's affirmative signal, she started pouring a bag of white sand in a small circle at the center of the room.

A few moments passed and nothing happened. I was about to start complaining that this whole mise-en-scène she was creating was silly, when a strange guy appeared out of thin air inside the circle of sand. I gasped loudly, but when I looked around, Tristan and Celeste were acting as if it was the most normal thing in the world.

The man had a beautiful, ethereal face and the most haunting black eyes I'd ever seen. My wrist started to throb as though sharp, hot needles were stabbing into my flesh. I let out a groan of distress, because the pain was steadily increasing, and that made the strange man glance up. His dark eyes were focused intensely on me, like they were piercing into my soul.

He took a step forward but halted midway, as if something was physically preventing him from continuing, and he frowned, glancing down at the floor to look for the reason he was being held back.

"Oh, dear God, my apologies!" Celeste hurried to him in a fluster. "I forgot to break the line for the concealment spell. I didn't mean to lock you up in there. I'm so very sorry!" She stomped her feet quickly over the white line, seeming mortified at her embarrassing faux pas.

"I can't believe this. It worked!" I exclaimed to Tristan, who had been standing calmly beside me. "Did you see how he showed up like an apparition? Is he a ghost, too?" My eyes were as wide as saucers.

Tristan turned to me, the corner of his lips twitching upwards in amusement. "I forgot you're scared of ghosts. He's not an apparition, though, so calm down. He's here to help."

"Is he an alien, then?" I gasped in realization. "Aliens can teletransport like that! I've seen it in movies!"

"I guess that's one way of seeing it. He's definitely not from this world, so . . ."

The guy began walking our way, after exchanging a few hushed words with Celeste. He stopped in front of us and greeted Tristan in a polite manner before he turned to me, searching intently for something.

"Hello, Joey. I was told you are momentarily devoid of the faculty to retrieve information right now. Is that correct?"

What was up with this guy, and why did he speak so weirdly?

"Y-yeah, they are telling me I have amnesia."

"In that case, let me introduce myself, since you probably have no recollection of meeting me before. I am a former Gray Hood Bearer. But you can call me Vigil. That is my human name now." And he extended his hand for me to shake.

I hesitated for a second, but then reached out and took his hand. The stabbing pain stopped immediately, and I sighed in relief. I made a motion to end the handshake, but he held on to my hand.

"It is better if we keep it this way," he explained. "It will prevent you from hurting. While there is contact between us, you will feel no pain."

"What? Really? Why?" I asked, puzzled.

"Vigil, do you think you can help get her memories back?" Celeste interrupted, glancing at our holding hands with a slight frown.

"Let me see what I can do." He closed his eyes in concentration.

I felt a light tug inside my skull and my recurrent headache paid yet another unpleasant visit. "Ugh! God, can you guys please stop giving me headaches?" I protested, letting go of his hand to rub my temples. My wrist began to hurt on cue, and I grunted in double protest. "First it was Celeste, now it's him. Stop doing whatever it is you guys are doing to me. I beg of you!"

"I am sorry. It was not my intention to cause you more pain, Joey," he apologized wholeheartedly, and I suddenly felt bad for snapping at him. He looked genuinely worried. "Sit down, please. Let me try to make amends."

I slumped down on the couch and he sat next to me, once more taking my hand in his. My wrist stopped hurting again, and he pressed a thumb over my forehead, making my headache subside until there wasn't any pain left.

"Do you feel better?" he asked.

"Yeah. Thanks. I'm sorry for snapping at you. These headaches make me a bit grumpy," I apologized.

"I understand. I experienced this illness when we switched our powers. It was very aggravating."

"Why do you think she's having these headaches, Vigil?" Celeste asked, coming to stand next to us, in front of the couch. "The same thing happened when I tried to prod inside her head."

"It seems like it is some sort of defense mechanism. Her mind is trying to protect itself, I think. But she is doing this without proper training, and the headache is the result of this unprepared effort."

"Do you think you can retrieve at least some of her memories? Maybe the one before she blacked out?" Celeste asked. "It would help us figure out what happened."

"I am afraid I may not be of assistance to you. Her psyche is blocking any outside intrusion," he continued. After a pause, he proposed: "I can try to make a more assertive advance, if you wish, and try to unlock her memories by force. But I am not completely sure if this will be a good course of action. It could trigger an even stronger reaction from her, and deteriorate her memory even further. Or cause her more pain. Or both."

"Oh, goodie," I grumbled under my breath.

"What do you think we should do, then?" Tristan asked.

"My advice is that you leave her be. The human mind usually heals quickly, and I think she will soon start to remember things on her own. It is better not to rush her recovery."

"That's what I told them," Celeste said.

"You are a very wise woman, Celeste," he agreed with a soft smile.

She blushed faintly.

"Vigil, we think Joey's amnesia could be linked to some mysterious attacks going on around here," Tristan said, interrupting the moment. "Maybe it could be magic related. I thought perhaps you could try to scan the place for any paranormal activity? Maybe you can catch whoever is doing this."

"Very well. Let me see . . ." He closed his eyes and concentrated again. "There are magical ripples signaling all over this place. It is everywhere."

"Oh, we are having a witch Gathering here," Celeste explained. "You must be picking up on them."

"Yes, that explains all the signals I am catching. The heavier concentration is in this room, though." He opened his eyes and they flashed briefly with a soft white glow. "Must be because of you, Celeste. You are a powerful sorcerer. And, of course, there is always Joey with her powers, and Tristan with his."

"Tristan has powers, too?" I asked, surprised. He'd forgotten to mention that tidbit of information to me. He was full of surprises.

"Yes, of course. There is also his paranormal background. He is a strong magical broadcaster." Vigil regarded me in silence for a moment, before turning to Tristan. "Does she really not remember you? After everything . . ."

I sensed Tristan tensing up beside me, and his arm wrapped around my shoulder, pulling me closer to him. "No. But she will. I'm sure of that. Our connection is still strong, even though she has no memory of it."

"Yes, of course," Vigil said in a cryptic tone.

It looked like there was some sort of unresolved feud going on between them, as they stared at each other, exchanging silent messages. Then a fleeting image of Vigil staring unblinkingly at Tristan flashed into my head: *Black fathomless cold eyes stared deep into piercing bright gray ones. They both looked so angry, and then Tristan's voice echoed in my memory: 'It. Is. Never. Going. To. Happen.' He said it slowly, deliberately and with the most absolute certainty.*

"You do not need to worry." Vigil's voice made me snap back to the present.

"I'm *not* worried." Tristan's tone was slightly clipped now.

"You know my main concern here is her wellbeing, Tristan. It has always been so."

"I know, Vigil. Thank you for coming and for your advice. I'll watch over her, until she is back to herself."

Vigil stood up and gave a slight bow to Tristan and me. Then he turned to Celeste. "If you need me again, you know how to contact me. I am always at your service, Celeste Harker."

"You are very kind, Vigil. As always. Thank you."

"I look forward to our afternoon tea. It is still on, I presume?"

"O-oh. Y-yes. Of course! If you still want to. I thought

you were busy with your travels and such. I didn't want to be a bother."

"I have a few pieces of unattended business to take care of first, but as soon as that is over, I will return to schedule our tea, yes?"

"O-okay," she said, all flustered, with cheeks tinting red as he took her hand gently and kissed the top of it.

"Oh, and Celeste," he added, before letting go of her hand, "you are never a bother." He smiled softly, dipped his head and vanished away.

"Holy crap! He did it again! That is so creepy!" I exclaimed, my eyes wide. "He is a charmer, though, huh, Celeste?" I teased her, wiggling my eyebrows at her. There was clearly something going on between those two, even though they were both so incredibly awkward around each other.

"I'd prefer it if you keep 'creepy' more in mind than 'charmer', if you can, please," Tristan muttered, standing up from the couch in a grumpy mood. "And please, mind your language."

"Sorry. So, what do we do now?" I asked, grinning so broadly I was almost biting the tips of my ears. I'd noticed Tristan didn't like when I cursed. He seemed to dislike foul language of any kind, so I realized I should start minding my tongue around him. But it didn't sound like he was grumpy because of my bad manners. It felt like he was jealous and I had never had a good-looking guy like Tristan jealous over me before. It was kind of thrilling.

Tristan paused for a moment before turning to me.

"Well, there is something we still haven't done."

Chapter Twenty-Two
Pieces of Puzzle

"So, the plan is we go inside and try to fish for anything suspicious about this Craig fellow, is that it?" I asked Tristan, as we stood at the head of the side road leading to the caretaker's cabin, observing it from a distance.

We had left Celeste's room and the main house, and followed the trail up to Misty Lake Camp's entrance gates. We were told at the reception desk in the lobby that Craig's cabin was down a track near to the main gates, and that we should find him resting there. It seemed his blackout had taken a lot more out of him than it had me, and he was still trying to recover.

The receptionist in the lobby, however, thought the caretaker was only slacking on the job and trying to get away with as many free days off as he could bluff from this incident. Arice was sure thinking the same way, since she had been stuck with a lot of his duties, and had been doing the camp rounds for the past couple of days: she was not amused by his "slow recovery".

He could be lazy or lying. Either way, we wanted to go

talk to him and ask him some questions. Maybe he'd give us some clues that would help us solve all the mysteries going on in the camp.

"Yes. I want to ask him a few things," Tristan said. "He was the only one with you when the last attack happened and you lost your memory. Maybe he can tell us something new about that, something the Harkers missed asking him."

We hurried to his cabin and knocked on the door. It took the guy quite some time to open it, but when he did, we realized the reason for the delay. Craig was a short, chubby, middle-aged man, typically dressed like a camp instructor in his khaki outfit. But right now he looked as if he'd been dragged out of hell, his face dead pale, big purple bags under the eyes, hair in disarray, and he looked as if he was in a lot of pain, too. Maybe he wasn't slacking on the job, after all.

"Yes? What do you want?" he grunted at us.

"Hello, Mr. Simms. Sorry to bother you. My name's Tristan, and this is Joey. I don't know if you remember us; we are staying at the camp for the week," Tristan said politely, introducing us. "We were wondering if we could have a few words with you, sir? About what happened to you and Joey at the main house."

"I can't help you, son. I don't know what happened." He motioned for us to come inside. "All I know is that I woke up with a big chunk of my memory gone."

"Oh, so you are suffering from memory loss as well?"

He slumped tiredly on to a chair, grabbing a damp cloth from a table next to it and pressing it against his forehead. "Why? Who else is not remembering things?"

"Joey can't remember a lot of things, too. Since you two were attacked at the main house—"

"We were attacked? By whom?" he asked, visibly startled.

"That's what we are trying to find out, sir," Tristan explained patiently, and we both sat down on a sofa next to Craig.

"I don't know about any attack. Like I said, son, I woke up and can't remember anything. But that's not even the worst part. Is the girl having these inhuman migraines, too? Because I feel like my skull is about to split in half, here. Every time I try to force myself to remember anything, it gets worse. I gave up trying. I just want this pain to stop."

"Yes, she has them, too. Not as strongly as you, I think." Tristan glanced at me for confirmation, and I nodded to reassure him I was fine.

"It was real bad in the first hours after the attack, and it comes back when I try to remember things, too. But I'm fine now," I said.

"Someone bashed us on the head, is that what happened?" Craig asked, squinting his eyes as if the light in the room was hurting them.

"We don't know, sir. We were hoping you could tell us something that would help solve this mystery."

"I'm sorry, kids, but I can't help you. I don't even know what I'm doing in this place. Three girls came over a couple days ago and told me I'm filling in for the usual caretaker for the summer. They'd better start looking for a substitute, then. As soon as this blasted headache ends, I'm leaving this place and checking in to a hospital. All this pain can't be normal."

"I'm sorry to hear you're not feeling well, sir," Tristan said.

"Excuse me, I gotta go to the bathroom. Head is getting worse and I'm feeling a bit sick now. Hold on," he muttered, and stood up on wobbly legs, dragging his feet to the bathroom and closing the door behind him.

"Quick, keep an eye on him while I snoop around," Tristan whispered, standing up from his seat.

"What are you looking for?" I whispered, scooting over to the door through which Craig had disappeared, while Tristan looked around for clues.

"I guess I'll know when I find it," he whispered back, quickly riffling through some drawers and cabinets.

"Do you think he's lying, Tris?"

"I don't know. He might be, or he might not even remember that he is. Do you think he knows about the Gathering happening here at the camp? Or knows about magic at all?"

"He doesn't look like he knows," I murmured. "Celeste said he's just a temporary caretaker." I strained to hear what he was doing. It sounded like he really was being sick inside that bathroom. Yuck.

"Well, in that case, he's definitely lying," Tristan said.

"Why?" I turned round to see him holding a piece of paper he had taken from a leather briefcase lying in one corner of the living room.

"Because if he doesn't know about magic, why would he have these magic symbols in his briefcase, then?" He waved a scroll of old paper with some weird faded symbols scribbled on it.

"What are those symbols?"

"I don't know. I've seen a few of them at the Harkers' occult store, though. It's definitely magic related. He's up to something, but he's clearly forgotten about it for the moment. Or, who knows, he could be lying that he doesn't remember."

"But—" I didn't have time to finish what I was about to say, because the bathroom door was suddenly flung open, and Craig shuffled out, looking even more worse for wear than before.

"I'm sorry, kids, but I'm not feeling well," he muttered, pressing a fresh cloth over his eyes to block out the light, while Tristan quickly shoved the paper into his pocket. "You can come back later, if you want, but I need to lie down and rest now."

"Okay. I hope you feel better, sir. Thanks for talking to us," Tristan replied smoothly, grabbing me by the arm and pulling me along with him outside.

"Did you by any chance catch anything from him, Joe?" Tristan asked, as soon as we were out of earshot down the trail.

"What do you mean by 'catch'?"

"Did you see anything suspicious in his eyes?"

"No. He was barely looking at us, what with the migraine and that cloth pressed over his eyes. He looked genuinely in pain, though. I don't think he was lying about that. That's all I got. Sorry."

"If only you had your memory back . . . You would've known how to squeeze the truth out of him back there," Tristan lamented, as we headed back to our cabin.

"How would I do that?"

"You were very good at catching people's lies and turning them against themselves, and making them confess stuff. I guess we're going to have to do the detective work the good old-fashioned way, then. Come on."

Chapter Twenty-Three
Finding Clues in a Wasp Nest

We were debating whether we should go to Celeste with the paper Tristan got from Craig, when we arrived at our cabin and found the boys huddled outside the front door, waiting for us.

"Finally, there you are!" Sam was the first to shout at us.

"What's going on, guys?" Tristan asked, as we approached them.

"We are sick of doing nothing in our cabin. This lock-down is stupid! We are coming out. I don't care if there's a real wolf out there or not," Harry said, exasperated. He was the most hyperactive of all the boys, and being forced indoors for days on end was starting to put him on edge. "We were supposed to be doing hikes and exploring the forest and swimming in the lake. I can't stand one more second inside that cabin, and poor Rocko's practically going nuts."

"Plus, you two don't seem to be bothered about any of that danger talk. You've been prancing up and down this camp without a worry. Where are you going now?" Josh asked.

"Yeah! Cos we are coming with you," Harry added.

"Right now, we need to talk to Celeste," Tristan told them. "We just found a very important clue and we need her input on it. But a thought just came to me . . ." he mused, changing his mind. "Before we head for the main house, maybe we should take a quick detour. I want to check on one last thing before we go to Celeste. The more clues we bring her, the better, right?"

"All right! Let's go, then. We'll help you hunt for more clues," Josh volunteered, while Harry jumped up and down in excitement.

"What are we doing here, again?" Seth asked, looking nervously around and rubbing his arms. He wasn't as excited as the boys about going outdoors. Especially outdoors that had real wolves in it.

"I thought maybe we could try to find a clue about what's happening in here," Tristan said, peering at the dark waters of the lake. "I know we usually rely on Joey's skills to solve these situations, but with her memory gone, we are on our own, guys. We have to try to get to the bottom of this ourselves. The two first attacks happened in the area by the lake. Maybe there's something the Harkers didn't see here . . ."

"Yeah, but Joey said she didn't exactly see a wolf that night, remember?" Seth said, joining him us the shoreline. "It could have been anything."

"Yeah, it was mostly weird sounds that scared her," Harry added.

"So there's nothing to worry about, right?" Seth asked, voice full of hope.

"Well, there's the thing in the lake. Joey has marks on her ankle to prove it's real," Josh pointed out.

"And there's her amnesia, too. There's definitely someone behind this," Tristan said.

"But who?" Seth asked, looking confused.

"That's what I'm trying to find out, guys," Tristan reasoned, looking intently at the shoreline. "And now we've discovered some suspicious evidence in Craig's cabin. Maybe he has something to do with this. He was spotted in this area that night, according to Luna. And he was with Joey when she lost her memory. I want to check this place and see if he could have left a clue behind."

"But we looked everywhere! There's nothing here," Sam grumbled.

"I still think you're all overreacting," Seth argued. "I don't think it's anything supernatural. The thing chasing after people must be a raccoon, or something. They make a lot of a ruckus, those pesky little buggers. I'm sure it was only looking for snacks in people's pockets. And the thing in the lake could be a big fish . . . or a crocodile? They can drag people down, can't they, Harry? You watch those animal TV shows all the bloody time, give us some input here, will you?"

"Yeah, they do. They usually latch on and pull their prey down until it drowns. It takes less energy to kill that way than fighting them. But if it really were a croc, Joey wouldn't have survived. Once they bite, they don't let go. And the marks on her ankle weren't bite marks. They were finger marks, dude," Harry reminded him.

"Plus, if it's nothing supernatural, what do you think caused her amnesia, then, smarty pants? Crocodiles?" Sam asked, his voice full of sarcasm.

"I don't know! It could have been coconuts falling on their heads, or something," Seth tried to reason.

Harry tried to be helpful and added. "Do you know coconuts kill fifteen times more people than sharks?"

"Were there killer coconuts around Joey when you found her unconscious outside the main house, Hal?" Josh asked.

"Not that I can recall, no."

"Well, then. Your palm tree conspiracy is busted, Fletcher," Josh mocked.

"All I'm saying it that forests have *a lot* of scary things in them, and maybe there's nothing supernatural about these occurrences," Seth retorted, annoyed. "You never listen, but I'm telling you, nature only wants to kill you in the most—"

". . . slow, torturous way possible," the boys chorused in unison. "Yeah, we know, Seth."

"You may be right, man. But I still think we need to investigate this," Tristan said, searching the treetops at our back. "I'm not sure, but something doesn't feel right, here . . ."

"How about the poltergeist attack in that kid's cabin? How do you explain that?" Josh asked. "This has supernatural written all over it, dude!"

"Joey usually knows if it's supernatural stuff or not . . ." Harry muttered to the boys. "If she had her memories back, she would've known for sure. Her intuitions were always spot on."

"It's not her fault she can't remember, Harry," Josh said.

"I know that, I'm not saying it is. I'm worried, though. What if she never remembers stuff? It has been a while since last time she remembered something new."

"She will remember, Harry," Tristan assured him, and glanced at me. "You *all* have to be patient."

I glanced around, trying to search for a clue, but there was nothing out of the ordinary, not in the lake, on the shore or the in forest at our back. Everything looked pretty normal. And I didn't feel anything suspicious at all in the air.

"I'm so sorry, guys. I wish I could be of more help. I feel like such a useless, good-for-nothing drag," I mumbled, kicking a pebble in the sand in frustration.

"Don't worry, Joey. We're here and we're going to help you," Josh promised, giving reassuring taps on my shoulder.

"All right, there's nothing to see here. Let's get back now. I want to talk to Celeste and see what she'll have to say about this paper I found in Craig's cabin," Tristan proposed, and walked towards the trail leading back to the main house.

We were halfway up the trail when we bumped into Simon heading towards the lake. "What are you doing here?" Tristan was the first to ask, his expression guarded and full of suspicion.

"Why? Are these woods your damned property? Do you own the whole camp now? I can't walk around any more without you barking at me?" he snapped, on the defensive.

"No, I don't 'own the camp'," Tristan replied, irritated. "But I want to know why you're around the exact same place where my wife has been attacked. *Twice.*"

"I was attacked here too, you know!" Simon protested.

"What are you doing roaming around here, then?" Josh interrupted, stepping beside Tristan and crossing his muscled arms in a very intimidating way. Sam joined in with the intimidation at the other side, and Harry and Seth glared at him from the back. It was too much pressure, and Simon's bravado instantly vanished.

"I . . . I just th-thought about going back to the lake to look for some clues. I don't see the Harkers striving to find out what's happening here! All they do is ask people to stay inside their rooms or in the main house. How's that going to help solve anything?" he complained. "And I thought maybe if I looked around and discovered who's doing all these things, I could help Joey get her memory back. She saved my life. I owe her. I'm trying to help."

"What a Good Samaritan you are," Josh sneered, not really believing him.

"Guys, stop it. You're like angry drones, harassing the poor boy!" I intervened, before their bickering went any further. "I appreciate you trying to protect me, but you're overdoing it."

"She's right. Take it easy, Josh." Tristan stepped in and turned to Simon. "We just came from the lake. There's nothing to see back there, though. You're free to go check for yourself, but it's a waste of time. We're heading back to the main house now. Come on, guys."

Tristan put a protective arm around me and pulled me next to him as we continued walking up the trail, the boys a few feet behind us. I was wondering if Simon had continued on his way down to the lake, or if he'd decided to follow us, when I heard his voice coming from behind Tristan.

"What were you all doing at the lake, anyway?" Simon asked, hurrying to keep up with Tristan's long strides.

"Same as you. Looking for clues," came Tristan's clipped reply.

"I had been wondering about a few things . . . How did

you know there was something happening that night by the lake?" Simon questioned him. "Nobody knew we were in trouble, except you." His tone was borderline accusatory.

"What are you trying to imply, here, Simon? That I'm trying to hurt Joey, is that what you're trying to say?"

"No. But you are a very jealous guy. I can't get one foot closer to her without you barging in, puffing out your chest like a bloody alpha male."

"So I'm jealous and trying to kill her, is that it? Yeah, that makes total sense," Tristan scoffed, with a roll of his eyes.

"Well, all I know is that you wouldn't have had time to get to the lake so fast that night, unless you'd already been lurking around. You were also close by when she lost her memory. She was talking to some other dude at that time. Maybe you got jealous and aimed for the guy, but overdid it and got her, too. And you were all smug when that ghost thing happened in my cabin. Maybe you were trying to scare me, just so you'd look good in front of her. It all makes a lot of sense, if you ask me."

"A lot of sense. Right. Then, please, enlighten me: Why was I trying to drown her in that lake?"

"You could have been playing hero, there, and arranged that prank just so you could arrive in the nick of time and save the day. And make me look like shit."

Tristan halted and turned to Simon. "You made yourself look like shit, pal. You did that all on your own." He huffed angrily, his patience finally ending. "Don't try to put the blame on me for your cowardice. If you get scared all the time, it's your fault, not mine."

"Halloway doesn't do tasteless pranks like these!" Josh barked, coming to Tristan's aid. "Plus, he couldn't have been in two places at the same time! He couldn't be pranking you in the lake and arriving to rescue her a second later. If I were you, I'd watch this bloke, Hal. He looks very shifty to me, trying to put the blame on you. I smell a rat here."

I stepped between them. "Hey, stop it!" I warned, as the rest of the boys caught up to us and joined in the argument. Even though everything that Simon had said sounded logical to a degree, I knew in my heart that Tristan would never do any of those things, for any reason, not in a million years.

"Listen, shut up, everybody! This is stupid," I said firmly. "You are fighting for nothing! We are *all* trying to figure this out. If we stop bickering with each other and work together, we might have a chance to crack this thing, okay?" They all grumbled under their breath, but conceded in the end. "All right, let's get back to the main house, then. Celeste will help us solve this. Come on."

I turned round, and was about to take a step forward, when Tristan reached out, forcefully pulling me back.

"What?" I asked, startled, but he shushed me and made a signal for the boys to stop talking as well.

"Everybody quiet," he hissed urgently, his eyes flashing in alarm. He had his eyes fixed on a tree that was invading part of the trail.

"That's weird. I don't remember this tree so near to the track . . ." Seth mused, and Tristan glanced worriedly at us.

"Did you happen to notice the giant nest of angry wasps dangling precariously from that frail branch in that same tree?" he asked in a low, cautious tone.

Everybody looked slowly upwards, eyes widening in

realization. It was the biggest wasp nest I had ever seen, buzzing loudly, with a swarm of angry wasps on top of its crown. The big hunk of wood pulp and mud swayed in the wind, making the branch it was hanging on creak ominously, threatening to give at any second.

"Oh, shit," Seth squeaked quietly beside me. "If that thing falls, we're so dead." And then, after a pause of pregnant terror, he added, "I hate nature so much."

"Sorry for making fun of your fear of insects, man," Sam whispered next to Seth. "I wish you'd brought your bug spray now . . ."

"I don't think any amount of bug spray could handle this, Sammy. Look at the size of that thing! It's ginormous!" Harry murmured, enthralled by the magnitude of the nest. "Did you know some wasps do not sting?"

"Are those by any chance that kind?" Seth asked, nodding at the nest.

"I don't think so. Look at the size of their ovipositors. I'd say these wasps are highly venomous," Harry said in awe.

"Of course they are," Seth grumbled darkly.

"Guys, how about everybody shuts their pie hole and steps slowly back and far away from that thing?" I hissed in exasperation. "We can walk off the trail and find another way back to main house, yes?"

"Yes, please," Seth whimpered, already shuffling to the back of the group.

"That is so weird. I don't know how we could have walked past that thing before and not noticed it . . ." Harry mused, still observing the wasps with an intrigued expression. "They are very loud; we can hear the buzzing all the way from here. It must be mad busy inside it. I'm sure we walked down this exact trail. How could we have missed it? It doesn't make any sense . . ."

"Harry, can you please reason about this some place else?" I said, tugging at his T-shirt and trying to pull him back with me. Everybody had already retreated a few meters away, leaving only me, Tristan and Harry behind. "That thing looks like it's about to fal—"

I didn't get to finish the sentence before a gust of wind swept fiercely through the trees, and the frail branch where the wasp nest was suspended gave way, taking it to the ground. The bulky nest crashed and split into many pieces on the grass, releasing its angry dark content with a vengeance. The buzzing swarm spilled outside, ready to swipe at everything in its wake.

"Everybody, run!" Tristan shouted, grabbing my hand and yanking me back. "Stay together! That way! Go! Go!" he ordered, and the boys took off running back to the lake, with Tristan, Harry and me at their heels.

We ran like mad people, with Josh taking the lead, but somehow he started to derail from the main track in his attempt to swerve around some bigger trunks, and before we knew it, we had lost the path.

"Shouldn't we be reaching the shore by now?" I panted, trying to keep up with the boys. My lungs burned and my legs were complaining about the strain, but I kept running until the vegetation suddenly gave way to a barren, rocky cliff. Everybody halted in surprise, gasping for air and looking for a way off or around the cliff. We were cornered.

"Wow. That's steep," Seth said, peeking cautiously over the edge of the cliff.

"Look!" Simon pointed to an almost vertical slope at our right. "That was the same boulder we fell off last time,

Joey. I can still see the trail marks we left on our fall! We need to get off this cliff! The only way is back through the forest," he realized, eyeing the dark waters of the lake with terror. We could hear the buzzing coming from the trees at our back, approaching scarily fast.

"We can't! We'd be running directly into the wasps, Simon!" I tried to pull him back, but he yanked his arm away. "I don't care! You're thinking about jumping, aren't you? No way! Are you insane? I'm not going back into that lake!"

"It's the only way, Simon! We'll be safer in the water."

"No! No, I won't! I'd rather face those wasps! Anything is better than the lake! Anything! I'm not jumping! You can't make me!" he yelled madly, already running back to the forest.

"He's running towards the wasps, Tristan!" I cried out, terrified. "He's going to die!"

Tristan cursed loudly and was preparing to run after Simon when a dark buzzing cloud broke from the trees, heading our way.

"It's too late! We have to jump! Now! Go! GO!" he ordered, and Josh promptly obeyed, grabbing Seth and Sam by the arms and pulling them along, while Tristan did the same with me and Harry, and we all jumped off the cliff and into the lake.

The cold water hit me hard, taking all the air from my lungs. I pulled myself quickly upwards, sputtering out water as I reached the surface. One by one, five heads slowly poked through the surface of the water, sputtering and coughing as they struggled to catch their breath. Everybody looked up towards the top of the cliff, to check if we'd managed to escape the wasps, which apparently we had.

"YES! The wasps stayed up there!" Sam cheered in victory. "They are not following us! Whoop!"

"I don't mean to rain in your parade, but maybe it's too soon to be cheering, Sammy," Josh countered, looking in alarm at the water around us.

"Why? The wasps aren't coming near the water!" Sam said, flicking his wet curls of hair out of his face.

"No, but the mystery creature slash murderous crocodile might be," Harry pointed out, splashing closer to him.

"Oh, God! Out of the frying pan of deadly wasps and into the water with killer crocodiles," Seth wailed in despair. "Seriously, I frigging hate nature so frigging much!"

"Perhaps it would be wiser if we started swimming to the shore as soon as possible, guys," Tristan suggested, looking around cautiously to find the right direction.

"It's that way," I told him, even though it was not visible through the mist swirling over the water's surface. "I don't know how or when, but I remember swimming away from this boulder that way."

"Come on, swim that way! Quick!" Tristan motioned for everybody to get a move on.

I think we broke a swimming speed record then, as we ploughed towards that shoreline. Seth was a blurry human propeller ahead of us, while Sammy, Harry and Josh kept circling at my flanks, with Tristan guarding at the back. Pretty quickly we were stepping out of the water, adrenaline kicking into overdrive in our systems as we slumped, completely drenched, on to the sand.

"I . . . can't . . . believe . . . we made it out . . . of that lake . . . alive," Seth wheezed, in between labored breaths.

"I don't mean to be a party pooper, here, but we are kind of back at square one, guys," Harry muttered, standing up. "How are we going to get to the main house now?"

"We could try going up a different trail," Sam suggested.

"Those wasps could be anywhere now. How will we know what's a safe trail?" Seth asked, looking scared.

"We are going to have to risk it, Seth," Tristan told him.

"What do you guys think happened to Simon?" I asked, worriedly. "You think he's still alive? He might need help! Maybe we can start a search and look for him?"

"I don't think it's wise to run blindly through these woods looking for him now, Joey. We don't know our way around these parts; we don't even have a map. We'll get lost and surely bump into those wasps again. We should go back and call for help," Tristan advised wisely. "Come on, the sooner we leave, the faster we'll get there."

Chapter Twenty-Four
Beneath the Starlight

"Are you happy now, Harry?" Seth grumbled to his grinning friend, as we left the main house. "Is this enough outdoor excitement for you?"

"Hell, yeah!" Harry yelled happily. "That was epic! Can we do it again?"

Sammy and Josh laughed out loud, while I shook my head, listening to their silly banter. Harry had certainly had his dose of adventure for one day: running all over the woods, jumping off high cliffs and having a good dip in the lake. He surely couldn't complain about the lack of activities today. That was more than I had bargained for, though, and I was glad we had all left the forest unscathed, including Simon.

As soon as we'd arrived at the main house, the Harkers were already on alert by the front steps, organizing a search party, which wasn't really necessary since we'd managed to get back safe and sound at the eleventh hour.

Simon had preceded us, having had a good head start when he ran madly back to the forest, miraculously managing to escape the angry swarm of wasps. Tristan and the boys eyed him from afar in the main lobby, filled with suspicion and distrust. His *I was so lucky to escape* speech wasn't flying with them at all.

"We need to get him alone somewhere and pressure him until he spills, Hal. That guy is hiding something," Josh had whispered quietly to Tristan, as we left the main house.

"We can come back tomorrow and talk to him," Tristan had agreed. "It's a shame we have nothing to show to Celeste now," he said to me, pulling a crumpled, sodden piece of paper out of his pocket. The paper fell apart in his hands, and he sighed in regret. "We should have come straight to her when we had the chance. I don't know what I was thinking when I made us go to the lake to try to find more clues. Now we have nothing."

"Oh. Pantaloons," I grumbled and Tristan raised an eyebrow at me. "That wasn't cursing! It doesn't count as a curse word. You can't get mad at me because of Pantaloons!" I protested.

"That's veiled cursing, Joey. But I'll let you keep this one because it's more funny than offensive," he reasoned.

"Thank you," I said with a grateful smile. "Anyway, can't you try to draw by memory some of the symbols you saw on the paper?" I suggested.

"I don't know if I can . . . I'm sorry."

"It's okay. We'll figure out something else. At least we told Celeste about Craig having this paper. She said she's going to pay him another visit today. Maybe she can find another clue. You can rest assured that tomorrow we'll have more information on him."

"Yeah, *tomorrow*," Seth piped up. "But right now, can we please go back to our cabin?"

"And what should we do until tomorrow? Sit and wait for my memories to come back?" I asked, as we walked up the hill to our cabin. "We need to keep trying to make me remember, right? Or have you guys given up on that?"

"Pft. We are Lost Boys. We never give up!" Harry boasted beside me.

"Although, we are kinda running out of options . . ." Sam muttered close by.

I glanced at Tristan. He seemed to be deep in thought about something, but then he caught me looking his way and the creases in his brow softened as he gave me a smile, his gray eyes twinkling with mischief.

"About that . . . I have an idea for tonight."

I stared for a while in silence, trying to figure out a better way to ask him this. I decided eventually to go for direct, blunt honesty.

They say honesty is the best policy, right?

"Okay, fine. But what are *you* doing here?" I asked the blond boy sitting cross-legged at the bottom of the bed.

"I am here because you're getting ready for your very first date with the big guy – it's kinda your first, anyway, since you don't remember any of the old ones – and you need support during this exciting, yet nerve-wracking time. I am also here on Tiff's behalf," Seth said.

"Tiff?" I asked, puzzled.

"Oh, yeah, you don't remember her, either. I mean Tiffany. She's the one who usually helps you do all the stuff girls do to get ready for dates. She's your BFF, and as Tiff's boyfriend, I'm here as her stand-in," Seth explained, while he fumbled with his phone. "I am actually trying to get her online to see what advice she'll have for me, but the internet connection here is the worst! Just pretend I'm a blonde supermodel with a lot of attitude, ordering you to wear heels or something incredibly uncomfortable that you'll hate putting on, and we should be fine. I think . . ."

"All right. So you're here as my BFF's stand-in. What about them? What are they all doing in here?" I asked, gesturing to the three other boys loitering around the bedroom.

"I am here because I am your best 'guy' friend. Tiff is your girl, I am your guy," Harry stated proudly, spreading out on the bed while the other boys booed and threw stuff at him. "You can boo all you want! You know I'm right! I'm her bestie and that means she loves *me* more!" he shouted, while a tidal wave of more things was thrown at his head.

"I am here to gather priceless material. There are so many golden jokes to be made of this situation, and I cannot miss any of them." Sammy barked out a laugh, but then Harry kicked him on the shin and he looked up and saw the expression on my face. "Only not right now, because making fun of you now would be very insensitive of me, of course. Jokes will only be allowed *after* you've fully recovered. Pinky swear," he vowed solemnly.

"And I'm here for moral support. You're my band-mate. I've got your back, bro," Josh said, thumping his chest lightly.

I shot him a weird look. "Okaaay. Thank you, 'bro'. Look, I appreciate all the support, guys, but I think I can manage to stay in the cabin on my own. You can go, you know – do whatever you want to do – I'll be fine. But thanks again. For the support. I'm good, though. You can leave now."

"She's giving us her *I think y'all are a bunch of weirdos and I can't wait to get away from you* speech, Seth!" Harry protested, with a scowl.

"Harry, we *are* a bunch of weirdos. She needs time to get acclimatized to us, is all," Seth said sagely.

"This amnesia sucks! What if she never gets her memory back, Seth? What then?" Harry complained, looking really upset. "It took her all these years to trust me to be her bestie! What if it's a one-shot-only deal? I don't know if I can do it again!"

"Look, I know this has been the most horrible experience for you, Harry. But try to see this from her point of view, will you? I'm sure you'll agree this has been an inconvenience for her as well. We are ALL her best friends" – Seth paused purposefully to shoot him a meaningful glare – "and as her best friends, we must be supportive. So let's all chill. And also tone down the weirdness, all right?" he said, and they all grumbled in agreement.

"Sorry, Joey. We'll try to be less weird from now on," Sammy mumbled.

"Look, guys, it's not the weird that bothers me, honestly. You are kind of funny with that. It's the level of intimacy you have at the moment, and I'm not used to it, because I don't remember all the years we've been together." I tried to explain how I was feeling, so they wouldn't feel so bummed about my reactions.

It was Josh's turn to speak up on their behalf. "Sorry, Joey. Guys, we should trust Tristan's judgment. He has faith that she'll get her memory back, so we should as well. The big guy is usually right about these things. Let's give him a vote of trust, yeah?"

"A vote of trust about what?" Tristan's head suddenly

poked through the doorway, his expression curious. "Is this about my idea for the next tour?" His gray eyes lit up in expectation.

"Noooooo!" they all chorused in unison. "We've told you that's not gonna fly, man. Forget about that, already!" Josh said, looking a bit peeved.

"Oh. All right, then. I know when I'm outnumbered . . ."

"Apparently not, since you keep bringing it up every chance you get," Sammy grumbled from his spot by the bed. "Let it go, dude. It's not gonna happen."

"Fine! I'm letting it go," Tristan said, and then turned to me. "So, my lovely fair maiden Isolde. Are you ready for our date?"

"Is it time, already?" the boys all gasped together.

"We hardly had any time to prep her!" Sammy complained.

Tristan had proposed we had a date tonight, to help me unwind and maybe fire up some memories from our time together in the past. I had been silently freaking out since I had agreed to this. I was trying to act cool in front of the boys, but I really appreciated their help. They had kept me so distracted with their silly comments that I had completely forgotten about freaking out, up until now, when Tristan had come back into the bedroom.

"You have been great keeping her company while I got some things done for our date outside, guys, thanks. But now you are released from your pre-date-prep duties. I can take it from here."

"Oh, but I'm not ready yet! I picked whatever dry clothes I could find in my bag, but I wasn't thinking about choosing an outfit for a date . . ." I flustered in panic, trying to stall for more time.

"Yeah! We didn't even get to help her choose some nice lingerie for the date!" Sammy protested, while I blushed profusely and Seth whacked him on the back of the head.

"You're being weird again, Sam! She doesn't know you're joking! Stop!" Seth ordered.

"Sorry. I'm stopping," he muttered, walking out of the room with his tail between his legs.

"That's okay, Sam. It was pretty funny," I said, as he passed by me. "Deeply inappropriate, but funny."

He grinned broadly and nodded before walking out of the room.

"Your clothes are fine. Don't worry about it, buttercup," Tristan reassured me, with a warm smile, and extended his arm for me to take it. "If you would be so gracious as to accompany me, milady."

I smiled shyly and took his arm. "What's with the medieval talk, if I may dare ask, dear sire?"

"Oh, when we first met, I used to joke and talk to you like that. Because of the book, you know?"

"Book? What book?"

"*Tristan and Isolde*." The tone of his voice was so sad, as if my question was hurtful to hear.

"Oh! I love that book!" I said, and realization finally dawned on me. "Your name! It's because of the book!" *And he looked sad because I didn't remember it.* "Oh, God. I'm so sorry, Tristan."

Way to go to start off a date, Joey – forgetting the reason for his name.

"It's okay," he said, still trying to be reassuring. "It's not your fault."

"What did you cook for her, Halloway? It smells a-mazing!" Harry exclaimed, sniffing the air. "Can I have a taste? Just a small bite! Just let me have a quick look inside the pan, then! Please? I swear I won't stick a finger in the food, this time!"

"Hold on a sec. If you'll excuse me, I have to take care of this first. You may not remember, but they will eat everything they can get their hungry little hands on, and leave us nothing, I swear. I must be swift and brutal about this extraction. Our meal is at stake," Tristan said, already dragging two of the boys by the arm towards the front door, and ordering the two remaining ones to follow him outside.

"All right. Where were we?" he asked, after shutting the cabin's front door with a loud bang and turning to me. "Oh, yes. Our dinner awaits, milady! Follow me, please."

I chuckled at his overly polite manners and followed him to the cabin's back door. "They are a fun bunch. A bit weird, but fun. I can see why we are close friends."

He paused before opening the door and turned to me. "They are not just 'close friends'. They are family," he corrected, before flicking a switch on. "That is why they are so gutted. It's like you forgot about your own brothers."

"Oh. I see. That really sucks. I'm sorry."

"I didn't mean to make you feel bad. I'm only trying to explain, so you won't think of them as weird." He pushed the back door open, extended his hand gently towards me, and, hand in hand, we walked outside.

"Oh, my God. This is so beautiful!" I gasped as I saw the small backyard. There was a wooden patio table beautifully set for us, with a rustic candle in the middle and some wild flowers in a tin cup. But the most beautiful of all decorations was a string of fairy lights hung above our heads, coming from the cabin and connecting the trees surrounding us. It gave a magical aura to the place, as if we had plunged into a fairy tale's summer night.

There was wine in a couple of glasses, and a steaming pot set next to the plates. Tristan, true gentleman that he was, pulled up a chair for me to sit down. "I made your favorite dish. You don't remember it's your favorite, so I hope you like it."

I quickly sat down, because I was swooning so badly, I might have started to float around at any second, with stars bursting from my eyes. It was the most romantic candlelit dinner anyone had ever prepared for me!

I really had struck gold with this guy.

"This is amazing, Tristan! You didn't have to go to all this trouble for me."

"It's no trouble," he replied charmingly, his beautiful gray eyes twinkling as bright as the fairy lights above us. He sat down in his chair. "Anything for my girl."

Major. Epic. Swooning. Here.

"I'm sorry, but I have to ask. What are you hiding from me?"

"I beg your pardon?" he asked, looking startled.

"I mean, what is your problem? Like, are you a psychopathic murderer, or something? You must have some serious creepy secret like that! No one can be as perfect as you are! It's not possible! I refuse to believe you're real, then."

He laughed heartily at my flustered face. "Trust me, I'm real, sweetheart. But I'm far from perfect. If you need to feel more reassured about me, you have my word that you don't need to worry. I have plenty of flaws and my fair share of secrets, too. You know them all and you have accepted them, too."

"Lucky for you, I can't remember either the flaws or the secrets."

"Yes, but despite them all, I truly am a man of my word. And I once swore to you that I would never lie to you. We always tell the truth to each other. So believe me, love, you're safe with me."

"Okay, fine. I believe you. I'll trust you that you're not perfect, even though it really looks like you are," I agreed playfully.

But as the night progressed, I was having trouble believing his protests. He had cooked me the most delicious pasta I had ever tasted in my life. Now I had to believe that this gorgeous man who could cook like heaven was not perfect? Yeah, right.

After we'd finished our meal, he put the dishes away and, when he returned, he turned the fairy lights off, leaving just the lights coming from the cabin. Then he pulled a blanket from a wood bench and unfolded it on the grass.

"What are we doing now?" I asked curiously, watching his silent preparations.

"We did something like this for our first date." He patted a place on the blanket for me to sit. "I thought maybe this might jog your memory. Come on, don't be scared. We're just going to lie down and watch the stars."

"We stargazed on our first date?" I asked, sitting down at his side.

"Yeah. The sky that night didn't have as many stars as right now, but I wasn't paying too much attention to the sky back then, anyway." He smiled at the memory. "I was so nervous, trying to impress you. I had promised you the best date of your life. It's a lot of pressure for a guy, you know."

I chuckled. "That's so sweet. Where did we go for the date?"

"Well, I kept it a secret while I planned the date, because I wanted to surprise you. So I fed false leads to the boys, knowing you'd harass them to tell you what I was up to. Seth ended up telling you I had dinner reservations for a fancy, posh restaurant near our school, and you bit the bait as expected."

"Oh, God. Really? I hate posh restaurants! I'm glad it was a false lead."

"I knew you hated them. I was trying to trick you. The main goal for that night was to surprise you."

"But where did you take me, then?"

He smiled, leaning back and resting on his elbows. "I picked you up a little earlier than I'd said I would, before you could put on fancy clothes and uncomfortable heels, and told you some bogus story about wanting to talk to you in private. I still can't believe I managed to fool you so easily, that day!"

"I was probably worried sick about not making a fool of myself in that fake posh place you'd pretended we were going, you trickster! But where did we go? Tell me!" I asked, eager to hear the rest of his story.

"I took you to this secret terrace in our old school. I thought it would be a nice, private place to have our date. I'd decorated it with tea-lights and lilies – you probably don't remember, but they were your favorite flowers – and had set out a couple of blankets, just like this one here, and I had a picnic basket specially prepared, full all sorts of junk food that I knew you loved, for our dinner. Oh, and an acoustic guitar so I could sing you a song later on."

"SHUT. UP! You didn't! That is the best idea ever!" I

exclaimed excitedly. "I can imagine my surprise. I must have adored it!"

He beamed broadly. "You did. More than I'd imagined you would. I was really nervous, because I wasn't so sure you'd like it. And I didn't have much money back then, so it was really the only option for me. I kept thinking you were going to laugh at my face for such a cheap date. I tried to act confident at the time, but I was worried sick you'd hate it."

I gasped in outrage. "I would never! That is the most romantic date I've ever heard of! I'm sorry, but even this amazing dinner beneath fairy lights on a summer night by a cabin by the woods is not as nearly as romantic as that date sounds!"

"I know. You told me you loved it, but I could already see in your eyes how much you truly did. I will never forget your face that night. You have no idea how happy I was. I couldn't believe my lucky stars." He lay down and crossed his hands under his head, watching the night sky with a contented smile. "And even though I was a nervous wreck, you somehow put me at ease so effortlessly . . . Five minutes into the date, I couldn't even remember why I'd been so nervous in the first place. It was like having a date with the love of your life and your best friend all at once," he confessed.

"I always thought you could only have the one or the other, you know? You have love *or* friendship." He reached out for my hand and interlaced his fingers with mine. "But with you, I have both. I am truly the luckiest man alive."

"Even now, with a wife that doesn't remember you?" I asked quietly.

"It's temporary, sweetheart." He squeezed my hand in reassurance.

Suddenly I felt so sad. How could I have forgotten a guy as incredible as Tristan? "So what else happened on our first date?" I asked, trying to keep at bay the tears that were prickling my eyes.

"Well, we lay on a blanket, just like we are doing now" – he pulled me down to rest beside him, and wrapped an arm around me – "and watched the stars for a while and just . . . talked. We talked about our plans for the future, our dreams . . . how we hoped we'd be still together when the year was over. It was the night I started believing that could really happen. You gave me true hope that night, Joey. I will treasure it forever."

"But the memory I treasure the most isn't of our first date. It's of our engagement party in Italy. In our hearts if felt like that was our wedding day. We exchanged vows and rings." He raised our clasped hands to show me the white gold wedding band on his finger. "And we celebrated with our close friends and your mom. I'll remember that day forever."

"I still can't believe I'm married. It seems so . . . unlike me," I said.

"Yeah, I know. It took a while for you to accept my proposal. You were dead set against a traditional marriage, but we made a very unorthodox celebration. There wasn't a priest, or a walk down the aisle or any of those traditional things. It was kind of crazy." He chuckled. "The only tradition you agreed was on the dress. God, when I saw you in that dress…" He paused, his voice shaking a little with emotion. "I don't even have words to describe it, Joey. You were radiant like the sun, the most beautiful I'd ever seen you. I couldn't speak or move, I was stunned by the sight of you.

"It was like all of who you are, your love, strength and courage had merged into a state of pure beauty. When you walked towards me dressed in that perfect white dress, your soul was shining so brightly and you looked so happy . . . I made a vow to myself then and there, that I would try to make you happy for as long as I lived, so I could always see you shining as you did on that day."

He glanced down, startled when he noticed me shaking. "Joey? Sweetheart? What's wrong? Why are you crying?"

"I'm so sorry, Tristan. I'm sorry I can't remember that date, the marriage or our life together. I'm so, so sorry!" I cried softly, while he sat up and scooped me into his arms.

"All those memories will come back to you, love. You have to be patient."

"How can you be so sure? How can you have this absolute certainty? How?" I protested, scared that I might never remember him again.

"Look, don't worry about this any more, okay? You're putting too much pressure on yourself, and that only makes things worse. We won't talk about the past any more. How about we just enjoy this lovely evening together, and think about nothing else? How's that sound?" he proposed, trying to calm me down.

"I'm sorry. I'm tired. And my head is hurting again. I want to go back inside and rest a little."

He hugged me tight before he agreed. "Okay. We can do that. Come on."

Chapter Twenty-Five
Welcome Back

Our date was officially over. Tristan picked up the blanket from the backyard and locked the back door behind us, while I shuffled tiredly into the bedroom. But I couldn't bear to see the resigned sadness on his face as he grabbed his pillow and started to get ready to sleep on the couch.

"The couch is really uncomfortable, isn't it?" I asked, moving quietly to stand in the living-room doorway a couple of minutes later.

He glanced up, startled to see me there. He thought I'd gone to bed by now. "Hmm, no, it's . . . all right."

"You said you promised never to lie to me."

He sighed. "Okay. This thing may be pretty, but it's goddarn uncomfortable. That's the truth. I was only trying not to upset you any more. I'm doing a terrible job so far, I know."

"You're not upsetting me, Tris. You've been wonderful and patient and perfect throughout all this . . . Look, you can sleep in the bed with me tonight, okay?"

"Really?" he asked, clearly surprised.

"Yeah. I feel really bad for not remembering our past; please don't make me feel even worse for making you sleep on this awful couch. Come on," I pleaded.

He hesitated, torn between giving me space and finally being able to have a good night's sleep in a real, decent bed. "Okay. Thank you," he said, grabbing his pillow and walking to the bedroom. "I promise I will stay on that side of the bed. Nothing will happen, you have my word. You can go to sleep peacefully on your side, okay?"

I nodded, seeing the honesty in his eyes.

"All right, then. Good night, Joey." He turned his back to me and snuggled his face into the pillow, while I stared at his broad, smooth, muscled back.

It took me a long time to relax and manage to drift into sleep, though. Tristan's warm presence next to me kept me on edge and made my heart beat faster.

How could I relax when the most handsome man I had ever seen was lying right next to me, in the same bed, half-naked and within arm's reach?

When I'd managed to quieten my frantic heart and finally drift off to sleep, my consciousness slipped to where lost memories were hidden in my dreams.

There was a glass castle in a glittery, silver ocean; an eerie gothic girl standing on a sand hill next to someone wearing a majestic gray hood, his eyes flaring with a cold white light, while snowflake crystals danced around his stilled frame. Then fireworks exploded in the night sky, and when I looked back down, the sand hills were gone and I was standing in a deserted cemetery. There was snow pilling over the tombstones, but as I twirled around, a warm light started to melt all the snow away.

I could hear boys' laughter and music playing in the

background. The music and laughter intensified, merging into one big chaotic cacophony of cheers, chanting and shouting in the distance.

I looked at myself and realized there were flames in my hands. The fire spread, running all over me, consuming me whole, like I was a born star. I felt big, invincible, as powerful as the sun. The whooshing sound of consuming fire filled my ears, and along with it came rattling chains and angry whispers. I cowered on the ground and shut my eyes, letting out an anguished whimper. The noise was maddeningly loud: too much for me to bear.

Just when I thought I couldn't stand it any longer, it started to slowly ebb away, and I risked opening my eyes: I was now sprawled over the cold cement floor of a dark warehouse. It was silent, but I knew there was a vile monster made of shadows in there with me, hidden out of sight. It was waiting, lurking and biding its time. "I will tear you to pieces and rip you apart," the shadows promised in an ominous whisper, and slithered across the floor in my direction. I cried out, startled, and in my hurry to get away from it, I tripped and fell back on the floor.

Then a river of blood crashed through the warehouse's entrance, flooding inside, painting everything with its dark ruby wetness, slippery slick and unstoppable. I was engulfed by blood, and then the dream changed once again.

I was gasping for air as I found myself standing by the steps leading up to the main house. Something very dangerous was close by. My heart pounded in my chest. I needed to flee, to run up those steps, straight to the top, where I knew I'd be safe, but my feet were rooted to the ground and I couldn't escape. A blurry dark silhouette loomed over me, ready to strike, and I raised my hands above my head, trying to protect myself. I screamed.

I woke up, struggling out of the sheets in alarm, my hands ablaze. Pieces of my dream merged with reality, and I couldn't discern what was real and what was not in the shadows of the dark room. I stumbled around, disoriented and in a panic, while the fire continued to burn out of my hands. I tried hard not to touch anything and burn the whole place down.

"Calm down, I've got you! You're safe! I'm here." Tristan's strong arms enveloped me, shielding me from the horrors of my nightmare.

"No, I'll burn you!" I shouted, and struggled against his hold, my hands pressed hard against his chest within his tight embrace.

"Your fire can't hurt me! It can't burn me, Joey, calm down!"

"I'm sorry! I'm so sorry . . ." I sobbed between labored breaths, slumping tiredly against him.

"It's okay, you're going to be all right. Everything is going to be fine," he soothed, cradling me in his arms.

"I-I had a nightmare . . . someone was attacking me, and I woke up like this," I told him, watching the flames dance on my trembling hands. "This is so crazy . . . Why is it not burning you?"

"I don't know why, but it can't hurt me. You need to calm down for it to stop. Can you do that for me? Relax, now, breathe and stay calm."

We both watched as the flames slowly faded away. I sighed in relief.

"I-I can't believe I can do this . . . I'm such a freak. I don't know how you put up with these things when you're with me." I gave him an embarrassed look, my hands still trembling a little.

"I have some 'ghost issues' that you have to deal with, too, so, you know, it all balances out in the end. I thought I was a freak once because of that, but you told me we're not freaks, we're just different." He held me and rocked me gently, as if we were slow dancing. It felt comforting and oddly calming.

"You're not a freak, that's absurd," I told him, and watched as a soft smile reached his eyes, making small wrinkles appear at the corners. "What's a guy like you even doing with me? You're . . . perfect. You could have anyone you want."

"I told you already, I'm not perfect," he said gently. "I have my flaws, like anyone else. But I do love you very much. That might be the reason I'm with you." He leaned closer until our noses were touching, the tips rubbing together in an Eskimo kiss. "As for having anyone I want, I already accomplished that when I put that ring on your finger, my love."

I smiled, feeling elated, wondering to myself how this amazing man could really be mine. I was enchanted by his gentleness and grace. Without realizing what I was doing, I closed the small distance between our lips. A distant memory of a kiss came back to me at the touch of his lips on mine.

We were wrapped in darkness, while fireworks hung frozen in the sky, and he placed a light feathery kiss on my lips; we were sitting on a stone wall in our school and he was kissing me, as gently and slowly as he was doing now. And then the memories of all our kisses rushed back, one after another, after another, until a last one where we were

*kissing each other before an ocean view. I was wearing a
beautiful white dress and he wore a starling-gray suit. We
were both crying as he put a white gold ring on my finger.*

"Joey? Are you all right?" I heard him ask, and I leaned
back, startled, blinking at his worried face. His thumb
brushed softly over my cheeks, wiping away my tears.

"I remember our first kiss . . . all our kisses," I
murmured, watching him in a daze. "I remember our
wedding. I remember you." I cupped his face, my hands
no longer trembling. I remembered his flaws, all his secrets,
the good and bad in him. I remembered all we'd been
through, our life together and also how much I loved him,
with all my heart.

"I remember *you*. All of you."

"I knew you would," he whispered in relief. "Welcome
back, my love."

I smiled when he kissed me again. "Hello, Coco Puffs,"
I said, the cute nickname I'd once given him finally popping
into my head.

"Oi!" he complained, but looked pleased all the same.

I closed my tired eyes as he hugged me tight. My head
throbbed, protesting at the overload of information that
had returned all in one go. The room seemed to spin,
shifting under my feet.

I felt Tristan's arms pulling me closer, and then a moment
later he was carrying me in his arms and I was back in
bed, resting.

"How are you feeling?"

"I'm okay. But my head hurts a lot."

"I can almost see your memories spinning inside your
head," he muttered, lying close to me. "Try to get some
rest now. You've had a long day."

"I'm so happy that I have you back."

"Me too, Buttons," he said, and kissed me. "You have never lost me, though. I'll always be here for you. I'm also very glad I can kiss you whenever I want again." And he kissed me one more time to prove it.

"Tris? What if I'd never remembered you? Weren't you worried, not even a little bit?"

"Honestly? No, I wasn't. I don't know why, Joey, but something in my gut tells me we will never forget each other. I suspect that is the reason I lingered in that cemetery for so long . . . I was waiting for you. I know that no matter what storms we have to face, we'll go through them together. And I know that with you, I can face anything. So, no, I wasn't worried. I'm a patient guy. I waited for you for years in that cemetery; I could wait again now. I knew it was only a matter of time until you remembered me."

"I'm so relieved, you have no idea."

"Do you remember what happened to you, before you lost your memory?"

I frowned in concentration. A lot of memories were coming back, but they were all out of order. I had a bunch of new pieces of the puzzle in my hands, but I still couldn't see the entire picture.

"I still can't remember everything . . . the parts of my life with you are all here. But the rest is still a blur."

"It's okay. Don't strain yourself. It will all come back to you sooner or later." He brushed my hair away from my face. "Hey, does this mean I can break my promise that nothing will happen between us tonight?" he asked, his voice ringing with amusement.

I buried my face in his chest to hide my embarrassment.

"Shut up! My memory was temporarily impaired! It's not funny!"

He pulled me closer, his light chuckle rumbling through his chest. "I'm happy to have my wife back. I was kinda missing her." He hummed playfully, planting soft light kisses all over my neck. "That forgetful Joey wouldn't let me get close. I was so gutted!"

I laughed and let him shower me with loving kisses. "Well, good riddance to that Joey. You can kiss me whenever you want and how much you want, starting now." I kissed him hard to make up for lost time, but then I paused, pushing him away with an upset frown.

"What? What is it?" he asked.

"I can't believe you left me behind like a helpless wuss while you went with Celeste to investigate that poltergeist all by yourselves!"

His expression softened and he shook his head, chuckling. "I know. I can't believe you stayed behind, either! You've never done as you're told before. I was more surprised than you when you obeyed me, believe you me!"

"Well, you better savor that memory, pal. Cos that ain't gonna happen ever again."

"I figured as much."

"Your wife is back, baby. And she's ready to kick some poltergeist's butt!"

Chapter Twenty-Six
Better Safe than Sorry

"So you remember everything? Just like that? All he had to do was kiss you and you got all your memories back?" Seth asked, looking slightly bemused, the next morning.

"Well, not everything. I remembered about Tristan, but apart from that, it's all a big blur. And I still can't figure out what caused the amnesia . . . but at least the parts of my life with Tristan are all back," I said happily.

"Just one kiss from the guy and you remembered him. Unbelievable," Josh mused, shaking his head. "Sometimes, you guys are sickeningly sweet, I swear."

"You know what they say: true love's kiss can cure it all," Tristan stated smugly, wrapping one arm around my shoulder and pulling me closer for a kiss, just to annoy Josh.

"Okay, you can stop now. I'll get diabetes here at this rate," he complained, making a face at us, while everybody laughed. Even Rocko yelped from underneath the table, where he was usually found, waiting for scraps and crumbs of breakfast to fall to the ground.

"And your kiss is not curing 'it all', pal. She still doesn't remember us," Sam grumbled. "How are we going to make her remember us, guys?"

"I think our top priority should be getting these mysterious attacks solved, Sammy," Tristan said. "Whatever it is that caused her amnesia, it's still roaming freely out there."

"Fine. We can make her remember us later, then. Mystery attacks come first."

"So what are we going to do now to solve these supernatural mysteries? The clock is ticking, dudes," Harry said.

"I thought you were scared of these things, Harry?" I said.

"Oh, I *was*. Scared shitless. But now I know supernatural adventures are so freaking cool! It's like we are in our own scary movie, here," he said excitedly.

"You realize the idiots are always the first to go in scary movies, right? I'm sure you know that you are our blooming idiot, Harry," Seth joked.

"What? Pfft, no! Sam's our idiot, everybody knows that!" Harry laughed. "I'm the eccentric dude, not quite as buff and heroic as the main lead guy, but equally awesome and very likely to be amongst the last ones standing."

"No way. The crazy eccentric dudes always die early on," Sam protested. "If I'm dying, you're going right after me, pal!"

"Okay, guys, *no one* is dying, here!" I said. Harry poked his tongue out at Sam, who blew a raspberry from the other side of the table. "I don't know about you guys, but I'm sick of this amnesia! I want to know who did this to me. We need to go to the main house right now and ask

Celeste if she's found out anything new about Craig. Maybe she has some clues that can help us solve this thing."

"And we can also try to squeeze some things from that fishy kid Simon," Josh remembered. "He knows about things he's not telling. I'm still not convinced about the way he ditched those wasps yesterday."

"All right. But hang on, before we leave, I need to go fetch something. If you'll all excuse me," Seth muttered, clearly not pleased to be heading outside into a forest filled with scary supernatural creatures on the loose, wandering free and wreaking havoc all over the place. He returned holding an iron poker that he had retrieved from the fire-place in the living room.

"Okay, we can head out. Now I have some protection," he said, twirling the metal bar to test his grip on it. "There could be friggin' wolves out there! I'm not taking any chances. You wanna know who's likely to survive in horror movies? The guy armed with an iron poker, that's who."

Josh gave a shrug and nodded. "Better safe than sorry: that's what they say, eh?"

"All right, then. Let's get a move on, guys," Tristan said, motioning us quickly to the front door. "Are you bringing Rocko, Sam?"

Sam looked hesitantly at the excited dog, who waggled his tail, but after Seth fake-coughed the words "wolf snack", he decided to let him stay in the cabin. "He's too young to be a wolf snack," he said to Harry, who grumbled in reply, "I'm too young to be a wolf snack, too."

We walked down the graveled road with hurried steps. Seth was in the lead and was still very skittish about being outdoors, wanting to get to the main house as quickly as possible. His grip on the iron poker was firm as he took a strategic position, walking between Tristan and Josh, the strongest blokes of the bunch.

When we stepped inside the main house, we found Celeste in the lobby, arguing over something with a member of the camp staff. There were a lot of people ambling around the entrance hall, since everybody was still on lockdown because of the weird attacks in the camp.

"So you're telling me we have to cancel the whole Gathering, just because there's no caretaker at the camp any more?" Celeste was saying when we approached them.

"Unfortunately, yes, Miss Harker. For safety reasons, we can't continue receiving guests here until we find a replacement. Usually, here at Misty Lake Camp, the caretaker is the one responsible for handling emergencies. If something happens now, we won't know what to do, whom to call, etc. And it seems a lot of strange things have been happening already. The camp manager isn't taking any chances. You'll have to call your reunion off. I'm very sorry," the man said, and quickly came up with an excuse to skitter away.

"Can you believe this?" Celeste turned to greet us. "We're going to have to cancel the Gathering! Just because the caretaker is leaving." She harrumphed.

"Craig is leaving?" I asked in alarm. "He can't leave!"

"Yeah. I went to his cabin and talked to him yesterday. He said he'd be resigning and leaving today."

"But did you find anything suspicious in his cabin?" Tristan joined in. "Or is he still saying he doesn't remember anything?"

"I didn't find anything, Tristan, sorry. He's claiming he doesn't recall what happened before he blacked out, and that he's leaving to have his head checked over. He's been having awful migraines since he woke up. I guess his blackout was a bit more serious than Joey's. How are you feeling, by the way?" she asked me.

"Well, the good news is that I got some of my memories back!" I said triumphantly. "The bad news is I still don't remember what happened to me on the front steps. We were hoping that maybe you would have discovered a new clue from Craig that could help explain everything . . ."

"No, I got nothing from Craig, sorry. I tried to see if I'd catch anything suspicious in his cabin, but there was nothing out of ordinary in the place. I also couldn't find any traces of magic there. He kept repeating he didn't remember a thing. If you'd been there, maybe you would have been able at least to see if he was telling me the truth or not . . ." She sighed in disappointment.

"I can go talk to him one last time before he leaves, and see if I can catch him in a lie," I proposed in a thoughtful mood. "Do you know when he's leaving?"

"Oh, well, he said he'd probably be leaving by the end of the day."

"Okay. We've got a little time, then. I'm really sorry about the Gathering cancelation, Celeste."

"Well, maybe this is for the best. Parents and mentors have been calling non-stop, asking for explanations. Maybe it's best just to cancel the Gathering this year. Plus, there have been panic outbreaks around the camp the whole time, people running scared, claiming they've had wolf sightings round every damned corner," she grumbled, looking irritated. "I can't take another false alarm. I'm serious. The next person that comes running to me with a wolf story is going to have a slap on the back of the neck! Yes! I'm looking at you, Miss Collins!" she berated the blonde girl who was hovering nearby with a group of friends.

"It's not my fault, Miss Harker! How was I supposed to know that it was a badger? It was tricky to see inside that shrub!"

"It wasn't a badger, Felicia, I've told you already! It was a raccoon! How can you not recognize a raccoon? God!" her older sister grumbled, with an eye roll.

"Well, you all went running off and yelling that it was a damned wolf. I didn't stick around to check what it really was!" she snapped back. "It was an honest mistake."

"You see what I have to deal with here?" Celeste complained, rubbing her temples. "They have taken the 'cry wolf' tale to a whole new level, I swear. When it is really a wolf, no one will be giving a damn . . ."

"Well, raccoons are kinda dangerous too, right? They can be very aggressive, and I hear some might have rabies," Seth pointed out, always nervous about any wildlife, no matter how small it turned out to be.

"A tiny, hungry raccoon is not the same as a pack of vicious, snarling wolves, boy," she argued.

"You have a point, there," Seth conceded.

"You really don't remember a wolf attacking you, Joey? It would be very helpful if you could describe it to us. We don't know if it's the same wolf showing up in all these places, or if it's different wolves . . . or no wolf at all," Celeste said.

"I'm sorry, I really don't remember, Celeste."

"Oh, all right. No point complaining about spilled milk, I suppose. We'll keep everyone inside the main house until this rumpus is resolved. Soon they'll all be leaving, anyway, so we won't need to worry about that for much longer."

"So this means camp's over? We are leaving, then?" Harry asked.

"Tristan." I grabbed Tristan by the arm to get his attention, and stared intently at the front doors, while Celeste and the boys began arguing with each other about what to do. "Look! Isn't that Simon over there, sneaking outside?"

He turned round quickly, just in time to see Simon shuffling slowly through the doors, his whole stance very suspicious and shady, as if he was trying his best to walk away unnoticed.

"Come on." Tristan grabbed my hand and we hurried outside to catch Simon before he could slither away from us.

Simon was not pleased when Tristan and I caught up with him at the bottom of the steps.

"What now? What do you want from me?" he grumbled, obviously in a bad mood.

"We just want to ask you a few questions," Tristan said.

"Look, I've answered a million questions already about those wasps. Ask the Harkers, they'll tell you everything you need to know." He made a motion to leave, but Tristan stepped in his way, preventing him from going any further.

"Why are you trying so hard to get away from us, then? Hiding something, are you?" Tristan suggested, crossing his arms.

Simon glanced at me, then quickly averted his eyes, but I still caught the flicker of fear in them. "Yes, he is," I said. "He's afraid and he's hiding something."

He took a step back, feeling cornered. "I-I don't know what you mean . . ."

"Come on, man. You know she can tell when you're

lying. Please, stop denying everything," Tristan berated him.

"What are you trying to hide, Simon? Is it about those wasps? Were you the one behind that?" I pressed on.

"No! No, I had nothing to do with that! I swear!"

"Then what is it?"

"Well, if you really want to know, I think we should start by asking what *you* are trying to hide, Gray," he snapped back defensively.

"What?"

"My brother just called and asked me all sorts of questions. More stories about the camp have reached him, and he was very curious to know what is going on here. He kept repeating one particular question: if I had seen anything strange, anything involving . . . *fire*." He stopped and gave me a pointed look. "He let out one more tidbit of information, and it happens to involve that Jonathan Gray you were so coincidentally asking about the other day.

"You know how everyone in the Top League has a distinctive ability?" Simon said, staring directly at my baffled face. I vaguely recalled that, but I had no idea where he was going with this. "Apparently, Jonathan Gray could create fire. Funny that, huh? It's very a rare, very special ability. Could even be hereditary."

"I don't understand . . ." I did, but I needed to stall for time. Even though I couldn't remember all the facts, I knew that I had been asking around about my father and this Top League. Now I knew this League had something to do with magic and people with special abilities. I also knew I possessed this one very particular ability involving fire. And so did my father, apparently. The puzzle pieces were starting to come together, and I was finally starting to get a glimpse of the bigger picture now.

I'd had so many things to worry about since my amnesia hit, that I'd forgotten to ask Tristan why he had lied about my father when we were in Simon's cabin. But how had Simon connected fire to me?

"This Jonathan Gray . . . you're related to him, aren't you!" Simon continued. "The fire in the lake – it was you, wasn't it?"

"What fire in the lake?" I asked, baffled.

Tristan's expression was tense and urgent. "Look, let's not jump to conclusions, here. A lot of strange things have happened around this place, Blaine."

"Are you going to tell me she's got nothing to do with that?" Simon accused deliberately. "Who's lying here now? You tried to pin it on me, but it was her all along! Now you've got the League's eyes on this place. That is never a good thing, believe you me."

"What did you tell your brother, Blaine?" Tristan asked, looking really worried.

"Why? Scared that I told about your wife's little secret, are you?" he jeered back, in the same accusatory tone Tristan had used with him. "I know what you are trying to do. You are trying to accuse me in order to keep your wife away from the crossfire. I'm not taking the heat for her, man. No way. You can quit what you're doing."

"She's not causing these attacks, Simon!" Tristan protested. "Someone or something is really attacking her. In the forest, in the lake, here at the main house and at your cabin, too. All I'm trying to do is keep her safe, I swear to you!"

"B-but who's—" he began to ask, but was interrupted

by the boys running down the steps, calling out for us.

"Joey! Tristan! Celeste just got a call at the lobby. It's that Craig fellow. He's packing up and getting ready to leave this place right now! This is our last chance. If we want to get to him, we'd better run," Harry said.

I glanced anxiously at Tristan. We were running out of time arguing with Simon, here, when Craig – who could be our last chance to find out what was happening – was leaving Misty Lake Camp. He could hold the key to solving this whole mystery.

"Let's run, then," I said.

Chapter Twenty-Seven
Chasing a Hunch

"We have to hurry, if we want to catch him," Tristan instructed. "Come on, his cabin is up that way."

We all bolted uphill, following the trail to Craig's cabin, afraid that we wouldn't make it in time to see Craig before he left. We were halfway up the track when someone shouted from behind.

"Hey! Wait up!" Simon called out, running after us. "I-I need a minute . . . to talk to you . . ." he panted, out of breath.

I stopped for a second and turned to face him. "We're kinda in a hurry, here, Simon. Can't we talk later?"

"What I need to tell you is urgent, too! I don't think you understand how serious this is. You're not listening to me. I mean, about what I told you back there."

I eyed him cautiously, but once I saw the level of distress on his face and the urgency in his eyes, I agreed to listen to what he wanted to say. "Okay, hold on." Then I turned to the boys, who hadn't noticed I had stopped and were continuing to hurry up the trail. "Guys, wait up for me for a sec!" I shouted.

Tristan halted and said something to the others, before tracking back towards Simon and me. "What's going on?" He stopped next to us and crossed his arms, making it clear that he wasn't going to leave me alone with Simon, not even if he was only a few feet away.

"Listen, I don't think you realize this," Simon began, looking very distressed as he passed a shaking hand through his blue-tipped hair, "but you have to stop whatever it is you're doing. The more weird things that happen here, the more attention you're drawing to this place. They will come for you!"

"Them? Who?" I asked, confused.

"The League! Are you not listening to what I'm saying? The League can send someone to look into these attacks! There are rumors flying around everywhere now. If they come, you're screwed! They are not what they seem. They are a threat. Why do you think they are so secretive? It's because they're up to no good!"

"Why? What can they do? What do they want?" I asked.

"They want whoever is causing these things around camp! If they come, they will take you with them."

"Me? What they will do to me?" He was really starting to worry me now.

"I-I don't know, something bad, okay? You have to believe me. Everyone that knows about them tries to stay the hell away. You should, too. You have to stop making these crazy things happen, please! You have to listen to me!"

"I can't make wolves, swamp creatures, poltergeists and wasps appear out of thin air, Simon! I swear to you, I can't," I told him firmly.

A few clouds rolled over our heads, filtering the warm

sunlight. Simon's eyes were flickering frantically towards Tristan then back to me. "No, it has to be you! You've been there whenever these things have happened. I saw the fire on the lake – I know that was you. Listen, this is serious! My brother *knows* something's up now. And he suspects it's somehow related to this Jonathan dude, because of all the questions I asked him before. All he needs to do is ask around a bit, and he'll figure things out! Everybody knows there's a Joe Gray attending the Gathering this year. He'll make the connection."

"Simon, what did you tell your brother about me?" I asked, feeling distinctly uneasy. The wind had picked up speed, sweeping our hair in all directions. It looked like a storm was approaching, unexpectedly and fast.

"Nothing! Of course I didn't say anything to him! They would have come immediately to get you, if I had!" he cried out. "You have to keep them away from you! You don't need to worry, I won't tell your secret, okay? But you have to be careful. If they find out—"

"Calm down, Simon," Tristan said, as he saw how agitated he was getting. More and more clouds were gathering in the sky, rumbling ominously, heavy and dark with the promise of a raging storm.

"Simon, you're overreacting, dude!" I told him. "These guys can't be as bad as you're saying. Even if they do come check things out, they can't do anything to us," I argued.

"No! You don't understand! When the League took my brother away, after that pool accident at home – the one I told you about – they did something to him. Cillian was never the same again. They . . . they changed him, he's been different – and not for the better. You can't let them get to you, Gray! They'll do the same to you!"

"What do you mean by 'different'? What they did to your brother, Simon?"

He hesitated, afraid to say something he shouldn't. "I-I can't . . ."

"You have to tell us, Simon, please!" I insisted.

"It's bad, all right? You have to trust me on this!"

"Bad, how? Tell us, Simon! What did they do to your brother?" I pressed urgently. "You can trust us. We won't tell anyone, I swear to you."

"Look, my brother was never the best to begin with, but after they took him . . . now he does whatever they want without questioning anything. He has no free will or even a conscience any more. They turned Cillian into this . . . amoral, unethical automaton. He doesn't care if what he's doing is good or bad. He doesn't care . . ." Simon grabbed me by both arms, shaking me lightly. "You have to stay away from these people! If they realize you can do the same as your father, they will come running for you. They will take you away! They will do the same to you as they did to my brother!"

I tried to wriggle away from Simon's grasp, but he was too terrified to listen, and his hands only tightened around my arms.

"Simon! Calm yourself and release her!" Tristan quickly intervened, pulling the boy away from me. A towering shadow flickered in and out of sight, looming right behind Tristan's back, as if there was a cloud of smoke over his shoulders, making him seem bigger, darker and more threatening.

Simon and I gaped in astonishment at the flickering shroud hovering over Tristan, but then in the blink of an eye, it disappeared.

"Hey, what's the hold-up?" Josh approached us with an upset frown, having seen the way Simon was manhandling me.

"W-what w-was that?" Simon asked me, eyes wide in fear.

I was about to reply, when a series of flickering shadows moved swiftly at Simon's back. Leaves and tree branches thrashed in the rushing wind, adding more dancing shadows to the bushes and the vegetation beneath the trees.

"It's you again, doing this, isn't it, Gray?" he accused, taking a slow step away from Tristan, Josh and me.

"Doing what?" Tristan asked, confused.

"Are you guys hearing this?" Seth closed the distance between us, his grip tight on the iron poker and his expression full of alarm.

Harry, Sam and Josh surrounded us in a circle, looking cautiously at the forest bordering the trail at our sides.

"Hear what?" Tristan and Josh asked, at the same time as a low growling rolled threateningly in our direction.

"Oh, no."

Chapter Twenty-Eight

Fearful

"Oh, no . . . not again," I groaned, as I watched the suspicious rustle in the low vegetation on the side of the trail where the growl had come from.

"It's the wolf!" Seth exclaimed, jumping in fright. "I think I saw it! Passing right behind those bushes!"

We all started to take small cautious steps back and away from the trail. "I told you, you have to stop doing this, Joey! Please!" Simon said in a shaky voice.

"Me? What? No!" I protested again. "I'm not doing this!"

"It's payback! You're doing this on purpose, just to scare me in front of your friends because I didn't go back to help you in the lake!" he shouted, stepping further away from us. "You think this is funny, don't you? Well, it's not! I'm here trying to help you, and this is what you do? Try to make me look like a coward? Stop doing this! It's mean and cruel and you can stop now!"

"Simon, I swear to you I'm *not* doing this!" I shouted back, while a threatening growl rumbled from the other side of the trail, and thunder rolled high up in the clouds in reply. The wind was slashing at the vegetation so hard that keeping track of whatever animal might be hidden in there had become increasingly difficult.

"Seth, pass me that iron bar," Josh ordered, since he was at the front of the group and the most likely to be attacked first.

"Ah, now you want my poker," Seth squeaked from the back. "I told you that you should all have come prepared, and you all laughed in my face. Who's laughing now, huh?"

"Seth," Josh growled, and turned to face him, a deadly look in his steely blue eyes. "This is no time for jokes. There's a frigging wolf right there! Pass me the poker. *Now.* Or do you want to tackle the thing yourself?"

Seth seemed to ponder that option for a microsecond, before hastily handing the iron poker to Josh. A rustling in a nearby bush made us all jump and turn in the direction of the sound. Josh gripped the poker hard, and swung it a couple of times, preparing to defend us. Tristan and Sam stepped forward to aid him in defense, while the rest of us stood waiting helplessly behind.

"What the hell do they think they're doing?" Simon hissed, watching the boys at the front.

"They clearly think they can beat the wolf with an iron stick. That's not very smart, if you ask me. The best thing to do is climb up a tree. Everybody knows wolves can't climb trees . . ." Seth reasoned, looking around for the most strategic tree to escape up, if push came to shove. "But that would only work if we are indeed facing a wolf, here, which we don't really know for sure," he continued. "I mean, this could be a bear. It's common to have bears in woods like this . . . If this is a bear, then trees won't be of any help. Nothing will be, to be completely honest with you. You can't escape a bear. Iron poker or not, bears are killing machines! They're better than humans at everything: running, climbing, swimming, ripping heads off . . ."

A few trees shook violently in a strange gale that passed by us, and the shadows lingering by the bushes seemed to grow taller, indeed reaching a bear's height.

"But if this is really a wolf, though, it's probably not alone. Wolves walk in packs. It's not likely to be just the one; there must be more around," Seth continued, rambling nervously. "And if that's the case, we are royally screwed, my friends. We don't stand a chance against a pack of wolves. They will eat us one by one, like a soft, tender, helpless buffet at their disposal."

Once again the trees shook, and now we could hear low howling coming from various directions in the forest all around us. Everybody started closing together in a tight circle formation, since we were clearly surrounded. Seth started to ramble even faster in his panic, too nervous to remain quiet.

"You all make fun of me because I'm scared of forests, but now you can see what I'm talking about," he blurted out, unable to stop himself. A storm gathered menacingly above our heads. "And bears and wolves aren't even the worst! I mean, they are the worst, but there must be scorpions and spiders crawling all over the forest, too, not to mention poisonous snakes and—"

While Seth rambled about every little thing that could kill us, the wind kept sweeping incessantly and the shadows lingering by the trunks started to move oddly, as if hundreds of insects had just come alive, sprouting from every crack, nook and crevice of the trees around us.

A wolf howled from far away, and what sounded like a bear growled and huffed, dangerously nearby. I gasped in shock when I saw hundreds of tiny little spiders and black scorpions storming to the ground, crawling to meet slithering snakes by the roots of the trees.

Everything that Seth had been talking about was becoming dangerously real. Tristan was also looking at the forest with wide eyes, just as I was, and he too seemed to realize what was happening.

"Seth! Would you *shut the hell up!*" he ordered urgently.

Seth halted, startled by the sharpness in Tristan's voice. "Why? All I was saying was—"

"STOP! Just don't . . . Stop talking! Everything you're saying is coming true!" I shouted in panic, as we all watched nervously as a wave of black insects descended to the ground.

"W-what?" Seth stammered, looking around in a panic and finally registering the black mass swarming out of the trees.

"It's him, then? He's the one causing all this?" Simon asked, scared. "Why is he doing this to us? Make him stop! Make him stop or I will!" He advanced in Seth's direction, with his hands in fists and a threatening glint in his eyes.

"Seth's not doing this!" I shouted, stepping between the two boys. Harry and Sam hurried to my side to block Simon's path. "Everybody calm down!" I commanded, my arms spread wide as I tried to restore some order.

"If it's not him, and it's not you, then who is it?" Simon snapped angrily, spit flying from his mouth. He was so terrified that he looked on the verge of doing something really stupid, like beating us up to make it stop. "Oh, God!

It's coming for us! It's all coming for us!" He pointed to the moving mass that was creeping in our direction now.

"Get a grip on yourself and calm the fuck down, man! It's like you're scared of your own shadow!" Josh shouted at Simon, pissed that he had threatened Seth a second ago, even though he'd reacted out of fear.

And that small comment was the key that unlocked the puzzle and made everything fall into place inside my head. It all made sense to me now.

Fear. That was the explanation.

"You are scared of *everything*." I exhaled in realization. "It's *you*. You're the one doing all this." But neither Simon nor anyone else had heard me. Everybody's attention was fixed on the giant shadow of a bear slashing down a tree trunk, making it crack and crumble in our direction.

"Everybody move!" Tristan shouted, pushing me, Simon and Harry out of the way, while Josh pulled Seth and Sam to the other side.

The tree landed with a loud thud, missing us all by an inch.

"Everyone okay over there?" Tristan shouted to the other side of the huge trunk, where Josh, Seth and Sam had jumped out of the way.

"Josh is crushed under a heavy branch, man! His leg is stuck! He can't get out!" Seth yelled back in panic, making Tristan and Harry jump hurriedly over the tree to help set Josh free.

I peeked over the other side and saw Josh squirming under a big branch, his leg stuck at a weird angle, while the boys tried to lift the branch off him. Crawling spiders and black bugs started to spill from the base of the fallen tree and swarm over the trunk towards the boys. Harry and

Sam had taken off their flannel shirts and were trying to swat the closest bugs, while Seth and Tristan helped Josh.

I turned round and ran after Simon. He was the key to making all of this go away. I found him crouched on the ground, freaking out badly, both hands over his head while he rocked back and forth, mumbling incoherent words to himself. He looked on the verge of a psychotic breakdown.

"Simon! Please, listen to me!" I shouted, shaking him by the arms to try to force him out of his panic attack. "It's you who's doing this! You're making the shadows turn into your worst fears! You have to calm down and make it stop!"

"I'm not! I can't! We're all going to die here!"

"Simon, look at me." I grabbed his face and made him look up. "Remember when you told me about your brother? You said he could curse people. What if his ability is really about instilling fear? What if *you* are the one who can make things happen?" I tried to explain to him as fast as I could. "If your brother can put fears into people's minds, maybe you can make those fears come true! Think about it. Every time something has happened, you were there. Someone mentions things that scare you, and suddenly it becomes real. The wolf only showed up after that girl mentioned it, and the ghost in your cabin after Tristan and I talked about it. Even the lake creature – that might not be your brother's curse, after all. It could be your fear of water making it real."

"No! It wasn't me! I swear it wasn't!" he denied in panic.

"But it makes sense, Simon," I persisted. "Those wasps appeared after you heard me scolding the boys, telling them they looked like drones harassing you. It might have been the suggestion you needed to create the wasp nest. You felt threatened by the boys. And it was the same thing with Tristan just now. The second he pulled you away from me, you felt scared, and then we saw that shadow shrouding him. Remember? You made him look bigger and scarier than he really was, because you were afraid. And now everything you heard Seth suggesting, it's happening! The more scared you are, the worse it gets, Simon."

"N-no! No! It can't be me! It can't be!" he wailed, rocking even harder on the ground. "I can't be doing all those things! If it's me, they'll come to get *me!*"

Every tree around us trembled violently, as if shaken by an invisible hand. Leaves, twigs and branches crackled loudly as they fell down, and the shadows that had once moved like insects now shifted and started to slither to the ground, morphing into silhouettes of big, tall, muscled men in dark cloaks.

I widened my eyes as I realized what I had done.

I had given Simon his biggest fear.

He was now creating shadows that resembled the members of the Top League.

I could see him losing control. I could see panic rising and taking over every inch of his mind, flooding uncontrollably out of his eyes. I had given him the one thing he feared most in his life: being taken away by the same men that had taken his brother and changed him into something horrible . . . the men who had marked and scarred his family for ever.

And now Simon thought they were coming for him, too.

"No, no, no! Listen to me, Simon! This is not going to happen, okay? I won't let them take you!" I tried to reverse the situation, but he wasn't listening to me. His head was buried under his arms, and his knees were bent, while he rocked frantically on the grass, mumbling quietly to himself. "They'll take me away, it can't be me, they'll take me away."

"Oh. Crap," I mumbled, as I watched the dark shadows sliding menacingly my way. "Tristan! Help!" I cried out.

The boys had told me I had black belts in martial arts, but I still had no memory of that. I had no idea what to do or how to protect myself. I felt so impotent, so useless. All would be lost because I couldn't remember how to save us. I knew I had the means to do it, but I couldn't remember a damned thing!

Tristan poked his head from over the tree trunk, and his eyes widened in shock when he saw the new threat marching towards me. He leaped over the tree in one fluid movement and ran fast, trying to get to me before the shadow men did. But he wasn't fast enough. The dark figures were already upon me.

One of them detached himself from the mass of menacing shadows and swung a heavy arm, throwing me away from Simon with a hard blow. I crashed on top of Tristan, the force of the impact dragging us both to the floor.

"What the hell are those things?" Tristan grunted, untangling himself from me. He stood up quickly and pulled me up, stepping immediately ahead to shield me. A few of the shadow men had formed a defensive circle around Simon, enclosing him within their hold, while the rest turned to face us.

It almost seemed as if they had pushed me away from Simon because I was trying to get him to stop freaking out. If he stopped being afraid, all the shadows would disappear. It made sense for them to be trying to prevent that from happening. They wanted to hold on to their existence through Simon's continuous state of fear.

But I didn't have time to explain any of this to Tristan. More and more shadows were morphing into dark silhouettes of suited men, and now they were closing threateningly on the boys. But Josh, the most equipped to fight back, was stuck under that tree branch, unable to protect anyone, even himself.

Even though I couldn't remember my martial arts training, something inside me still jumped alert, ready to protect the boys. The thought of any one of them getting hurt made me react on instinct. I was jumping over that trunk and running to them before Tristan could even think about stopping me.

Chapter Twenty-Nine
Ring of Fire

"Guys! Watch out!" I shouted in warning, as I ran towards the boys.

Seth, Sam and Harry stood up and stretched their necks to get a better look over the tree trunk. As soon as they realized what was happening, I saw their faces grow pale. Seth immediately scrambled around, frantically looking for his iron poker. Sam crouched back down to try, with increased urgency, to dislodge Josh from beneath the tree branch, and Harry started to break a smaller branch off the tree in a hurry, with a view to arming himself.

"What? What's going on?" a clueless Josh asked, his words emerging in huffs with the effort of trying to help Sam release him from under the massive branch.

"Shit's about to get ugly, dude!" Harry shouted, finally pulling a branch off the trunk with a loud crack.

"There's a bunch of creepy shadow men closing in on us!" Seth wailed, grabbing the iron poker and hurrying to stand beside Harry in the defense line.

"How do you even fight off shadows?" Sam grunted

through gritted teeth, heaving at Josh's branch with all his might.

"Hell if I know! But I'm praying I can hit them hard with this!" Seth gripped his iron bar and swung it around in an attempt to make the shadows back away.

I reached the boys at the same moment Seth had hit one of them, the iron bar slashing the shadow man in half as if a gust of wind had brushed through a cluster of dense fog. The figure hissed loudly, its form breaking and dissolving on the ground in rolls of dark smoke. Before Seth could celebrate his victory, another shadow man detached itself from the group at the back, and stepped forward. He swung a heavy arm and threw Seth to land on top of Sam. The iron poker swirled and landed far away from anyone's grasp. Apparently, iron pokers could dissolve the smoky bastards, but also made them very, very cranky.

The line of shadow men advanced, prompting Harry to hold his branch aloft, in a fencing stance, as if he was about to challenge them to a duel with a silly wooden stick.

"Stop! Stay back!" Harry hissed, but the men continued advancing, forcing Harry into a slow retreat.

It looked like the shadows were trying to force us all away from Simon. But what would they do when they reached Josh, stuck under that branch and unable to move? Would they tear him out, even if it meant ripping his leg off in the process?

I had to do something, and fast, before they could get near Josh. But what could I do? Seth's iron bar was gone! I had no weapons to fight them with! If only I could remember how to create fire again, I could try to blast these shadows to hell.

Tristan had followed at my heels, and was trying to help Seth and Sam back to their feet, while Josh cursed the extra weight their bodies added to the branch pinning down his leg.

When one of the shadow men took another step closer, and started to get ready to strike Harry down, I reacted on instinct. I ran towards him with my arms outstretched and my hands wide open, palms up, trying to stop the blow. That thing was going to hit Harry. I couldn't let that happen!

The thought of Harry being hurt made my blood boil. But then, as my heartbeat raced and blood rushed through my veins, a memory of a dream came back to me. *I looked at myself and there were flames in my hands. The fire spread, running all over me, consuming me whole, like I was a born star. I felt big, invincible, as powerful as the sun.* The sound of crackling fire caught my ears, merging with the urgent shouts of the boys in the background. Yellow, bright flames burst from the palms of my hands, a warning sign that anger was taking over.

"STOP!" I shouted at the top of my lungs, and stood defensively in front of Harry, the flames now enveloping my whole hands. I could hear Harry gasping in shock behind my back, while the shadow man retreated and hissed, cowering in pain as if the flames were actually burning him.

"J-Joey? W-what's happening?" Harry stammered, eyes wide as he stared fixedly at my hand. "H-how are you doing that?"

None of the boys knew about my ability, except Tristan. Oh, well, I guess that metaphorical flaming cat was out of the burning bag now.

"I can explain this later, Harry," I grunted, concentrating

on my anger so the fire in my hand wouldn't vanish. I needed to stay angry. I needed that feeling to keep the fire going, so I could protect everybody.

The shadows retreated in unison, backing away from my burning hand, but they quickly began to slide sideways and move to our back. They were forming a circle around us. I couldn't protect everybody, not if they decided to attack from every side, all at the same time. It seemed that was their plan. Tricky, smart shadows.

Was that Simon's doing? Was he thinking up all these strategies? I couldn't see him any more, not over the huge tree trunk and the wall of shadow men blocking the view. Was he still cowering on the ground, head stuck in his arms, mumbling in fear all this time? How long would his panic attack last?

"Shit! They are coming from behind now!" Harry warned, turning round when he heard the others shouting to get our attention.

I tensed again, the imminent danger fueling my anger. As I stared at the flames in my hand, trying to think of a way to get out of this, another memory drifted back to me: *The whooshing sound of consuming fire filled my ears, and along with it came rattling chains and angry whispers. The noise was maddeningly loud, but this time I knew I could bear it. For Tristan and the boys' safety, I could control this. For them, I could do anything.*

A rush of images filled my spinning mind, and all my memories returned to me all at once in a fierce torrent: the boys, all the moments we shared together, the brotherhood we had, their support and love whenever I needed strength or help; Vigil, all the struggles we'd been through that led us into the friendship we had now; magic and the wonders it brought to me; my life since I first met Tristan and everything that has happened after that point. I remembered it all. It seemed the release of my fire powers had unlocked the rest of my memories along with it. I frowned in concentration and remembered Vigil's words echoing in my mind in one of the many lessons he gave me about controlling these abilities when we had switched powers: *You can be fierce like a blazing sun and gentle like a candle flame. It is you who controls this power; it does not control you. You cannot let it rule over you.* And then I remembered the key to making this power come to life.

Let it burn.

I let heat consume me from inside, rushing within me, taking over my soul. The sound of crackling fire was loud inside my head, deafening my thoughts. But I would not let it rule over me. I had to make this fire bend to my wishes.

Let it burn, something whispered seductively, urging me to unleash all this force building inside of me. It would take only a slip for me to fall prey to these suggestive whispers. I frowned harder and focused all my attention on this energy, taming and ordering it to form a circle around the boys and me.

Flames sprouted from the grass, running like wildfire around us. It looked as if I had struck a match and cast it onto a line of gasoline, which was now forming a circle of fire around us, safely enclosing us inside its burning walls.

The boys and I had protection now.

They all watched the circle of fire with awestruck eyes, including Tristan, who also seemed startled by it. Slowly, they started to huddle together in the middle, trying to stay away from the flames.

"Oh, my God, is she doing this?" I heard Seth gasping at Tristan, his voice shaky and scared. I knew this would frighten the living daylights out of them. That was why I'd wanted to keep this a secret all along. The boys would never look at me the same way again after this.

The shadows outside the circle hissed loudly, angry at the sudden obstruction. It was pretty obvious they hated fire. But it looked as though the fire I was making wasn't strong enough to hold them back. They began to stretch out, looming over us like giants made of dark smoke. One of the shadow men risked taking a giant step forward, his long leg passing easily over the ring of fire.

I stomped my feet on the ground. "NO!" I yelled angrily. "You can't get in here!" And I let the whispers inside my head grow louder, allowing the heat to spread and the need to burn grow stronger inside me. I unleashed it all.

The fire wall sparked up, flaming higher and higher, licking at the sky. That seemed to do the trick. The shadow men weren't advancing any more; we couldn't even see them on the other side, the fire was too high.

"Ugh!" I grunted under the stress, beads of sweat rolling down my face. To maintain this level of constant fire was taking a lot of energy and all of my concentration. I didn't know how much longer I could keep it up. Probably not very long.

The fire licked at the fallen tree trunk and started to spread through the wood, finding a new source of fuel to feed on. I frowned and concentrated harder, forcing the fire to retreat back to the circle I had drawn in my mind. It should stay in that line, not run wild, or it could burn the boys to a crisp.

But fire has a will of its own. It was eager to spread

and take over, to run free through the forest. The urge was too strong, the force too big to be contained only by my wishes and concentration. It started to inch back to the wood again in tentative strokes, waiting for me to get tired and lose control.

I realized in shock that the fire could soon take over the trunk completely, and get to Josh, burning him, since he was still trapped beneath that blasted branch. I wouldn't be able to keep it constrained for much longer. I didn't have much time. To save Josh, I would have to put the fire out. I needed to will it to go away. But then those shadows would strike at us again.

"Tristan!" I shouted through gritted teeth. "Tristan . . . the fire . . . can't hurt you," I gasped between labored breaths. "You need . . . to get to Simon. He's making the shadows . . . come to life. You need to . . . go to him!"

"What? Simon?" Tristan asked, shocked. "He's the one doing all this?"

"Yes!" I grunted. "Hurry . . . I can't keep this up . . . for much longer!" I felt my legs start to wobble, threatening to give way under my weight. I was getting weak. "When you get close to Simon, use your fading!" I said, the realization suddenly coming to me. Tristan hardly ever used his fading any more; we sometimes even forgot he could still use this special trick he had acquired back in Ghost Land. "Fade and pass through the shadows protecting him . . . and then hit him! Knock him out! If he's unconscious . . . this will all go away!"

Tristan turned to face the fire, creases on his sweaty forehead revealing his doubt. The wall was impressive, and for a second he seemed uncertain. Then he turned to me, gave me a firm nod, and walked right through the fire, his whole frame engulfed as he disappeared into the flames.

I heard the boys calling after Tristan in panic, but I couldn't risk losing concentration now. I couldn't stop to reassure them everything was fine and that Tristan was okay. I needed to focus on the ring of fire and keep it locked in place. I wobbled dizzily again, and almost fell, but I managed to regain my balance just in time. My chest felt so heavy, as if there wasn't enough air to breathe. My trembling arms were open and outstretched, fingers spread wide to command the fire around me.

But Tristan was taking too long! My strength was running out, and every second felt like torture to me. Then a dark silhouette appeared in the fire and Tristan walked right through, his brow beaded with sweat and peppered with soot, and his T-shirt a bit charred.

"It's done! He's out for the count! Everything is okay now!" he exclaimed, running up to me. "It's all vanished, like you said it would."

I sighed in relief and forced the fire to slowly shrink and disappear into a swift warm breeze. All that remained of the flames was a large charcoal ring on the burnt grass.

My arms dropped to my sides, and a second later, my knees gave way. Tristan was at my side as fast as an arrow, his arms wrapping around me, holding me and not letting me fall.

"I've got you," he assured me, while he helped me sit down on the grass to rest.

"I know. You always do," I murmured, with a tired smile.

"How did you come up with that crazy plan? I can't believe it actually worked!" he said, looking impressed. He kneeled down next to me.

"Tris, is Simon okay?"

"Well, as far as he can be. He's been knocked out, after all."

"Can anyone help me get the hell out of here now, please?!" Josh shouted as loud as he could.

"Go help Josh. He needs as many pairs of hands as possible to get him out of there. Go!" I told Tristan.

"You sure? How are you feeling?" he asked, hesitantly, torn between helping our friend and staying with me until he was sure I was really all right.

I pulled him close for a deep kiss to answer his question. He stared at me, surprised and slightly confused, after we broke apart. "I'm totally fine, Tris! And I have all my memories back," I explained ecstatically. "Every last one. I remembered everything when I unleashed all that fire. I have them back now – you, the boys, our life together, everything."

"That's wonderful, Joey!" He grinned happily, but the boys' voices caught his attention and he turned his face in their direction, getting worried again.

"Go help them. I'm tired, but fine. Go! Josh needs you more than I do."

"Okay. Hang in there, I'll be right back."

Chapter Thirty

Memories Out

*"There was mention of fire breaking out, down by the lake,"
I remembered Craig saying . . . How had he known about
that? There was definitely something fishy about Craig; I
remembered the shifty look in his eyes.*

*"What is it that you want to ask me?" I had said, full
of suspicion.*

*The main house front doors had been only a few feet
away. If I could walk that small distance up those steps,
I'd known I would be safe again . . . But Craig had known
that I sensed he was a threat. His cover had been blown.*

*The hit had come unexpectedly, and I hadn't been
prepared for the blunt force of a surprise mental attack.
My knees had caved and I'd hit the ground, grabbing my
head in pain. I could hear Craig a few feet away from me.
He had hit the ground the same way I had. We'd locked
eyes for a split second. In his eyes I'd seen surprise. And
fear. But something else . . . realization.*

* * *

I realized I was more exhausted than I'd imagined, because soon after Tristan had left to help Josh, I blacked out, and it was only when Tristan gently shook me awake that I gathered I'd been unconscious.

"You said you were fine," he harrumphed as soon as I blinked awake.

"I am fine. What happened?"

"I went to help Josh, and when we came back, you had passed out."

"Oh. Well, I did say I was pretty tired," I mumbled, groggily, sitting up on the grass. "How's Josh's leg?"

"I'm all right," Josh said, limping out from behind Tristan, with Sam right by his side, providing a shoulder to lean on. "Leg's kinda painful, though, so I might have broken something. But it doesn't hurt too much. I reckon I'll be walking normally in a few days," he said bravely.

"We have to get you back to the main house as quickly as possible and check your leg properly, Josh. That tree branch looked pretty heavy," I said anxiously, but was relieved to see my friend safe from creepy shadows – and from burns, too. Well, to see that *all* my friends were okay, I registered, as Harry and Seth approached, also safe and sound. "How long have I been out?"

"Not long. Ten minutes or so," Tristan said, crouching next to me. "How are you really feeling, Joey? You scared us half to death! I didn't know you had it in you to create a wall of fire like that. It was impressive . . . and kinda scary."

"Yeah, and since we're on the topic, I'd like to ask something, here," Harry interrupted. "What the hell was that about?" he asked in a freaked-out voice. "One minute you're Joey, the next you're Miss Pyromania, blasting fire everywhere! Care to explain that?"

"Yeah, I almost pissed my pants when I saw what you were doing!" Sam exclaimed. "In a very manly way, I mean . . ." he added.

"*You* pissed your pants? What about me, stuck under that highly flammable piece of wood? I was practically a bonfire waiting to happen!" Josh said.

"Oh, erm, it's . . . sorry, guys, I was trying to keep that a secret for now . . . you know, because I didn't want you thinking I was some sort of freak of nature," I mumbled.

"Ah, come on, Joe! You know we would never think that of you!" Seth said. "Haven't we all supported you and Tristan through the weirdest things ever? The witch stuff, the ghost issues, *Vigil*, your eye thing. When did we ever think badly about you?"

"Yeah, Seth's right!" Harry huffed indignantly. "That's not a good reason to keep secrets from us! You know we will always support you, no matter what!"

"Come on, you guys! I saw the way you were all looking at me when you saw the, erm, fire and all . . ." I argued, shuffling my feet guiltily.

"That was only cos you took us by surprise, is all!" Harry countered. "We don't care what weird stuff you can do. Just give us a heads-up first, so it won't scare the shit out of us when it happens."

"Yeah, you do know you can trust us with everything, right?" Seth asked, his tone conciliatory now.

"Of course I do. I'm sorry for keeping this from you, guys. Really, I am."

"Okay, then." They accepted my apology, although still looked slightly miffed.

"Tristan!" I straightened up, suddenly realizing something urgent. "We still need to go see Craig! He could be leaving the camp right this second!"

"W-what? Why?" he asked, looking confused "We've figured things out already. It was all Simon. We don't need to see Craig now, do we?"

"Yes, we do still need to talk to him! I've remembered our last talk by the front steps. This amnesia has something to do with him. I think he's the one who caused it but I don't know why. And he kept asking about the fire on the lake, too. He knows something. We need to know for sure what he has figured out, and before he leaves the camp!"

"He could have left already, Joe."

"Yeah, but we have to find out, Tris. Maybe he's still here! I'm sure there's something he has realized about me, I swear! We have to go find out what it is. Simon has already made the connection between the fire and me; I can't have Craig blabbering about it, too! I need your help now, boys," I told them, turning very businesslike. "Sam, can you wait with Josh until we send help? Josh, if Simon by any chance wakes up, knock him out again, would you? You know how to do it without hurting him. He has to be unconscious until help arrives, or he could make those shadows appear again."

Sam and Josh nodded, shuffling quickly to where Simon had been left sprawled on the grass.

"Seth, go grab your iron poker and keep guard over there. Keep them safe, okay? And Harry, you need to run down to the main house and get the Harkers. Tell them what happened to Simon. They will come to help," I instructed them quickly. "I'm going to run with Tristan to Craig's cabin now, okay? There are things we need to find out before he bails."

"Okay, but Joey, are you sure you don't want us to go with you? For backup and all?" Seth asked anxiously.

"Don't worry, man. I've got her back," Tristan reassured him.

"Well, I reckon you do, tough guy. Since when can't you get burned, anyway?" Seth asked curiously. "That was majorly impressive! I thought you were going insane, walking through fire like it was nothing!"

"Yeah, well." Tristan scratched the back of his head, looking embarrassed. "I think it's another ex-ghost ability. The first time it happened, it scared us like hell, too, until we realized it couldn't hurt me. Sorry you had to find out that way."

"You almost gave me a heart attack, but it's okay. I don't think anything can surprise me any more after that . . ." he mused, looking at the large, dark, smoking ring on the grass.

"Okay, guys. We need to hurry. Seth, I need you to be taking care of things here now, okay?" I interrupted, because we were running out of time. Craig could be leaving at this very second! "Please, tell Celeste that whatever she's planning to do, not to call that pompous secret Top League. That's Simon's biggest fear; he'll lose it all over again if he suspects they are coming to get him. Tell her that, please. It's important, don't forget!"

"Got it, don't worry. I'll tell her," Seth said.

"Oh, and please don't mention to anyone about me making that fire wall!" I remembered at the last second. "I want to keep that between us; it's best no one knows about that, okay?"

He nodded before backtracking to the place he had last seen his iron poker.

"Come on, Tris. Let's go!" I urged, hoping Craig had not left yet.

We only had this one last chance to get some real answers before the guy disappeared without a trace into the world.

Chapter Thirty-One
One Last Thing

Craig's pickup truck was heading down the road, tires spitting gravel, before it stopped only a few inches in front of us. We were halfway through our hike up the trail that led to his cabin when we bumped into him driving away.

I had been right to be in a hurry. We would have missed him if we had arrived only a minute later. Craig cut the engine and slowly stepped out of the car. He wasn't wearing his usual khaki shorts any more, just jeans and a long-sleeved shirt, though with his round-rimmed glasses perched as ever on the end of his nose.

And he didn't look ill: his face wasn't pale and his eyes weren't puffy as they had been before.

"Miss Gray," he greeted, with a nod, his eyes fixed on me. "What a surprise, bumping into you on my way out of camp."

"Cut the crap, Craig! I've got all my memories back. I remember everything," I snapped, irritated, my fists balled at my sides. I was exhausted and in a foul mood, and Craig was still pretending, right in my face. I had had it with his deceitful lies!

"Ah. I see." He didn't seem surprised by my little outburst; his expression had remained cool and collected since he'd left the car. He watched me in silence for a moment, taking what felt like all the time in the world before he continued, "You are just like your old man: charging in without thinking, letting your anger dictate your moves. Typical Gray."

"What's that supposed to mean?" I snapped, taken aback.

"It means you are not being smart. It is very easy to connect your father's *flammable* personality to yours. You act the same way as him, thinking you're being bold and brave, but actually you're only impulsive and stupid."

I pursed my lips and forced myself not to lash out. "How do you know my father?"

He paused and watched me squirm in doubt before he replied. "Oh, we were colleagues once, a long time ago. I assume you not only inherited his passionate temper, but his ability as well, am I correct? The boy looks like he's stepped right out of a fire. I imagine that's probably because of you?" He nodded at Tristan.

Even though my flames couldn't hurt Tristan, his skin being immune to the fire, his clothes hadn't been so lucky and there were a few holes burned through his slightly charred shirt.

I felt Tristan's hand taking hold of my arm and squeezing with gentle pressure to let me know I should tread lightly.

"I don't know what you're talking about." I decided to take Tristan's silent advice and go for a deflective approach.

Craig tilted his head, watching curiously how Tristan's hand on my arm had so easily been able to restrain my impulsive advances. "I see that you are different from your father, since you have someone to help you. It's a pity Jonathan didn't have anyone to keep him from his reckless ways. You're lucky to have the boy taking care of you."

He got that right on the mark. Tristan was the epitome of prudence and caution, and had helped me handle things calmly more times than I could count.

"What is he, by the way?" Craig asked, his eyes flicking away from me to observe Tristan in scrutinizing detail.

"He is my husband," I stated, with my chin up in defiance and my eyes flashing a silent warning to stay the hell away from Tristan, or there would be hell to pay. I'd make sure of that.

The pressure of Tristan's fingers increased slightly on my arm, warning me to stay quiet. He shouldn't worry so much. It was not like I was revealing any breaking news, here. I had told Craig I was married when we'd first arrived at the main gate, but I hadn't told who was the husband. Everyone at camp knew Tristan and I were married, though, and even if they didn't tell Craig, he was bound to find out sooner or later, from some magazine or gossip TV show. Our faces were all over the news right now.

"Oh, so he is the famous husband you had mentioned before," Craig said.

Ah, so he did remember things. Why was he still calling me Miss Gray then?

"But once a Gray, always a Gray," Craig told me, in answer to my unspoken question. Even though he" – he gave a cursory nod at Tristan – "is now your husband. But that's not what I meant. I want to know what he *is*. I'm positively sure he's not entirely human . . ."

"Excuse me? I'm certainly very human!" Tristan said, offended on more than one count.

"Oh, no, you're not. Want to know how I know that? It's the eyes, boy. They give you away. Plus, your mind is like a fog filled with muffled whispers. I can't understand a damned thing," Craig said, squinting at Tristan.

"Are you saying you can read minds? Is that what you did to me by the front steps? Did you cause my amnesia?" I asked, stepping protectively in front of Tristan. Whenever something – or someone – ever threatened Tristan or the boys, I completely lost it and charged in without thinking.

Once again, I felt Tristan's hand resting gently on my shoulders, telling me to calm down and keep my center, so as not to give anything away.

"Yes, I can read minds. That's my special ability," Craig stated, crossing his arms over the chest. "What? Did you think you were the only special one in this world, Miss Gray? Or Mrs. Halloway, if you insist. Did you believe you were the only one with abilities? Our numbers are not many, but I'd like to think all good things come in limited edition. It makes it that much *more* special, don't you think?"

"Is that how you knew Jonathan Gray is my father? By reading my mind?" I asked defensively. "You surely haven't assumed that on the basis of my name alone."

"Actually, no. I've had my suspicions since the incident by the lake, but I didn't know for sure. Well, not until now, when you've just confirmed it for me. Thanks for clearing that up, by the way." He chuckled smartly.

I gritted my teeth, silently cursing my big fat mouth. "You're saying you can read minds, but you didn't know for sure? That's bull! One of those statements is a lie."

"I didn't say I can read *everyone's*," he corrected, tutting playfully. "I can read *most*. But I can't read his, for instance, whatever he is." He pointed at Tristan. "And I certainly learned my lesson when I tried to read yours, didn't I?"

"W-what?"

"Oh, you know. The blackout by the main house. That was all you, sweetie pie."

"You're lying. I didn't do anything! It was you!"

"I'm not lying. I didn't know about your empathy-sight. Jonathan didn't have that, so I wasn't expecting you to have it. Shouldn't have tried probing your mind. If what people are saying is right, you're a strong empathy reader. Tell me, then, *Mrs. Halloway,* am I lying now?" He locked his eyes on me, squinting ever so menacingly.

He wasn't lying. I could see it in his big round bespectacled eyes.

"That doesn't make any sense. Why would she cause herself amnesia?" Tristan said, deciding to join in the interrogation.

Craig sighed, getting tired of having to explain everything to us. "I tried to get a full read on her by the front steps." He paused and turned to look at me. "You were running away, I didn't have much time, so I barged in with too much force, you might say. You reacted on instinct. It was very raw and crude, very untrained, too, but I can't say it wasn't effective. That backlash of yours gave me quite the headache, dear. I haven't had one like that in decades. You even knocked me out cold. Only very few can do that. It was very impressive."

Glad you think so, you smug bastard.

"The memory loss was a side effect. You tried to block me from getting to your memories, and locked them up, causing your amnesia. Sorry about that. If I'd known you'd react that way, I wouldn't have tried to take a peek. I won't be making that mistake again, trust me. My head's still hurting . . ." he complained, rubbing his temple. "I've never had migraines as strong as these before. If it weren't for your empathy-sight, you wouldn't have suspected anything, and wouldn't have been so alarmed when I tried to read you. That was my biggest mistake," he confessed. "I should know better than to try to read a mind when there's all sorts of alarms and shields on. It's a surefire recipe for a bloody migraine, that's for certain."

"Well, it serves you right," I retaliated. The bastard had got what he deserved for barging into my head like a damned troll.

"Hah! That's rich, coming from you. The pot calling the kettle black!" he scoffed. "How's that wrong for me, but you can read people as you please and it's all good and dandy?"

"I only do it for my own protection! I don't purposefully try to pry into others' personal thoughts with shady motives, like you do," I protested, but felt a bit guilty all the same, because he was kind of right. When it boiled down to it, we really did almost the same thing. "And you said you couldn't remember anything, when we went to your cabin to ask you questions. You were lying about that, weren't you? You didn't have amnesia at all!" I accused.

"I couldn't remember things for the first day, but by the end of the night my memories returned. The migraines I had afterwards were so bad I couldn't do anything, anyway. You saw how I was; that wasn't an act," he protested darkly. "I tried peeking inside the boy's head when you came over to interrogate me, but like I said, it's like trying to listen to whispers in a fog. And I sure wasn't stupid enough to try anything again on you, that's for damned sure."

"Why did you want to read my mind so bad in the first place, anyway?"

He rubbed his thick moustache, mulling over the question. "Well, there was the connection with Jonathan Gray that I was trying to uncover," he began slowly. "I peeked inside that kid's head, Simon. There were all sorts of jumbled thoughts, but you know what was the most interesting thing to fish out of there? A memory of fire over the lake. That caught my attention, fast. I knew you were somehow involved, then. Fire and 'Gray' in the same sentence is never a coincidence, I know that much. I tried to read your mind to confirm my suspicions, but it backfired on me – no pun intended."

"How do you even know about Jonathan Gray and his connection with fire?" Tristan asked.

"Yeah! How?" I joined in, full of suspicion. Even my mother didn't know about that, and they were together for a good few years. I didn't think my father would have boasted about his fire powers to anyone, if he hadn't even trusted his own wife with the secret. It wasn't likely that he would have shown it to a kid in high school, or wherever they had met.

"Ah, well, we studied and then worked together a few times on field missions. But that was a long time ago, twenty-eight years back. We were just starting out in the League, fresh and young and full of hope."

"You were in the Top League, too?" I asked in alarm.

"I am. Present tense, kiddo."

I didn't even need Tristan's grip tightening on my arm to warn me about the danger in those words. All sorts of red flags, neon signs and flashing alarms were let loose inside my head as soon as he mentioned the League.

"We were assigned to work together in the first years we joined the League. But then he got too important to be with the likes of me, once he'd started to hang around the popular circle. Then suddenly he didn't have time for me any more," Craig continued, his tone filled with resentment.

"What was this job that you two worked on together? What did you do in the League?"

He paused and regarded me critically. "I'm sure you know. Your father must have told you all about the important job he had at the League when he was younger, before he quit and went off grid."

"He never told me anything," I said through gritted teeth. He couldn't have, on account of having died when I was three years old.

"I doubt that very much. Jonathan Gray was always the cockiest and smuggest bastard around. I'm sure he couldn't have kept himself from bragging about this to his own daughter."

"I've heard about the League, but not from Jonathan," I said in a clipped tone.

"So what are you doing at this camp, anyway?" Tristan asked Craig. "You said you only suspected there was something related to her father after you probed Simon's head, and only then did you decide to investigate. What brought you here in the first place?"

"I came here to check on a 'Joe Gray'. Your name has been bleeping on our radar for a while. I thought you were a boy, though. They thought Jonathan must have slipped up and was being careless, letting his son show up at a Gathering now. They were betting on a cocky boy taking after his daddy, showing off his powers to his friends."

"They? The League sent you, then?"

"Of course, who do you think? You don't just disappear one day, never to be heard of again – not in the League, you don't. We've been trying to track him down forever. But your father, oh man, he's good! He didn't leave a single trace, not one track that could lead back to him. For more than twenty years he's kept away. But he wasn't counting on his reckless offspring blowing his cover, was he? He's going to be mighty pissed with you, kid, when he finds out you've been 'playing with fire', for all the world to see, without Daddy's consent. That's karma at its best: the most reckless guy I've ever met getting grief over his daughter's negligence now."

"What does the League want him for? Why go to the trouble of sending people here to investigate his where-abouts after all this time? Why can't they just leave him alone?"

"*Fire*, Mrs. Halloway. Jonathan was a fire charmer, like yourself. That is a rare ability and very precious to them. They never stopped looking for him because of his fire." His voice was laced with envy now. "They don't care for *silly* mind powers like mine. To get recognition in that place you have to demonstrate tactile, invasive brute force that can be used in battle. They don't appreciate subtle, much more efficient ways, like mine, oh no. To them it's all about brutality. Your old man could only conjure up small flames in the palm of his hands, back in the old days, yet they fucking loved him for it. I was pushed aside, irrelevant, just a useless piece of furniture to them." He sneered, full of venom. "They tried to train Jonathan, to make him practice his abilities, make his power bigger, stronger, but he was too undisciplined, stubborn and he lacked concentration . . . He never applied himself to his training. But maybe he could have been practicing by himself all this time. They think maybe now he's gotten better at it. That's why they sent me here to look for him again."

I couldn't help but notice the similarity between Celeste's evaluation of me and Craig's breakdown of my father's problems: undisciplined, stubborn, lacked concentration and application to studies. I guessed the apple really didn't fall far from the tree.

Craig continued with his rant. "Even hating his pretty little guts for leaving the way he did, they still want him back. Jonathan was always a gigantic pain in their collective ass, yet they are still crazy to get their hands on him and take him back."

"Why was he a pain in their ass? What did he do?"

"Let's just say obeying orders and dealing with authority were never his forte. But they don't have to worry about that any more. Can you imagine what they'll think when I tell them about you? When I tell them there's a younger, female, more subdued and mellow version of Jonathan? They'll think they've hit the jackpot!"

Tristan snorted loud at hearing that. "Oh, sorry. I thought you were throwing jokes at us," he said, when Craig shot him a quizzical look. "If they think Joey is a 'mellow version' of anything, they'll have a good surprise coming. I'd bet good money she's more stubborn, fierce and brave than her father ever was, and then some."

I smiled proudly at Tristan for coming to my defense. You go, hubby!

"You think just because she's a woman, it'll be easy to control her? Think again, pal," Tristan added with a scoff.

"It doesn't matter, anyway." Craig gave an uncaring

shrug. "They'll sure come after her, easy or hard. If what I saw in that kid's head is really true . . . It wasn't just a small flame in the palms of your hands, was it, young lady? It was massive. So much potential for so much destruction . . . I can almost see the party they're going to throw for you."

But I suspected I knew exactly what sort of "party" those people in the League were about to throw for me. Simon had been very incisive in his confession about how dangerous they really were, how they craved slaves they could control and use and abuse.

I remember the look in Simon's eyes, how real the fear was in them. Anything was better than being "recruited" by those men, I knew that much. Now I also understood why my father had never mentioned them, why he'd never told my mother about his old life, and about magic. He'd wanted to get away from them, at all costs, even if he'd had to deny part of himself, deny his magic.

He'd kept it a secret to protect us from this League, to keep his family out of reach of their hold. And now I had ruined everything, drawing attention to myself – and my powers.

"You can't tell anyone!" I took one step in his direction, pleading. "Craig, please, you can't. I know you don't like my father, but this is not his fault. It's mine, okay? I didn't know any of this. I didn't know I was supposed to stay out of sight. No one ever told me about this damned League! Please!"

I think it was the crack in my voice that made him falter, or maybe the tears brimming in my eyes. He uncrossed his arms, relaxing his unyielding stance, for once. "Look, kid. It's out of my hands now. I have to report this. They are expecting me to contact them any time soon. They are hearing a lot of strange rumors coming from this place, and they want to know what's going on. I have to tell them."

"You could tell them you found nothing here," Tristan suggested. "It's mostly rumors of animal attacks, anyway . . . they would buy that story."

"It's not that simple. They are not stupid, boy! They know there is something supernatural going on at this camp! That Simon boy is going to blabber about the fire he saw on the lake – you know that, don't you? His brother works for us. In fact, Cillian Blaine was the one supposed to come here to investigate. They switched to me because I insisted on coming to check this out. They know how much I despise Jonathan, and that I would do anything to get my hands on him. I was their best choice for this job. I'm the best at tracking people down without too much fuss: I'm quick and clean about it, whereas that Blaine kid leaves a mess wherever he goes. Not that I've ever heard a word of appreciation for any of my talents," he complained, looking hurt. "But it's only a matter of time before Simon tells his brother about the fire and they connect it to you, same way I did. I'm sorry, but I have to tell them what I know."

"No! Please. You can't," I begged.

"Actually, I can't wait to see how Jonathan will wriggle out of this one. I'll bet it will be with some trick. He was always so full of annoying, smart tricks. This will be an irritation to him, but he deserves it, trust me. He's made me look like a fool plenty of times before. I'll tell him to consider this payback," Craig boasted, but then he saw the despair on my face and his eyes glinted with guilt and remorse. "Hey, I'm sure your father will take care of this, kid. He disappeared on us completely once; he can do it again. You don't need to worry so much, he'll look after you."

"No. He won't. He can't. My father, he's—"

"No, Joe! Don't!" Tristan cut in, stopping me from telling the truth. "If they know, they will think you're unprotected."

"I have to tell him, Tris. He may sound mean, but he's not. I can see it. He's not a bad person." I turned to look Craig straight in the eyes. "My father is dead, Craig. He died when I was very little. It was an accident; he wasn't expecting it. He thought he had all the time in the world to tell me everything when I was older and could understand things a little better. He never got to tell me about any of this stuff. I didn't know I should've stayed away from magic. I didn't know. But now that I do, I won't ever use my ability again, I swear to you."

Craig seemed completely stunned, shock marking his features. He closed his eyes and exhaled, seeming genuinely surprised and even saddened at the news. "I'm so sorry, Joe." It was the first time he'd addressed me by my first name. "Your dad, well, he was an arrogant prick, but he didn't deserve to die. I guess he was only trying to protect his family . . . that's why he went off grid. It makes sense now. He was trying to keep all this away from you, and to have a normal life," he mumbled in realization.

"You have to help us," Tristan pleaded. "They can't know about her! No one can know."

"I'll quit magic, like he wanted me to. I'll stay away, for good. I promise. The League won't ever know about me, if you don't tell them. Please."

Craig started pacing in front of his car, clearly having an internal debate, but then he reached a conclusion. "Okay, look, this is what we'll do. I'll tell them you're a girl. That should throw them off your track for a while. They are expecting a boy Gray, not a girl. If you keep your word, stop casting fire and . . . well, and continue being a girl, maybe it can work," he said thoughtfully, wringing his hands nervously. "You are really a girl, right?" He stopped pacing to raise a skeptical eyebrow at me.

"No. I'm a plant. Duh."

"Sorry, I had to be sure. These days, you can never be quite certain . . ."

"What's that got to do with anything? You're talking nonsense," Tristan said, looking confused.

"Well, hmm, there's this one other thing you should know about your dad's family, the Grays," Craig began to explain. "For about eight generations, maybe even more, there have only been males in that family."

"What? That doesn't make any sense. And it's impossible. How can they have descendants, then?" I asked, baffled.

Craig rolled his eyes. "They marry women outside the family, but the offspring are always males. Like, *always*, really. Not one single kid has been born female in that family. Ever. You're the first one that I've heard of."

"You're joking!" I gasped, my eyes opening wide in astonishment.

"I'm serious, kid. I almost packed up and left the day you arrived at Misty Lake Camp, and I saw you were a girl. Like I said, I was expecting a boy named Joe Gray to attend the Gathering. Then you showed up, obviously very female. I thought, well, investigation's over, that is not the Gray boy we are looking for. But then weird things started happening and I got a peek into Simon Blaine's mind, saw the fire, connected the dots . . ."

"I can't believe this, but . . . it actually makes sense," I said, deep in thought.

My mother used to tell me old stories about how they'd decided to name me Joe.

She told me that the second my father knew she was pregnant, he was absolutely sure it would be a boy. She used to say he didn't have an inkling of a doubt that the baby was going to be anything other than a boy. He just knew it.

It had always been that way in his – our – family, which is how he was so sure.

My mother used to say he spent the entire nine months calling me Joe. The name had been picked on that first day and stuck like glue. He even told Mom to skip her ultrasound scans, as there was no doubt in his mind about the sex of the baby. He had assured her a million times, with such certainty that she'd started to believe it herself.

They were both shocked when I popped out with all the "girl parts". Mom said he'd cried a lot when he held me for the first time, calling me his special little miracle. She didn't realize how accurate that was.

I really was a miracle in the Gray genealogical line.

By the time I was born, they'd gotten so used to calling me Joe, it didn't sound right to change the name, Mom said.

So they kept it. I was Joe. A girl named Joe.

Now it all made sense.

"He thought I was going to be a boy. That's why he named me Joe," I said, turning to Tristan. "It wasn't that he only *wanted* a boy; he just wasn't expecting his baby to come out a girl."

"Oh," Tristan said softly in realization. "That explains quite a lot, actually."

"Yeah, I know." I felt light-headed from too many groundbreaking life revelations in just one day. It was overwhelming, to say the least.

"But I'm not entirely sure they will believe this lie for long, though," Craig interrupted. "They will still suspect something's up. I mean, people are talking about wolves, ghosts, lake creatures . . . all sorts running wild around here. They will look for answers. If they dig enough, they will bump into stories of fire. If they look closely enough, they are bound to figure it out."

"All this weird stuff going on at the camp – it's Simon's fault," Tristan blurted out, before I could stop him. "You can tell them it's all down to Simon, not Joey."

"Tristan, don't say that!"

"No, Joey. It's the truth. Soon Celeste is going to have to contact his parents and let them know. It was serious what happened back there, Joey! He could have seriously hurt someone. He's out of control! She has to tell his parents. Soon everybody will know about it. I'm just speeding up the flow of information, here."

"So you think tossing him to the lions in my place is the right thing to do?" I argued, upset. "He's terrified of this League, Tris! They can't know about Simon! They will take him away!"

"They can't know about you, Joey!" Tristan argued back. "I'm sorry, but we can't save Simon! That ship has sailed. But we still have a shot at saving you!"

"Simon's the one doing this?" Craig said in surprise.

"Well, then I'm afraid the boy is right, Joe. If Simon is really the one responsible for all the supernatural occurrences, you might have a chance to duck under their radar . . ."

"Yes, he is. He's making his fears come to life," Tristan explained.

"Well, then Miss Harker really does have to inform his parents. And if I know the Blaines, they will report it to the League right away. They did it with their first child; they will surely do it again. The decision is out of your hands, kiddo."

"I can't believe this," I huffed, feeling frustrated.

"I think this can work out," Craig said slowly. "They'll have Simon to focus on, and you'll be off the hook. If Simon doesn't tell on you, that is. If he tells about the fire he saw, then all bets are off. But if he keeps quiet, I can make it look like it's all related to him. If he can create wolves and lake monsters, he can create fire, too, I'll suggest."

"You can't blame Simon for something he didn't do! It's not right!" I protested.

"It's the only way we can make this work, kid," Craig countered. "Look, I promise I'll do what I can to convince them that there's nothing to see here," he proposed sincerely. "I'll throw them off your track, okay? I'm not as good as your dad at fixing things, but I'll try. I know what it's like to have no one to take care of you. I'll do my best to help you." And he extended his hand for me to shake.

I slumped my shoulders. "Okay. Thank you, Craig. I owe you one." I shook his hand, my heart filled with a mix of remorse and apprehension. I could see in Craig's eyes that, deep down, he was an honest man, and that he would try hard to keep his word. But there was still Simon to worry about.

"And you . . ." Craig turned to Tristan. "Keep her safe, all right?"

"Will do, sir," Tristan promised, shaking the hand he was offered.

"Okay, then. I need to get going now," Craig said, walking back to his car. He turned the engine on, and was about to shift gear and set the car in motion, when I called out to him.

"No, wait! Craig!" I shouted, suddenly realizing I wouldn't have the chance again to ask him anything more. There was so much I still wanted to know, so many things about my father that Craig knew and could tell me. If I missed this chance, I'd never find out any of it. This was my one and only shot. I couldn't pass it up that easily! "You can't go!" I said, planting my feet firmly next to his car. "There's so much I need to ask you. Is there anything else you can tell me about my father, Craig? Anything at all you can remember . . ."

I hardly knew any stories about my father's past, about how he'd been with his friends, what his work was like, his life with my mom . . . My mother ended up so depressed whenever she started reminiscing about life with my dad that, as I grew up, I'd begun to avoid asking any more questions. I didn't want to make her sad, and she often got sad whenever Jonathan was mentioned. So I stopped asking, and I stopped mentioning him.

The truth was that I barely knew my father. But Craig did. He could tell me a few precious gems, some old stories – he could share them with me now.

Craig wound down his window. He seemed taken by surprise at my question. "Hmm, we did work together, but it was a long time ago. To be honest, I didn't know much about his private life . . ."

"Yeah, but what about the work you did together? What else can you tell me? What was he like back then? I mean, besides the fact he was an undisciplined, arrogant prick. We know all about that already, right?" I said, with a snort, trying to lighten the mood.

"Joe . . . I only said that because, well, I don't know why . . . Please, forgive me. I was being petty and jealous. Jonathan was in the popular crowd and I was the lame, loner nerd. I said all that stuff out of spite, I'm sorry . . ."

"Oh, you don't need to apologize. I don't mind if you have bad things to say about him. I just want to know the truth – how he really was – good or bad, I don't care. I just want to know."

The look he gave me held so much pity, as if it broke his heart to hear what I'd just said.

"Honestly, we only worked together on a couple missions. We barely talked, then; we weren't that close. Everybody liked him, though. I guess that's why I resented him so much . . . He didn't even have to try, people just . . . liked him, unconditionally." For a second, he seemed lost in his thoughts, but then he shook his head and glanced up at me. "I can tell you he was a major pain to the headmaster when we were at school, always disobeying orders . . . too headstrong, you know, rushing into things without thinking first. But he was very good at what he did – sort of reckless, but he got things done, and that was what mattered in the end.

"He did show me his trick with the fire ball, this one time . . . after I'd badgered the hell out of him to let me see it." He chuckled at the memory. "It was a neat trick. Very pretty. The fire danced in the palm of his hand, like it was floating. Made me remember that magic can be about beauty, delicacy and grace, too."

Out of the corner of my eye, I could see Tristan giving me a meaningful look, a faint, knowing smile ghosting his lips, while Craig continued talking.

"He would be proud to see what you can do now, how far you've come without anyone to guide you . . ." He trailed off, turning his head away from the car window, staring pensively ahead. After an awkward moment of silence, he cleared his throat and said, "I don't know much else. I'm so sorry."

"That's okay. You've told me so much today. Thank you, Craig. It means a lot to me."

He paused, seeming to be mulling something over, and then leaned across to shuffle through papers in the glove compartment. He found a pen and, after quickly scribbling on something, he handed it to me through the window. "Here. Take this." It was a small white card. "It's my contact number. I keep it strictly for emergencies; no one knows this number, not even anyone in the League. You call me if you're ever in trouble, okay?"

I nodded and took the card from his outstretched hand.

"And stop playing with fire, kiddo. For your own good, yeah?"

"I will. Thanks for everything, Craig. I won't forget your help."

"No problem. You're a good kid. Take care, you two," he said, before winding up his window and driving off down the graveled road, leaving Tristan and me standing still, watching the pickup disappear.

"So, what now?" I asked Tristan, after a moment of silence.

"Now we make sure Simon won't tell on you," Tristan said, his expression filled with resolution.

Chapter Thirty-Two

Happy Normal Ending

"You look like you're about to pass out again. Let me carry you the rest of the way there, please," Tristan urged, full of worry.

We stopped first at the clearing where we had left the boys, but there wasn't anyone there, so we quickly headed to the main house to see if we could find them.

"I'm fine, Tristan. Stop treating me like a damsel in distress all the time. I'm really not that helpless." I dismissed his offer with a stubborn scoff.

I wasn't injured; I was just tired. There was no need for him to overreact like this. I knew most people thought that boys carrying girls in their arms was romantic as hell, but to me it wasn't. It only made me feel pathetic and helpless.

Neither of which I was, thank you very much.

"You're surely back to your old stubborn self," Tristan muttered, shaking his head.

Yes, I was sure back: good as new and stubborn as ever.

But the walk was turning out to be excruciatingly tiring

and I was already exhausted to the bones. I forced myself to keep walking, but after tripping over my own feet for the second time, I decided it was time to give in a little.

"Fine. You can lend me your arm for support for a little while, okay?" I compromised, leaning all my weight on him. "How do you think we can convince Simon to keep quiet?" I asked, to divert Tristan's attention.

"Well, he promised that he wouldn't tell anyone, remember? He didn't want the League anywhere near this place," Tristan replied.

"Yeah, but that was before his ass was on the line," I countered, slightly out of breath as we finally approached the main house. "When he finds out his parents are going to be called, and that the League will be notified, too . . . he might not think the same way. He could change his opinion to: 'What the hell – if I'm going down, I'm taking everyone down with me.'"

Tristan pursed his lips, none too pleased with that possibility. "We're just going to have to convince him, somehow. We'll talk to him and figure it out."

There was a big commotion at the front of the main house, with people bustling out of the building, bidding farewell to their friends, packing things into the trunks of their cars and preparing to leave. A car swerved to pass Tristan and me in a hurry, while another car following behind stopped right next to us.

Alicia Collins was driving, with her sister in the passenger seat and two of her girlfriends sitting in the back.

"Wow! What happened to you? You look awful!" Alicia exclaimed, eyebrows rising towards her hairline as she gave us a thorough once over. I was sure I must be quite a sight: a sweaty, disgruntled mess dragging my exhausted bones along the road. "I don't mean you, Tristan. You look a delight, as always," she quickly corrected, treating him to a flirty bat of eyelashes.

"Excuse me. Could you stop hitting on my *husband*, Alicia. I'm right here."

"What? I'm merely stating facts: you look bad; he does not," she argued smartly.

"Oh, ouch. That hurts. I think I might even cry now. Boo hoo," I mocked.

"I can see that even though you may have amnesia, you still remember how to be rude."

"My memory is absolutely fine now. You can stop worrying about me. It's giving you horrible wrinkles," I said, pointing at her face.

I didn't even care about wrinkles, to be honest. People shouldn't get upset about getting old. It's a natural thing to happen to every living being on the planet. But Alicia seemed like the superficial type that would get wound up by such a stupid comment; she looked like she worried a lot about appearances. Right on the money, I watched as she gasped in outrage.

"I don't have wrinkles!"

"It's not what I'm seeing from here," I provoked. She was getting on my nerves, and my patience was non-existent at the moment.

"Ladies, please, can we *not* do this now?" Tristan interrupted, with a long-suffering sigh.

"I was going on my merry way. She's the one who stopped to throw out insults and flirt with you!" I pointed out, irritated.

"Me? I was just trying to leave camp! She was the one strolling along the middle of the road like she owned the damned place. It was either stop or run her over," Alicia complained to Tristan, then turned to me. "What are you still doing taking strolls, anyway? The Gathering is over, haven't you heard? Celeste has told everyone to pack up and leave. Which is so stupid! Just because there are a few strange things going on, it's no reason for her to panic and abort the whole reunion!"

"It was not her choice. The camp owners are closing Misty Lake until they can arrange for another caretaker. And I'm sure Celeste is only thinking about everyone's safety, Miss Collins. There's always next year's Gathering," Tristan reasoned calmly.

"Well, this one has been a complete fiasco, I'll tell you that," she grumbled, but her gloomy mood quickly switched to happy when she looked up at Tristan. "Except for your presence, of course. Will we see you again next year, Tristan?"

"I'm afraid neither my wife nor I will be attending any more Gatherings, Miss Collins."

Her face fell in disappointment. "Oh, why is that?"

"We have a pretty busy schedule with the band, and all. You know how it is. I don't think we'll be able to come again, unfortunately."

"That's such a shame." She gave him her best pout.

"Yeah, yeah. I'm sure you are all going to be crying freaking rivers. Now, if you'll excuse us, we have to get going," I interrupted rudely, tugging at Tristan's arm to make him follow me. "You have a nice life, Alicia. And take care of those wrinkles!"

I flashed a big fake grin at her outraged face before hurrying away, dragging Tristan with me.

A black SUV was parked at the entrance to the main

house, its doors wide open and a burly man packing some bags inside.

Celeste was at the front steps, talking to a stern-looking woman dressed in a somber, dark suit. We were approaching them when Simon walked down the steps, carrying a few more bags to hand over to the burly man by the SUV.

"Look! It's Simon." I pointed him out to Tristan. "That woman must be his mother. They are leaving the camp! Hurry!"

"Celeste!" we both called out. She turned round with an annoyed frown, but when she realized it was Tristan and I calling, her expression changed.

"Oh, there you are." She greeted us calmly, but her eyes held an edgy, worried look. "Mrs. Blaine, this is Tristan and Joey Halloway, the couple I was telling you about. They were with your son when this last 'episode' happened. Guys, this is Simon's mother. She was staying at a holiday lodge nearby with Simon's stepfather. They came as soon as I called them."

Mrs. Blaine turned to greet us properly. The resemblance to Simon was very evident: they both had the same dark hair and facial structure, along with the same tall, slim physique.

"Oh, Celeste told me what you did. Thank you so much, Mr. Halloway, for your help. If it wasn't for you, things could've gotten way out of control . . . I mean, more than it already has." She shook her head, a tired look softening her stern features.

"Yes, I've told Mrs. Blaine about Tristan's quick presence of mind, and how he found a way to stop Simon's hallucinations before someone got seriously hurt," Celeste cut in.

I frowned at her odd spin on the latest events, but she

gave me a warning look and the message flaring in her piercing blue eyes was loud and clear.

Keep quiet. Let me do the talking.

"He's very sorry for having to knock your son unconscious, Mrs. Blaine. Mr. Halloway is completely against any kind of violence. You can ask any of his friends and they will tell you the same. But it was the only way to make him stop," Celeste continued.

"Oh, I'm sure he did the best he could at the time. I understand completely," Mrs. Blaine agreed, giving Tristan a weak smile.

"I'm very sorry for your troubles, Mrs. Blaine. I'm glad to see Simon is okay now," Tristan said, looking at Simon standing a few feet away next to the SUV.

"We had to sedate him, to prevent any more 'episodes'," Mrs. Blaine explained, noticing Tristan's glance. "I'm afraid he's not quite himself at the moment. He's been walking round like a sleepwalker since the sedatives kicked in."

I glanced over at Simon, too. He really did look like a sleepwalker, his movements automatic and his eyes emotionless like a robot.

"There had been some signs that an ability could be emerging, but . . . well, I thought I was overreacting and imagining things. I shouldn't have left him on his own. But he had so insisted on coming to this Gathering. I thought it was normal for a boy his age to want his independence, so I let him come. If I had been with him, maybe none of this would've happened."

"What is going to happen to him now, Mrs. Blaine?" I asked, ignoring Celeste's warning looks to keep quiet.

Mrs. Blaine gave me her first genuine smile since we

were introduced. "It is very kind of you to be concerned about my son, dear. He'll be all right, don't worry. We'll get the best people to help him."

"Are you talking about the Top League, Mrs. Blaine? Are you taking Simon to them?"

She gave me a puzzled look then, clearly not comfortable with my direct question. "W-well, I still have to call his father and tell him about this. He lives in Russia, you see. We need to discuss things before we decide anything, but the League is the best place for people with Simon's abilities. He'll learn to control himself with them."

"No, Mrs. Blaine! You can't let him go to them!" I pleaded, raising my voice. "You have to keep them away from your son! You're his mother, you have to protect him!"

"W-what?" she stammered, confused by my fervent protests.

"Simon is terrified of those people in the League. And he loses control when he's scared. You can't let him go to that place! It is his biggest fear!"

"Joey, I'm sure Mrs. Blaine knows what's best for her son," Celeste tried to intervene.

"Please, say you'll let him stay with you, Mrs. Blaine?" I insisted again. "I know it is not my choice to make, but I promised him I wouldn't let them take him. I have to at least try to make you see. The best place for him is with *you*!"

"I'm not sure if staying home right now is the best thing for Simon, dear," she said at last, after a moment of tense silence. "From what Miss Harker told me, he's very unstable and a danger to himself and everyone around him. I know he almost drowned you in the lake because of a monster he created from his fear of water. And there's also a friend of yours with a broken leg as a consequence of this last episode. I don't know if I can handle this by myself. Things could get out of control again, and I'm not equipped to stop him. But I will weigh up everything you've told me, Joey, before I decide anything."

It wasn't the answer I was hoping for. I opened my mouth to protest, to argue one more time, to try to make her understand, but Tristan's hand on my shoulder pulled me softly back while he answered for me.

"Thank you for considering Joey's advice, Mrs. Blaine. I know it's not our place to intrude in your family problems." He stepped forward and placed his hand gently on top of hers. "We only ask you this because we care about Simon's wellbeing. We're concerned you might turn to the League because you may fear there is no one else to help Simon, and that maybe you have no other choice. But Miss Harker and her sisters can help, as can Joey and I, of course. You and Simon should know he's not alone in this. I know for a fact that problems feel less scary, and difficulties seem less hard, when you have friends by your side. The League is not your only option, Mrs. Blaine. We are here for you. We only want you to know that," Tristan said, his voice soothing and reassuring. "And I know you will choose what is best for him: you are his mother, after all, and you know best."

She gave him a faltering smile, the hope and trust in Tristan's eyes weighing down on her shoulders. "Thank you all for your concern, but I do have to go now." She turned quickly and almost crashed into Simon in her hurry to get away from the pressure of Tristan's expectations.

"Oh, it's you, Simon. We're leaving, son. Say goodbye to your friends."

Simon looked at us, his eyes vacant and unresponsive. There was no emotion that I could pick up in there, nothing I could read. He extended his hand for me to shake, in an automatic goodbye gesture.

"I'm sorry, Simon. We tried. I hope you will be all right." I looked at him, searching for a sign that he was listening, that he understood, but no answer came. Feeling deflated, I sighed and shook his hand. "Take care of yourself."

He slipped a piece of paper into my hand without anyone noticing and turned away from me, walking back to his parents' car with wobbly steps, his mother right at his heels.

It was only after their car was a long way down the exit road that Celeste risked talking again. "You know, for someone who's the best empathy reader around, you sure can't pick up on my warning glares."

"Oh, I picked up on them, all right, Miss Smarty Pants. But I had to try to talk to his mother. I gave Simon my word, Celeste. I couldn't just let her take him straight to those League bastards!"

"Bastards?" She frowned. "Why would you say that? You continued to ask about them, didn't you? Even after I specifically told you not to!"

"Well, yeah. And I found out that they are utter bastards, and that I don't want anything to do with them!" I said snippily.

"That's exactly why I told *you* to stop asking questions!" Celeste berated. "If only you'd listen and let me handle things, for once!"

"There's nothing to handle any more. I'm quitting, anyway."

"You're quitting your investigations?"

"No. I'm quitting magic. I'm done with it. I'm not studying it, practicing or talking about it. I don't need you to be my tutor any more," I told her firmly.

"What? Why?"

"I hope you don't take this the wrong way and think I'm ungrateful, Celeste. I appreciate everything you've done for me – all your patience and willingness to teach me – I truly do. But I've realized magic has brought me a lot of trouble, and I don't want it in my life any more."

I decided not to tell Celeste about my recent discoveries. The fewer people who knew about my father and his secrets, the better. And I'd keep quiet about my fire ability, too, so that people wouldn't end up making the same connection as Craig had. I had to disappear now, just like my father had once done.

"What? It was not only *trouble*! You helped a lot of people with your magic," Celeste countered. "Like Tristan, for instance. And Vigil – you helped him solve a lot of problems."

"Well, Tristan is the one true good thing to come out of all this, you're right about that. But Vigil has retired now; he doesn't need me any more. I'm not even sure I helped him that much. You saw how his last job turned out. I brought him more trouble than help in the end."

"You just need practice, Joey, that is all. You'll get better at it."

"It doesn't even matter any more. I've been thinking about magic a lot, lately. How it has a good and a bad side. But this incident with Simon . . . the boys almost got trampled in the middle of it. That's the bad side, Celeste. They could have gotten hurt pretty badly in the forest. And it would have been my fault."

"Aren't you exaggerating a little, Joey? It was Simon's fault, really—"

"No, Celeste," I cut in. "It's my fault. The boys are at this camp because of me. And that's the thing, don't you see? They will always be in my life. If it's not Simon, it will be some other danger that's bound to happen. I've learned that magic always comes with a price, and I'm not willing to make someone else pay for it. I want others to be safe from all of this. If I have to let go of magic, so be it. The most important thing is that Tristan, my mom and the boys are safe. They are my family. And family matters more than magic. They are all that matter to me."

"I understand that you worry about them, Joey. But I'm not sure that you can banish magic from your life. It is *in* you. You can pretend it's not there, but it will still be a part of you."

"I know that. I'm not trying to pretend it doesn't exist. But I can choose to stay away from it, stop using it. I can stop being involved in this world. The less I know about it, the better I will be. I want out. I want a normal life for me and for the people close to me. No more trouble, no more danger or magical messes." I wrapped an arm around Tristan's waist and gave a reassuring squeeze.

"Even if you're running from it, magic seems always to be at your heels," Celeste mused. "I'm not sure if you can will it to stay away. It will find a way back into your life again, whether you want it to or not."

"I'll have to be faster and not let it catch up to me,

then," I said firmly. "And if trouble still finds me, I'll just have to deal with it the good old-fashioned way."

Celeste mulled that over for a while in silence, and when she spoke again, she seemed to have come round to the idea. "All right, Joey. I still think you could achieve great things with your magic – I have an intuition that, with time and practice, you could have been the greatest – but if this is what you truly want, I respect your decision. I am proud to see that you really understand the cost of using magic. Most people only see the power that it can bring, the rewards, the gain. Very few understand what it truly means and how much it can take from you. You are wise for choosing this path. I won't insist any more. You have my blessing and my friendship always."

"Thank you for understanding, Celeste. It is the right thing to do, trust me. I would never forgive myself if anything ever happened to Tristan or the boys because of me and my magic. Speaking of which, have you seen the boys?" I asked, and looked around. "I'm worried about Josh. He got his leg squashed by this huge branch, but he wasn't where we left him."

"They are all inside the main house in a restricted room, so people won't bother them," Celeste said. "Josh is in good hands. Arice is tending to him now; she's an excellent healer. But I think he'll need a splint for that ankle; Arice says it seems to be broken."

"Oh, God. I hope he's going to be okay," I said, full of concern. "He said he was fine! I don't know why he has to do the tough guy act all the time!"

"Yeah, I don't know where he gets it from," Tristan scoffed, amused. "For someone who prefers to pass out rather than let me carry her back here, you really shouldn't be mocking someone else's tough act, you know."

"I was not acting tough!" I protested, despite knowing he was right. "And I'm not 'mocking'; I'm worried about him! That's the point of this whole conversation. I don't want to see my friends getting hurt!"

"He'll be fine, stop fretting. He splints his ankle once every trimester. He did it during our last show of the tour, remember? And before that, in his martial arts class."

"Don't worry, Joey. He is going to be fine," Celeste reassured me, and extended a hand to me. "Well, I guess this is farewell for us, then. Take care, you hear? And if you need me, I'm always a phone call away."

"Thanks, Celeste." I pushed her hand away and gave her a tight hug instead. "You're the best." She chuckled and hugged me back.

Another car arrived and she hurried off to greet a set of worried parents, while Tristan and I stayed by the front steps. I glanced down and remembered the small piece of paper that Simon had handed me. "Simon slipped this into my hand, right before he left." I showed Tristan the folded note.

He eyed the paper with a frown. "What is it?"

I opened it up and, inside, found a message written in shaky handwriting:

I won't tell.

"I guess we don't have to worry if he's telling on me, then," I murmured, staring at the crumpled note.

"You think we can trust him?" Tristan asked, still not convinced.

"We don't have a choice. We're just going to have to."

"I guess so." He nodded pensively. "So, what are you really going to do now?" he asked, watching me with intent silver eyes that sparkled in the sunlight.

"I guess I'm really quitting magic," I told him, as firmly as I had said to Celeste. "From now on, I will try to stay out of trouble, and most importantly, keep out of sight and off the radar, like my dad wanted in the first place. And I'll focus on our band, the concerts, the new album, the boys and you. I want to live a normal life, Tris, I really do. I mean, sure, magic is thrilling and exciting, but we can still have a good life without magic being involved, right?"

"Yeah, but . . . I think Celeste might be right, Joey. You can't really quit magic. It's a part of you. You can't quit having it, in the same way as I can't quit having gray eyes, or fading or being an ex-ghost. Magic is a part of us. Believe me, because I've learned this the hard way: Denying what you really are won't bring you happiness."

"I'm not denying what I am, Tris. I've accepted magic into my life and have embraced it fully without question for all these years. But I can't let it rule over me or control my life any more. It is my choice to use it, and I'm choosing not to. I know we can't be normal, but we can live normal lives."

"Hey, you don't need to sell me the idea. I'm all in favor of normality!" He chuckled and leaned in to give me a playful peck on the lips. "But we did a pretty good job back there in the forest using our magic, with my fading and your fire wall. Are you really okay with giving that up?"

"Yes. I'm serious about what I said: I don't want anyone

hurt because of this. The more I think about it, the more it sounds like the right thing to do, Tris. These abilities will only put the people we love in danger. It's not worth it."

"I have to confess, though . . . it was pretty exciting using my fading today," Tristan said shyly. "The guys were looking at me like I was some sort of superhero. For the first time, I didn't feel like a total freak. I felt – I don't know – *important*."

I held his hand, gently. "You are important, Tristan. It's not your fading that makes you so. Make no mistake about that: your fading doesn't define your worth. It's your heart and what's inside it that does. But hey, I get it. Using it does give you a kind of rush. It's a deceitful feeling, though."

"What do you mean?"

"Well, I mean . . . I know that, at first, using these powers makes us feel incredible, ecstatic, like we can do anything. But that sense of control is an illusion. We're deceived into believing we can control the magic, but we can't, not really. It takes over in the blink of an eye. I almost couldn't restrain it today, Tris. That fire could have burned that whole tree trunk to ashes, quick as lightning. With Josh underneath it."

"Oh." He exhaled in recognition of the danger our friends had been in.

"How can we know for sure what will happen when we use these abilities? How do we know when I might lose control and my fire will break free and run rampant? How do we know what you might be bringing back from the place you go to when you fade? It is something given to you from the dead. Do you know for sure the price that comes with it when you use it?"

"W-what? Do you think something bad can happen when I use my fading?" he asked, shocked at the idea.

I shrugged. "It could, some day . . . We may never know, that's what I'm trying to tell you. Whenever I cast fire, dark whispers run a little louder each time, inside my head, urging me to unleash it all, burn everything down. We have no control over this. It's foolish to think we do."

"But nothing has ever happened to me, though, when I used my fading."

"Because you hardly ever use it. Maybe that's why. You've been avoiding using your fading since the first day you discovered you had that ability. Maybe you've been doing the right thing all along. Maybe it's time for me to follow your example and stop using my powers, too."

"I have never thought about it this way," he said quietly, frowning.

"I'm only now coming to realize all of this, too. In the beginning, it was all so exciting and full of enchantment and wonder. That's the tricky part, I suppose. We fall under the spell of all the amazing things magic can do, how it makes us feel important, different . . . special. But then comes the price to pay for it," I said, trying to make him understand. "I almost died trying to get in contact with Sky in the first year we met. I have this mark on my wrist from my fight with Vigil that will never go away. I got away lightly with that; it could have ended very badly. I barely kept hold of my sanity during the power switch incident. I could have seriously hurt you with my jealousy when I had Vigil's powers. Back then in the forest, Josh could have been badly hurt, or worse, and the boys too. I'm telling you, Tristan, it's a risk I'm not willing to take any more. Magic is not worth it."

"But doesn't this decision go against our deal with Sky, Joey? You promised her a life full of possibilities . . ."

"Yes, and we will live by that promise. Just because magic isn't going to be in our lives any more, it doesn't mean we will stop having an interesting life, Tristan. That's what I'm trying to explain to you. Life without magic can still be amazing, don't you see? We still can have normal lives full of wonder, adventure and excitement. People don't usually see how much beauty there is all around, out there in the world. They think glamour, power and sparkly things will make it more special, but there is wonder in the ordinary, if you know how to look at it. Sky will still have amazing things to see in our lives, don't you worry."

I had come to Misty Lake Camp trying to find answers about my past and my father's history. I came to see if I could belong here, if there were other people like me in this place. I discovered those people were very unpleasant and dangerous. And that it was best to leave the past behind.

I'd realized I belonged with Tristan and the boys, my friends and family. I didn't need anything more than that. Magic was not going to bring me happiness: Tristan and the boys were. Magic wouldn't make my life better, easier or more special: their love and friendship would.

I guess that was the true lesson I'd learned from this Gathering. To cherish what I already had, and leave the tricks and illusions behind.

In the end, magic really was just smoke and mirrors, sparkly things that only made you lose focus on what really matters.

"So, from now on, we're just ordinary people living an amazing, normal life," I told him.

"Ordinary people who play in concerts in front of thousands of other people."

"Fine. We're not-so-ordinary-and-more-like-famous-people, then, living rock-star lives – but with no magic whatsoever. There. Happy?" I shot him a cheeky grin.

"That's more like it," he agreed, smiling.

"Now, can we go see how Josh is doing? Then we should round up the boys, go somewhere else and get started on the album and this normal life, ASAP. Shall we?" I proposed excitedly. "To a life filled with music, friends and normality!"

"To a normal life," Tristan cheered along with me, as we hurried up the front steps and into the main house, in search of the other Lost Boys.

"It's going to be a good life."

Chapter Thirty-Three
A Normal Future

"So far, how's your *normal* life going, then?" Tiffany, my best girlfriend in the whole wide world, asked me, resting cozily on my living-room couch.

It had been a while since we'd had any girls' time together, and today we were making up for it as we stuffed our faces with cupcakes, tarts, biscuits and every kind of delicious goodie we could get our hands on. The amount of food on the table was impressive, but even more impressive was our tenacious effort to eat it all up, every last crumb.

"So far, so good," I replied, sipping my pink champagne – Tiffany's special treat for the afternoon celebration.

"No bumps in the road whatsoever?" she asked, sounding skeptical.

The boys and I had been back from our road trip slash witchy boot camp for a week now, and Seth had been quick to bring his girlfriend up to date on the latest events. Tiffany had come to see me as soon as she heard about my resolution to quit magic, to "show support during these trial times", as she had gently put it.

"Road's been smooth and clear as ever," I replied, sticking half a cupcake in my mouth and trying to chew it all in one go, just so I could watch her wrinkle her pretty little nose in disgust at me.

Tiffany had been trying to teach me to be more civilized since the first year we met, but I stubbornly refused to learn. I knew that, deep down, she didn't really care. I wasn't as posh and fancy as all her other friends, but she knew that I loved her to pieces.

Plus, delicious cupcakes were made to be devoured like this. Everyone knew that.

"It's only been a week since I decided this, though. We might have to wait a little longer to see how it goes," I mumbled around a mouthful of cake.

"How's Tristan dealing with it? Is he having trouble coping with normality?"

"Even though he started to enjoy exploring his supernatural side during this last trip, he agrees that we should avoid using magic from now on. It's the best thing for all of us, really."

"I hear the boys aren't feeling the same way, though," Tiffany mused, with a chuckle.

"I know! Can you believe it? They've always freaked out whenever there has been any magic involved in my life, and now they are sulking because I've given up on it. Go figure," I grumbled, annoyed. "I reckon it's mostly because of Tristan. The way he walked through fire made quite an impression on the boys. They are looking at him like he's a superhero now."

Tiffany laughed. "If you think they're impressed with Tristan, you have to listen to what they're saying about *you*, then. Walking through fire isn't nearly as fantastic as making that wall of fire in the first place, girlfriend." She snapped her fingers, all sassy. "I wish I'd been there to see it. They think it was the hottest thing you've ever done, pun intended."

I chuckled at her. "That's probably Seth's talk. He thinks it's the coolest thing to have two best friends with supernatural powers. But real life doesn't work the way it does in the comics he reads all the time, you know."

"It's not only Seth. Harry was really psyched about your last adventure, too. He said he ran through the woods fleeing from angry wasps, jumped off cliffs, swam in a lake full of deadly crocs, fought against weird shadows . . . Did you guys really do all that?" she asked, her eyes wide.

"Yeah . . . but it wasn't quite so much fun when it was happening, though. It was pretty scary, actually. Harry might make it sound like it was cool, but it was really dangerous. So don't mind the boys and their excitement, Tiff. I'm doing this to keep us all safe, trust me."

"I know." She leaned closer and lowered her voice to a whisper. "And how about those League folks? No sign of them?"

"No. I think Simon and Craig have been true to their word and haven't told on me. Let's hope they keep it that way."

"Good, good." She nodded, resting back on the couch. "If anyone ever comes to bother you, though, you let me know. My family knows people who know people who are very efficient at making troubling people go away . . ." And she made a hand gesture of a knife slicing across her neck.

I raised an eyebrow at her. "Tiffany! Are you serious?"

She glanced at me. "I'm joking, silly!" she said, with a playful smile. "But they really do go away for good . . ." she muttered under her breath.

I chuckled at her over-protectiveness. Tiffany was as fierce as I was when it came to protecting friends. "Thanks, Tiff, but that won't be necessary. For now, it seems we're off the hook. I just need to keep it on the down-low, stay normal, and we should be fine."

"All right, then."

"It was really nice of Craig to cover my tracks at the camp. I think he may have risked a lot doing that. I wonder what this Top League might do to him if they ever find out he's been lying to them . . ."

"It's cool that he got to tell you all those things about your dad, too, huh?" she risked saying, knowing what a touchy subject this was with me.

"Yeah . . ." I fidgeted, toying with the cupcake wrapping. "Do you know that since recovering my memories, a lot of things that I didn't even realize I had been repressing have started to come back to me? Like, memories of my dad when I was very little. I've started to remember them now . . ."

"Really? That's really cool, Joey! What have you remembered?"

"I've remembered that he played the guitar to calm me down, and that he used to sing to help me go to sleep. That's why music moves me so much . . . he played to make me happy. I've loved music since I was a baby, because of Dad. I learned it from him."

"That's so lovely . . . All I learned from mine was merciless tactics and business strategies to crush the competition . . . oh, and Monopoly! It's all we played as I grew up. God, how I hated that bloody board game," she reminisced. "What else did you remember, Joe?"

"It's mostly fragmented memories of his face, his voice . . ." My throat constricted when I thought of his voice. It was my most treasured memory. Sometimes, if I closed my eyes and concentrated hard enough, I could hear him singing, as if he was in another room, far away . . . "Let's stop talking about him or I'm going to start crying," I said in a shaky voice, and gave her a faltering smile.

"Yeah, okay. Sorry." She dabbed at her own eyes, getting emotional seeing me emotional.

"The important thing is that I know about my father's past now, and have learned how important it is that I keep away from magic. No one will ever know about what I can do. We covered all tracks at the camp and left no clues . . . No one will ever know," I repeated reassuringly. "From now on, I will focus only on my music, my friends, Mom and Tristan. I really think we can live a normal life, Tiff. You'll see, everything is going to be fine."

"Well, let's drink a toast to that, then!"

She raised her glass to meet mine, and together we cheered a happy new magic-free life.

Epilogue
A Glimpse Ahead

An old man stared at the view through a big glass window, but his eyes were glazed over as his mind wandered elsewhere, in a time long gone a place far away from the two-storey mansion where he now spent most of his days.

The intercom buzzed, forcing him to pull away from the past and focus on the present matters at hand.

"Yes?" His voice was cold and collected, as usual.

Very few were capable of making him lose his temper, and he was proud to boast of his unrelenting self-restraint. But despite his cold demeanor, everybody knew about the destructive fury the old man concealed beneath that cool façade. If you were wise, you'd do anything not to be on the receiving end of his wrath.

He enjoyed seeing the fear in people's eyes as much as he enjoyed basking in the blind allegiance engendered by that fear.

"He has arrived, sir," the voice on the line promptly reported. The guard at the front iron gates had been instructed to call him the second the car passed by him, and so he'd dutifully called as ordered.

The old man put the phone back without replying. Now he had enough time to rein in his excitement and collect his thoughts, so when his nephew entered his office, he would seem in control, as he should always appear to be.

He tapped his gold pen impatiently on the carved mahogany table as he waited, but stopped immediately when he heard the knock on the door. Controlled people don't tap pens impatiently on their tables, after all.

"Come in," he ordered calmly.

He was pleased to see the boy had come straight to him – as instructed – and hadn't wandered around the mansion, wasting his time. The boy was already late as it was, and he pursed his lips to let that fact be very clear to the dark-haired youngster fretting quietly in the doorway.

"I'm very sorry about the delay, Uncle. I came back as soon as I had all the information you needed. Our informant was an hour late, you see. He said he had trouble getting out of his meeting with the headmaster."

"I hope he had interesting things to share to compensate for the time he's kept us waiting," the old man grumbled, irritated. He did not like to be kept waiting. It showed lack of respect, and he didn't appreciate being disrespected at all.

"He apologized profusely, sir. It wasn't his fault: the meeting took longer than he'd expected, and when it was over he had to linger behind at the compounds for a while so they wouldn't suspect anything."

"So what is the news, boy? What did he have to say? Spit it out." He let his cool façade slip for a moment, but quickly recomposed himself. "I have a lot of important things to take care of, here. Let's not waste more of my precious time."

"Yes, Uncle, of course. The informant told me all about the infiltrator's report on the Annual Gathering investigation . . ." The boy hesitated because he knew the news he had to share wasn't the best.

"Did he tell you who they sent to investigate?"

"I believe it was a Craig Simms who was sent, sir."

"Simms? Isn't he the one with the mind powers?"

"I believe he is, sir."

"And what did Craig Simms have to say?"

The boy shifted on the spot, knowing full well that his uncle was not going to like hearing what was coming next. "Well . . . it seems there's been a problem of miscommunication, sir. The person attending the Gathering was a *Joey* Gray, sir. *A girl.*"

"A girl?" The old man asked, surprised.

"She's a girl, not a boy. It's not his son, sir. Sorry."

"Are you sure about that?"

"Yes, sir. They have gathered a lot of testimonials from people attending the Gathering, to confirm the report. They all claim the same thing: Joey Gray is a girl, sir."

"And what did the informant say about all the strange rumors coming from this camp?"

"It seems they were all about this other kid, the youngest son of the Blaines. He was the one causing a stir in the grid. Apparently, he's started to develop abilities as well, like his older brother, Cillian Blaine. They are having trouble recruiting the boy, though. His mother is reluctant to release him into their hold. That was the major point discussed at their meeting."

"So this Joey girl had nothing to do with anything?"

"No, sir. The Blaine kid was present during all episodes. The girl was there for one, but at another there were some boys involved, and in another a Filipino girl, I think. Blaine is the only common factor in all occurrences."

"What is the boy capable of doing?" he asked curiously. It was always better to be up to date and prepared for the future. Information was the highest form of power in these modern times.

"He can make his fears become real."

"Hmph. What good can that do?" he grumbled in disappointment. "What a waste of ability."

He tapped the gold pen on the table, mulling over the information he'd just received. "What else?"

The boy fidgeted on the spot again. He hadn't been invited to sit, so he remained standing in the middle of the room, looking uncomfortably at his uncle on the other side of the huge antique desk. "Hmm, that's it, Uncle. There's nothing more to say. The informant said they were very disappointed to hear Craig's report too, sir. They had high hopes that this time it could be a real lead to Jonathan."

"The blame's on them. They trained Jonathan well . . . too well," he muttered in a grim tone, looking out of the window. "It's been twenty-one years without a clue. He surely must have had someone helping him cover his tracks during all this time. Jonathan was never good at being cautious."

"I've heard the stories," the boy said.

"Hmm, yes. Especially with his ability, he was bound to lose control . . . I thought that, sooner or later, we would hear about something, surely . . ."

"Maybe he decided to stop using it. That way none of you could track him down."

"Maybe," the old man murmured. "But I doubt it. Jonathan was also never good at self-restraint. I find it hard to believe he'd be able to contain himself all this time."

He stared at his laptop screen, deep in thought. He made sure that he mastered all new technology, determined not to be like his old friends, who refused to adapt and learn new things. The world belonged to the ones who knew how to adapt.

You stopped moving with the times, you ended up being engulfed by the world.

You stopped learning, you lost the game.

"There's something we're missing here . . ." He rubbed his chin and tapped a finger on the table. "Old Violet wouldn't just take this Gray girl under her wing for nothing . . . that's not like her. The old hag has never had interest in anyone before. And the Harkers wouldn't make an exception and take on a tutorship for just anyone, either. There's certainly something about this girl we're not seeing."

"It doesn't even matter, Uncle. She's not a boy; she can't be related to Jonathan. You know that. She has nothing unique or special about her. Craig confirmed this to everyone in that meeting room. She's just a dumb, poser girl, in a stupid goth band, is all."

"She's in a band?" he asked with a frown.

"Yeah, it's called . . . What was it again? Some Peter Pan bullshit thing," the boy muttered, feeling cross. He wanted to leave, already. He was getting tired of standing there, and tired of talking all day long. He wanted to get out of that office and go relax with his friends. His uncle's persistence on this subject was starting to get on his nerves, because the point they were discussing was moot: she was *a girl* and therefore could not be related to the Grays. It was stupid to waste time digging things up about her. He wasn't suicidal enough to tell that to the old man's face, though.

His uncle watched him sulk for a while, before finally

allowing him to go. "If there's nothing else you have to tell me, you may leave. I have a lot of work to do, here." He dismissed his nephew with a wave of his hand, and the boy left as quickly as possible.

"Let me see . . ." He then turned his attention back to the laptop in front of him, and typed a few words into a search engine. The search for "Joe Gray" and "Peter Pan" yielded a lot of links related to a current rock band named The Lost Boys, and he clicked on the first image link in the list.

He crossed his fingers under his chin and looked at the downloaded picture for a long time, as he tried to calm his thoughts and return to a level, controlled state of mind.

The photo of five boys and one girl, who was in the middle of the group, was open in his browser, taunting him. He did not care for the boys. They were mere background to him, unimportant scenery. But the girl . . .

She had inky black hair and dark eyes, as she should. All Grays were famous for that particular genetic trait, even though his own hair had long since gained a grizzled hue, due to his old age. She was very pretty, too. And she looked very determined and, he even dared say, fierce, in this particular photo.

He knew that look all too well, because he had seen it countless times, in his own son's face.

She was the spitting image of Jonathan Gray: a younger, female version of him, staring back at him through the laptop screen.

"Well, hello, there, Joe Gray," the old man said triumphantly, unable to hide a smile. "It looks like you are not a false lead, after all."

Also by Lilian Carmine:

THE LOST BOYS

**Fate has brought them together.
But will it also keep them apart?**

Having moved to a strange town, seventeen-year-old
Joey Gray is feeling a little lost, until she meets a cute,
mysterious boy near her new home.

But there's a very good reason why
Tristan Halloway is always to be found roaming
in the local graveyard . . .

**Perfect for fans of Stephenie Meyer and
Lauren Kate, *The Lost Boys* is a magical, romantic
tale of girl meets ghost.**

EBURY
PRESS

Also by Lilian Carmine:

THE LOST GIRL

Even Death can't keep them apart . . .

After falling in love with a ghost, Joey has succeeded in
saving her boyfriend from Death, not once but twice.

But then a mysterious and horrifying creature begins
stalking Joey – can Tristan save her before it's too late?

EBURY
PRESS